7/17

OBSIDIAN
AND
STARS

Also by Julie Eshbaugh

Ivory and Bone

OBSIDIAN AND STARS

JULIE ESHBAUGH

An Imprint of HarperCollinsPublishers

HarperTeen is an imprint of HarperCollins Publishers.

Library of Congress Control Number: 2016961162
ISBN 978-0-06-239928-1

Typography by Erin Fitzsimmons
17 18 19 20 21   PC/LSCH   10 9 8 7 6 5 4 3 2 1

First Edition

For Gary. Thank you for filling my life with music.

ONE

The day is so new, it's barely day at all. Yet we are already far out on the blue water, gliding under the blue sky. The first rays of the sun paint long stripes of light on the surface. I watch that light—watch it shimmer and ripple until the movement makes my head swim.

Either the movement or my nerves. Or maybe both.

That's the kind of day this will be—a day of movement and nerves.

I wriggle in my seat, unable to relax. I go back to the moment I last saw Kol, standing on the edge of the sea. I can see his warm eyes, his half smile. I remember every detail of that last good-bye—that last time he said my name and kissed my lips. I can still feel the heat of his breath on my cheek. I hold that image in my mind as the oarsmen stab at the water, bringing me farther and farther north, closer and closer to that very same strip of shoreline.

Bringing me back to Kol.

I wish I could get comfortable. This canoe is so narrow I feel the rock of every wave in the pit of my stomach. My clothes are new and stiff—each place where the hides of my tunic and pants touch me, they rub against my skin. At the back of my neck, in my left armpit, against my right hip bone and the backs of both knees. I have no one to blame but myself, of course, since these clothes are the products of my own hands, made from my own designs. But though I may have bold ideas for intricate patterns of dark and light— the brown of caribou stitched to the tan of sealskin stitched to the gray of otter—I am not always the most patient of tailors. I do not always take the extra time to make sure the fit is perfect. The design on the front of my tunic may draw praise, but no one would want to spend a long day wrapped in this discomfort.

Though that's exactly what I must do today.

This morning, as soon as I was dressed, I visited Ela's hut. I don't ask many people for their opinions, but Ela is one of our clan's healers, and I trust her. She had not yet seen the new tunic; this was the first I'd shown it to anyone besides my sisters. "It's supposed to suggest a meadow," I said. "The golden grass bending and turning in the wind . . ."

"Yes, it looks just like that, Mya." She smiled, the sort of smile that belongs to a girl with a secret.

"What?"

"I just never thought I'd see you looking so much like a bride."

"This is not the tunic of a bride," I said.

"Not yet." She laughed, and I shoved her, and I laughed, too.

She was right, of course. These are the clothes of a girl coming for a betrothal. If a promise of marriage is made, this betrothal tunic will be enhanced, and even more pieces of light and dark will be worked in. It will become even more ornate. . . .

It will become the tunic of a bride.

A wave tosses and lifts the canoe as I think of this—as I let myself imagine for just a moment a wedding to Kol—and my stomach flips as I brace myself against the sides of the boat. This trip to the Manu camp would feel long on the calmest sea, but today, on these choppy waves, it will feel like it goes on for days.

Before I left Ela's hut, I sat on her bed, held very still, and let her do my hair. Her hands are the hands of a healer—hands blessed by the Divine. Pulling my hair up and away from my face, her fingers quickly divided sections of strands. She wove tiny ivory beads into a fan of small braids that met at the crown of my head.

"The beads stand out like stars in a night sky," she said, smiling at the product of her work.

Now, out here on the water, I let my own fingers trace the beads in my hair. They are so similar to the beads that are strung on either side of my ivory pendant—the symbol of the Bosha clan I inherited from my mother.

Will my own daughter one day wear a pendant of bone, as I did when I was a girl?

I glance at the coastline. Short, stunted trees dot the cliffs, thinned out by the cold wind that even here, south of the mountains, begins to sting my cheeks. I think of Kol, somewhere on the other side of those mountains, and my head swims again. This time I cannot blame the movement of the boat or the light reflecting on the sea.

This time I can blame only my nerves.

Where are you at this moment? I wonder. *Are you out in the meadow—the meadow that inspired the design on my tunic? Will you recognize your meadow when you see these clothes?*

In front of me in the canoe sits my sister Seeri. Like me, she wears ornate clothes, and her hair is carefully styled, but on her, these things look less out of place. From her clothes to her hair to her easy smile, Seeri is so effortlessly charming. So different from me. But then, she's not the oldest girl. She didn't have to take on as much responsibility when our mother died.

But I don't begrudge Seeri her lack of responsibility or envy her charm. I'm happy for her, just as I know she's happy for me. This visit to the Manu camp will change both our lives.

This trip is so different from the first I made to Kol's camp, when I wore my simple hunting parka, the parka that had once belonged to my mother. When my brother, my sister, and I each paddled, sharing the work in one canoe. For this trip, with its more formal purpose, rowers have been employed—two to paddle this boat, and two to paddle the other. The second boat carries my brother Chev, High Elder of our clan, and my twelve-year-old sister, Lees. Her clothes are plain—this trip is not for her—but at least she is coming along. Chev had planned at first to leave her home, but she had pleaded and cried and pleaded some more, until he'd given in.

"How can you keep me away when my sisters are becoming betrothed?" she'd whined, and he'd acquiesced. He'd admitted that this visit was important enough for all of us to attend.

True enough, but I suspect Lees has another motive. By coming along on this trip, she will get to see the boy she hopes one day will be her own betrothed—Kol's youngest brother, Roon.

The spray from the waves grows colder as we press farther and farther north, and I look back over my shoulder at the boat that carries Chev and Lees, a few oar strokes behind. Chev's head is down, leaning into the wind, but Lees's eyes are raised, fixed on the ice-capped mountains that rise ahead of us, her lips curled into a smile, oblivious to the knife within the wind.

Or perhaps welcoming it, as it signals that we are drawing closer to our destination.

I wish I could welcome it, too. I wish I could welcome the cold and the wind, and all the other small signs that announce that I will soon see the Manu. A part of me does welcome it. Of course I'm anxious to see Kol's clan—to see Kol's family—but I am not anxious to be seen. I know that one glance at me will reveal my intentions, and I shrink at the thought of my private hopes displayed so publicly.

He already knows, I tell myself. *It's no secret how you feel.* And though I know this is true, it feels much more like a secret when it's whispered between a boy and a girl lying in the grass.

This will be much more public. Everyone will know my desires. I will have no secrets left.

As the shoreline bends to the west, the coast changes. Tree-dotted cliffs transform into bare bluffs of rock. Farther ahead, waterfalls of ice—blue in the bright sunlight—spill into the sea.

The sun is almost directly overhead—our shadows are tucked up tightly beneath us, the shining water seeming to give its own light—when the Manu camp comes into view. The southern point of the bay, an ominous mass of rocks and ice, passes to our right, and we leave the open water behind as we enter the shallows. The oars beat in unison, suddenly so much faster than they've beaten all day, or so it seems. My heart quickens, too. Tiny silver fish race by in the sun-heated water just beneath the surface, and I feel their wriggling motion in the pit of my stomach.

People stand at the shore, watching us come. There are only two. We draw closer, and I recognize Kol's brother Roon and his mother.

Our boat comes into shore first, and Roon hurries to the side of the canoe to offer a hand to Seeri. As he helps her step out, the boat pitches hard from left to right, and I grab the sides. The rower at the front—Evet, an elder of our clan who has known me all my life—jumps into the water and quickly offers his hand. I smile, taking hold of his outstretched arm with both hands as I steady myself and the rocking boat. "You're fine," he whispers. His wife, Niki, the rower at the rear, is suddenly beside me, holding the boat still to allow me to step out.

My face flushes with heat. I can usually trust my own legs to hold me up, my own feet to find steady ground beneath me. *What is it about this day—this moment—that makes me so unsure?*

As I grab my spear and climb up onto shore, my eyes meet the eyes of Kol's mother, Mala, and I know the answer to my question. The edges of her face soften when her gaze falls on me. She reaches out her hand, and I take it, expecting her to haul me up the steep bank. Instead, she pulls me into an embrace.

My body goes stiff in her arms. When was the last time a woman—not a girl—held me in this way? Was it my own mother? No, it was Ela's mother, right before she died, too, a year after mine.

"Kol told me about the battle in your camp, and how strong you were," Mala says against my ear. Her breath is warm, and the tension in my shoulders melts a bit as I slump ever so slightly against her. "He told me how you'd faced injury so bravely, how you'd tried to save Lo." Goose bumps rise on my arms and at the back of my neck. "I'm proud of you, Mya, and I'm so glad you're safe."

A memory shivers across my skin. A memory of my mother's voice. She is saying, "I'm proud of you," as she draws me into her arms.

Kol's mother pulls back, holding me at arm's length. Her eyes sweep over me, taking in the patterned tunic, the crisp newness of my pants, gliding over my face to linger on the beads in my hair. Her lips soften, smooth into a smile. Her eyes move to mine, and they touch something at my core.

I know she sees right into me, to the meaning of everything on the surface, to the secret in my heart. Not just that I'm here to be betrothed, but that I *want* to be betrothed. That I want to be betrothed to her son. She looks at me and I am known. More known than I've been in so long.

I lean away, just far enough that she loses her grip on my arms, and I drop my eyes. Kol's mother has seen into me, to a place I'm not ready to show. Not to her. Maybe not even to Kol.

Not yet.

Anger flares up in me like a flame—anger at myself for my selfishness. For my unwillingness to share myself. Kol gave me everything. He wanted me. He gave me the security and confidence of knowing I was wanted.

And I gave so little back.

But I've resolved to change that. I told Kol I trust him, and I do. And I want more. I want trust and everything else.

Beyond Kol's mother's shoulder, the path that leads to the camp is empty. I hear no shouts of greeting, no feet hurrying down the trail.

"They're hunting," Mala says. I notice all at once that my brother and sisters are behind me. Chev has just asked about Arem, Kol's father. "They left early this morning, and we're now past midday, so I'm sure they will be returning to join us soon."

Something inside me lurches sideways at the thought of this disparity—Kol out hunting, running, working with his wits and his weapons, while I stand here, expectant, dressed in these stiff, formal clothes, holding a spear like an ornament instead of a weapon.

I'm broken from my thoughts by the movement of the others up the path. Seeri gives my arm a small squeeze as she passes, and when I look into her face she beams as if a light burns inside her. I need to try to be more like her. Relaxed. Trusting. Willing to let people see that there's light and heat in me, too.

I told Kol I trusted him the day of Lo's burial, lying next

to him in the grass, his cool hand on my back, his warm lips on mine. That memory never leaves me. If only the trust I felt that day could be just as constant.

We travel in a quick procession up the slope to the center of camp, to the meeting place. The whole clan is out, readying the midday meal, and everyone jumps to their feet, calling to us, offering us each a place to sit and food to eat.

If they notice my clothing, my hair, all the hints to my purpose in coming here, they make nothing of it. The meal is mussels and roasted lupine roots, and the portions—though far from skimpy—are not robust. My mat is far lighter than at any other meal I've shared with this clan. My thoughts go to Kol and the hunting party, as I realize the pressure they must feel.

After we eat, Lees helps Roon gather empty mats before the two of them disappear into the kitchen. *Good for them*, I think, envying the lack of notice they enjoy. Chev seems oblivious to the preference they clearly show each other. Instead, he is caught up in speaking with Mala and other elders—Mala's sister, Ama, who brought in the shellfish, and a man I believe to be the High Elder's brother.

As they talk, the clan goes back to their tasks. Two boys sit down with Urar, the Manu healer, to help him sort sharply fragrant herbs. A group of women twist stalks of stinging nettle into twine. Mala talks and smiles, smiles and talks, but her eyes move frequently to the shadows of the huts, measuring their progress along the ground. The wind shifts, from a gentle sea breeze to gusts coming down from the east, and she shivers, even though it is far from cold. Her sister, Ama, moves to sit beside her, leaning close and saying something into her ear.

When the sun is hanging over the tops of the spindly trees that stand out in silhouette across the ridge to the west, my brother finally goes quiet. Mala's mouth draws down at the corners. Her eyes have darkened.

"We'll go and look for them," my brother says. "They do not know that we are here, so they take their time. We will go call them home, and help them bring in the kill."

"I should come to lead the way," Kol's mother says, turning in the place where she sits on a large stone beside the unlit hearth, looking over her shoulder toward the meadow as if she might have heard something. I look up too, but the only new sound is the call of geese passing overhead. There is nothing new to see but the even strokes of their wings.

"No need," says Chev. "You should wait here, in case they return by another route. I'm sure we remember the way into the hills since the last time we hunted with your clan."

Kol's mother falls silent. The chorus of conversation of those scattered around the meeting place goes quiet too.

How can any of us remember that hunting trip and not remember the saber-toothed cat that I killed, the cat that threatened to kill Kol? How can we think about any hunting trip between our two clans and not think of death?

We move quickly, and before the sun has brushed the tops of the trees on the ridge, Seeri, Chev, and I are ready to hike north into the meadow, then east into the hills. Lees and Roon will stay here. They are not too young to face the risks of hunting—Lees has hunted many times at home—but perhaps too young to come along on a trip such as this one, with so much uncertainty about what we might find. No one says this, of course, but everyone thinks it— probably even Lees and Roon.

I raise my hand to shield my eyes as I look back at them— Mala, Lees, and Roon—and the wind rattles the ivory beads in my hair. I had forgotten they were there. My hand moves to touch them, to trace over Ela's handiwork, and Lees lifts her hand and waves.

Roon waves too, and my mind catches on the sight of them, standing side by side. A thought leaps to me as I hurry to catch up to Seeri, who strides behind my brother up the sloping path.

Do not think of it, I tell myself. *Do not open a flap in the roof and let such a thought blow in.* And yet the thought is there.

Of the three of us—me, Seeri, and Lees—Lees is the only one who is certain to see the boy she came to see.

TWO

We take the trail we walked with Kol's parents, on that morning not long ago when the three of us arrived, uninvited, on the Manu's shore. The day we hiked to the meadow to meet Kol and his brother Pek.

The day I first saw Kol and first learned his name.

We hike in silence, except for the birds that nest in the grass, fluttering into flight as we shuffle by. When we are well away from camp the rising ground levels off, the north wind blows hard against our faces, and the tall grass mixes with wildflowers.

We've reached the meadow, and Kol is everywhere.

I imagine I see him as he was on that morning when we first arrived, the morning my heart overflowed with insult and contempt. He stood with Pek, watching us approach, and I felt his assessing gaze.

Or so I thought.

That day, I saw Kol and his whole clan as enemies—enemies of my heart and of my mind. I squint into the wind, and I see him in my memory as if he is standing there now.

How little I understood Kol that day.

Chev hesitates, looks east toward the mountains, and rolls his spear in his hand. Absentmindedly, Seeri does the same.

"Stay alert," Chev says. But we were all here that day. We all saw the cat I killed, and we all remember the danger.

We turn, following a faint track where feet have crossed into the hills. My eyes scan the sky and I notice fast-moving clouds, blowing down from beyond the snowcapped peaks in the northeast, turning the placid blue into something ominous and wild. I drop my eyes, not wanting to think what kind of sign these clouds might be. Instead, I watch our shadows move over the flowers under our feet—purple, blue, and white—and search their blooms for honeybees.

By the time we reach the gravel path that winds up into the foothills, I haven't seen a single one. Too cold, I think, as the wind swirls my hair around my shoulders.

We climb, hiking higher as the gravel underfoot turns to stone, then to slabs. The path twists as it winds around tall, jutting walls of rock. We arrive at the boulders that form a gate to the alpine meadow where we found the mammoth herd that day. Looking in, the field is as it was—windswept and lush—and the pool where the two streams meet remains wide and still. At its edge, caribou and elk graze between tall sedges.

But we find no mammoths and no hunting party.

Chev continues up the trail, and we follow without comment. I do not always like to let my brother lead—in fact, I rarely do—but today I'm happy to lag behind. I dread each new step forward, not knowing what might be found around each turn.

I can think of many things that might detain a hunting party. None of them are good.

We climb higher for a while, but then the path turns down, descending to a pass into a narrow canyon—a canyon surrounded on all sides by tall crags of steeply rising rock. The walls soar so high, and the sun in the west sits so low, a blanket of shadow covers the canyon floor. Standing above on the sunlit pass, looking down into the walled canyon, it takes a moment for my eyes to adjust to the contrast. Slowly, shapes separate from shadows, and I recognize what I see.

Inside the canyon, their backs to the towers of stone, stand the members of the hunting party—Arem, Pek . . . Kol. And between the three of them and us, blocking their escape to the pass, stands a herd of mammoths. They hold still, as still as the rocks that rise behind the hunters.

I count ten mammoths in all.

Our vantage point is lit by the sideways beams of the

evening sun, stretching our shadows toward the canyon like the fingers of a reaching hand. A hand reaching through the pass that forms the only route of retreat—the only way of escape. The mammoths are all attentive, all threatening, all waiting expectantly for the quick move, the sudden sound, the provocation that will send them surging forward to crush the cornered hunters.

The fingers of our shadows disappear into the gloomy light on the canyon floor, and I wonder if Kol and the others even know we're here. I don't dare call Kol's name or even raise an arm to attract his eye. Seeri and Chev hover beside me, as motionless as the mammoths.

Six humans, ten beasts. Sixteen hearts beating. And yet the only motion is overhead. The clouds race by, and a buzzard, anticipating, circles high in the sky.

The danger of Kol's situation sets a wide distance between us, so that he feels remote and far off, though in reality he is close enough that I can see his face clearly. The three of them are framed in light above the shade as if they wade in murky water. I notice the angle of Kol's body, one shoulder pointing in the direction of the pass, ready to block his brother Pek, just a few paces to his right, from an advancing mammoth.

What good could that possibly do? What help could flesh and bones offer against a charging mammoth?

My foot slides as I shift my weight forward. A stone rolls

out from beneath my heel and skitters along the gravel of the pass, sending small pebbles tumbling over a steep drop to my right. A long moment of silence is followed by the rattle of rocks against rock far below. The sound echoes against the canyon walls.

I hold my breath. A dark shape traces across the ground—the slanted shadow of the circling bird. He is expectant, ready, as we all are. I listen as the pebbles fall, each one a voice calling *No! No! No!*

And then the voices hush. Nothing else stirs. The mammoths hold their places like silent sentries.

The shadow of the bird sweeps across me, and I see Kol move.

His head tips back, ever so slightly, and he raises his eyes.

He sees me. I am revealed to him. Here, in this moment of held breath, of balance between life and death. I stand in the sharp light of the sun's clarifying rays, in my ornate tunic, my stiff, new pants, my dark braids woven with ivory beads.

He sees me, and I am known to him.

My heartbeat trips on the thought, but before it can tumble out of control, something in Kol's gaze catches me and sets me right again.

It's not that he smiles, though he does smile. But it's more than that. Something passes over his face—the opposite of the wildness of the fast-moving clouds and the ominous shade cast by the bird. Something like peace passes over his face, where there was nothing but wariness there before.

And that peace, just for a moment, comes back to me. For just a moment, it crowds out dread and fear.

I shudder. *What would be worse?* I ask myself. *We've seen each other, and we've understood. Would it have been better to have never been seen at all?*

As the sun drops lower and lower behind us, the wait—this painful, dread-laden wait—goes on. The darkness on the canyon floor deepens. Perception shifts. My eyes become unsure. *Is that movement? Yes, yes.* Pek, closest to the pass, has slid, almost imperceptibly, nearer. A step. A step. He comes closer, his feet pressing down softly on the gravel beneath them, his body rising higher, out of the shade and into the slanting light.

He is almost in the pass. If he were to run, he might make it out before they had him under their feet.

My gaze floats over the mammoths. There is movement there, too—the swish of a tail, the flick of an ear. A huge dark head tilts sideways, and an eye turns toward Pek before returning to the two gray shapes against the gray rock wall—Kol and his father.

At the back of the herd—closer to the pass, closer to Pek—a trunk rises. Then another. The sun catches two bright white tusks tilted toward the sky. Two spears in the light. The other mammoths listen, their ears alert. *Will there be a signal? Is this the moment?*

The tusks dip back into shadow. *Not yet*, the mammoth seems to say. *But stay vigilant.*

When my focus returns to Kol, he has moved.

He's come closer.

Cloaked in that moment of unbearable frailty, he took a chance. When the slightest shift might have sent the balance crashing into pieces, he let fear and danger serve him as a distraction.

Like Pek, he has reached the bottom slope of the pass. He's climbed high enough that his shoulders are now in the sunlight, his dark eyes squinting over a restless, tense smile—a smile sprung from the satisfaction of having achieved this small victory. He has gained a degree of safety, and yet the posture of the mammoths has not changed. Not yet.

But as I watch, changes take shape. Slowly, slowly. There are subtle shifts—the angle of a broad back, the turn of a head, the stomp of a foot.

Movement—small but meaningful movement—ripples across the herd. A few feet shuffle under the strain. Not a strain of fatigue, but of impatience—an impatience born out of inaction. Mammoths are active. Though these stand still, they are full of action. Ponderous, potential action.

My eyes shift to Kol's face. If a moment ago he felt a bit of satisfaction at his progress, that satisfaction is already gone. His teeth clench. His gaze presses on his father, and his hand rises, as he slowly, carefully, fans the air in a circle in front of his chest, bidding his father to come.

Come on, I think. *Follow your sons. Move toward the pass.*

He takes the first step, his first tenuous step toward escape. A slow slide of his foot.

I do not raise my eyes to the clouds. I do not look for the shadow of the buzzard. I do not need to. I know.

Everything—on the ground, in the air, far away beyond the camp in the bay—everything is still. The clouds could not possibly roll, the waves on the sea could not possibly stir while Kol's father edges his foot toward the pass. The sun does not sink. The wind does not blow. I do not breathe.

But then one mammoth takes a step—a hurried, urgent step forward—and motion returns. The clouds shiver in the sky, the buzzard swoops low, diving into the canyon, and I draw a deep breath. One mammoth tramples the rock beneath his feet, and nine mammoths watch him, the hides of their backs twitching.

My eyes go to Kol's father. He knows that the rules have changed. Motion has broken through, and he will make it his tool. In short even steps, he advances. He is steady, unwavering, full of authority. The mammoth whose feet had shown such impatience a moment ago reverts to his rigid posture. All eyes—ours and theirs—fix on Arem as he takes certain, measured strides.

The soft hides of his boots crush the gravel underfoot,

and a low whisper of assent rises from the ground. *Yes, yes, yes.* Twilight sends the shade of the canyon ever higher up the walls, but he is rising, too. Soon he has climbed to the foot of the gravel pass. Thin streaks of evening sun touch the top of his head, glowing blue in his black hair. He walks with his back to us—keeping his eyes on the mammoths as he draws away from them and moves closer to his sons—but as he climbs he throws a quick glance over his shoulder and meets Kol's eyes.

And something happens.

Beyond Arem, down in the canyon, the mammoth at the front of the herd lifts his tusks, spreads his ears, and lunges forward. A burst of sound flies from his raised trunk.

Stillness reigns as the echo grows and fades. And then everything moves.

Everything moves.

And everything . . .

Everything . . .

Everything changes.

THREE

The stillness dissolves like a snowflake on water.

As one, the mammoths turn and rush toward us, their feet carrying massive and twitching bodies over the ground. Chev, Seeri, and I clamber over the jagged boulders that border the pass, struggling to get out of the way.

As I climb higher I look behind me, my eyes sweeping the lower end of the pass. Pek scrambles onto the slabs opposite me, out of danger. Farther below I see Kol, and behind him—not far, maybe an arm's length away—his father.

At the foot of the pass, shadows ripple like water. Everything—the ground, the sky, the sun itself—trembles with the motion of the herd.

Kol does not slow, but he turns. I see him reach back, his hand open for his father. He expects him to take his hand.

I watch. He is there. He is running right behind Kol.

A sound knifes through me—a violent breaking of rocks.

I see Kol, his hand out, his head raised as he shouts to his father—and then the place he stands is washed out by a swiftly flowing current of broad backs and tusks and raised trunks. The herd runs by like a river, raging and churning after a storm.

And then the river runs dry. The mammoths are gone. Only the whisper of falling dust remains.

From my perch above the pass, movement catches my eye. A hand slides out from under deep shadows and broken rocks—Kol's hand. The same hand I'd seen him stretching out behind him toward his father.

He pulls himself up, and all I see of him is the top of his head. Even through the gloomy shade, I see his hair turning crimson as it fills with blood. I hear a voice call out his name—my own voice. I hurry down over the rocks, but before I can reach him, he's on his feet, stumbling forward.

He moves only three steps before he drops to the ground. I think he must have collapsed—light-headed from blood loss, or maybe something worse. I rush to him, and when I reach his side—when I drop to my knees at the spot where he fell—I realize that things are much worse.

Much, much worse.

Bright red blood runs in the gray dust. It pools, dark and thick, in a rut, cut into the ground beside a long, shallow ditch.

And in that shallow ditch at the edge of the pass, beside

a trampled and shattered spear, lies a trampled and shattered body.

The body of Arem, the High Elder of the Manu.

The body of Kol's father.

Kol leans over him, takes his head in his hands, and tries to raise him up. Words tumble from his lips. "Don't worry. Don't worry. I'll take care of you. I'll take care of you." Cradling his head, he pulls him to his chest. Blood flows like water over Kol's hands. If he notices, he doesn't let it show.

He rocks his father against his chest, and I realize he has no hope of saving him, and he knows it. He knows it is too late. His only hope now is to comfort his father as he goes.

He eases himself onto the ground beside the place where his father lies, still cradling him in his arms. For a short time, both chests heave, both men gulp in air. Both backs stiffen against the hard, cold ground.

But then Arem's hands slide from the places where they cling to Kol, his arms dropping into the dirt. His back softens and his chest stills.

But not Kol's. Kol's chest heaves as he lets the lifeless body of his father slide from his arms. He does not get up, but stays where he is, stretched out beside his father. He is in no hurry to leave his father's side. Instead, he lays his own head on his father's chest, and weeps.

Time passes, but the sun remains, squatting on the horizon. Its rays hug the ground, drawing the shadows of mountains from the smallest of rocks. This is the time of year when the sun dips below the horizon only in the middle of each night, when the Divine leaves the Land Above the Sky to feed its fire in preparation for its next trek into day.

I stand with Chev and Seeri, at least twenty paces from Kol, his brother, and his father. The body of his father. They've asked us to wait, to give them time.

So we wait.

As the sun sinks, its warmth flees, and a torrent of cold sweeps over the ground. It seeps through my tunic. Without the protection of the parka I would normally wear on a hunt, it soaks right into my bones. My teeth clench but still they chatter, rattling in my head.

The sun is half hidden behind the western hills when Kol and his brother get to their feet and remove their parkas. A shiver runs through me as I watch Kol, stripped from the waist up, crouch and slide his parka under his father's shoulders. Pek slides his own under his hips. When they tie the sleeves, they have fashioned a sling to carry the body home. Before they lift it, Kol runs both hands through his hair, shaking his head as if to clear it. Drops of blood splatter his bare chest, and his hands, still stained with his father's blood, are wet again, this time with his own.

At last, he turns toward me. His eyes are red-rimmed and damp. "Could you help me?" he asks.

Biting my bottom lip to hold in a sob, I nod. "Of course."

Kol squats at my feet and lets me look at the gash on the top of his head. Blood cakes his hair into clumps, but using water from my own waterskin, I rinse it away, careful not to let any drip onto his bare skin. It takes almost all the water I have before I can see the cut in his scalp. "It's not bad," I say. I let out a deep breath, relieved to see that this injury shouldn't need any special care. "The cut's a bit jagged but not long—maybe the length of my thumb. And not deep."

"Thank you," Kol says, but the words fracture and become a groan as he straightens to his feet. His left knee buckles, and he clutches my arm and holds on to keep from falling.

Looking down at his leg, I notice blood running from the hem of his pant leg and over his boot. Dirt mixes with it, forming a sticky dark mud. "Let me look at your leg," I say, but Kol steps away.

"It's fine."

"Kol—"

"There's no time right now. When we get back to camp I'll look at it—I'll let Urar look at it—but there's not enough time to worry about that now."

I want to argue, but I don't. He's right. Especially about

Urar. Kol needs a healer, and the sooner we return to camp, the better. Kol and Pek need to get back into parkas. The cold air stirs and I notice Kol is trembling. Seeri and Pek stand huddled together, her arms around him for warmth.

"Can I help carry him?" my brother asks. He stands away from us, closer to the body. His voice sounds strange, like I'd almost forgotten he was here. Chev usually doesn't stay quiet for so long, but I can tell by the look on his face that he isn't sure what to say.

"No, but thank you," Kol says. "Pek and I can manage."

The two brothers lift their father's body in the makeshift sling, and Kol nods for us to follow. Like this, they lead us out of the foothills. We walk in single file, Kol and Pek carrying their father's body at the head of the line. Arem's legs hang down, but his head is wrapped in the hood of Kol's parka. The laces are pulled tight and wound around Kol's hand in such a way that his father's head is supported by the sling.

I think of Kol attending to this detail, tying the laces beneath his father's chin, and my throat closes so tight, I can't swallow.

We reach the Manu camp after the sun has fully set and the sky is the blue-black of a summer night. Most of the clan is still awake, shadows huddled in the meeting place with Mala, but while we are still too far away to be clearly seen, she hurries to Kol and Pek's side. It's too dark to see her face, but I know when I hear the cry come from her throat that she knows what Kol and Pek carry. She knows her husband is dead.

The body is placed in the center of the meeting place, and everyone from Kol's clan crowds around. The fire burning in the central hearth had nearly gone out, but Urar adds kindling to help it grow. Kol's uncle carries wood out from the kitchen—this fire will burn throughout the night. Pek emerges from his family's hut wrapped in a clean parka and heads right to Seeri's side. Chev joins Lees and Roon among the mourners. I find myself alone, listening and watching from the edge of things. I hear Pek, Chev, Seeri—their voices overlap as questions swirl through the crowd. It's only when he touches my hand that I realize Kol is not with them.

"I don't want to bother Urar," Kol says. My hand burns where he touches me, though his fingers are cold. He hasn't pulled on a parka yet, and I notice the hairs on his neck standing up in the cold light from the fire. His breath mists the air. Through the din of voices, the healer's voice stands out. He's offering a chanted prayer over the body. Kol's icy fingers wrap around my hand and tug me toward him. "There's not much light, but could you come look at my knee? If you could clean the wound—"

"Yes," I say.

He drops his eyes, and I feel like there's something else he wants to say, but he doesn't. He pushes through the bear hide that drapes across the doorway to his hut, pulling me in behind him.

FOUR

He's right. There's not much light. An open vent in the wall that faces the fire lets in a shimmer of gold that dances across the hides that form the ceiling. In the center of the room, a wick of moss burns in a shallow stone lamp filled with seal oil.

The light from the flame explores Kol's skin, illuminating first the lines of his stomach, then the curve of his upper arms. "Are you warm enough?" I ask, all at once aware of my eyes tracing the light's path across his body.

"I will be," he says, reaching for a parka that hangs from a notch in the central post. Immediately I recognize it.

"That's the one I made for you."

"From the cat you killed when you saved me."

"Kol . . ." Shame burns in my cheeks. How many times have I let myself feel superior because I killed the cat that threatened Kol? As if I'd shown him some great courtesy.

"Anyone would have done that," I say. "You would have done it for me."

"I would have," he answers. "I wish I had."

Outside, a drumbeat starts. A chorus of voices takes up a low, dark melody. The whole Manu clan is singing a song of mourning. "You should be out there—"

"I know. I will be," Kol says, sliding his arms into the sleeves and wrapping the cat's warm fur around him. He drops onto a pile of pelts that make up one of the beds. "But I need your help first. I need to get the pieces out—"

His voice cuts off, replaced by a sharp inhale of breath as he tugs his ruined left pant leg up over his knee, revealing wide gashes pocked and wedged with fragments of broken rock. Clotted blood—not dry but thick and moist—covers everything like a layer of red algae.

"This . . . this . . . You need your healer. This is too much for me."

"It's all right. I'll ask Urar to look at it in the morning. But right now, I just need someone to clean it."

He exhales a long sigh, rolling back onto the bed. His eyes squeeze shut as he sucks in breath through his teeth, then lets it roll out as a groan. "I can't interrupt Urar right now," he says, his voice tight with pain. "And I can't let my mother see this. She's been through too much. My father . . ."

That's all he gets out before his voice breaks.

"Kol," I say. "I'll clean this. Of course I will."

I get up, searching in the dark for the tools I'll need. I find a waterskin on a hook by the door. Kol tells me to look in his pack for a soft, thin piece of well-worked hide to use to wipe away the blood. I work slowly, and as I do, Kol's body relaxes. His limbs stretch, uncoiling, tension dissolving. His eyes close.

"It's not over yet," I say, easing my knife from my belt. "I need to pick the small pieces out with this."

"I've been through worse before. When Urar and Ela cleaned the wounds from that saber-toothed cat. Remember?"

"I could never forget that," I say. I leave out that I thought he would die that day.

"Besides, I know you won't hurt me."

But I will hurt him. Though I begin to suspect that Kol won't mind, because he'd rather lie here and have me dig gravel from his knee with a sharp knife than join the mourners outside. Not because he didn't love his father, but because he did.

I know how he feels. I understand the desire to draw away from people when you've lost someone, to refuse to let anyone help.

Even with the lamp set right next to his leg, it's difficult to see the gashes. They split the skin across his knee, gaping open with the slightest movement. In places, the skin stretches and swells around bits of rock wedged into the wounds. These must come out.

I slide the tip of my knife into the first cut, and Kol stiffens. Blood pours around the blade. Twisting it no more than I must, I work a chunk of rock about the size of a child's tooth out from under his skin. His fingers dig into my shoulder, but he doesn't make a sound.

"That was the first one—"

"I'm fine—"

"There are several more—"

"I'll be all right. I appreciate your concern, but I'll be fine." He quiets, and I think he may be listening to the voices of the singers coming from the other side of the wall. The drum continues, joined by a rattle made of beads attached to a wooden rod, but I don't hear the flute that Kol's brother plays.

"Is Kesh not here?"

"He's at the Bosha camp, with Shava and her mother."

"So he doesn't know yet."

"I'll go in the morning and tell him," he says.

I work another piece of stone loose, and Kol winces. The song ends and another one begins. This one is sung by a single female voice.

"That's my mother," Kol says. He lets his eyes fall closed and turns his head toward the wall, though I'm not sure if he is turning toward the sound or turning away from me. I set to work on the next piece of stone. It comes out quickly—a tiny bead—almost like the beads of ivory in my hair. I start on the next one, but it's wedged more deeply in Kol's flesh. So much blood flows from the wound, it's impossible to see. I blot his skin. I can feel the fragment of rock move beneath my fingertips. Gently, I work it free.

"When my own father died," I say, speaking in a quiet voice that I hope will soothe him, "I was almost twelve years old. Old enough to know what death was. To understand the permanence of it," I say. I pause, looking for clues from Kol as to how he feels about me talking like this. He doesn't answer, so I go on. "I loved my father, but I was fortunate. I have an older brother. Chev slid easily into the father role in my life. He looked after me in the same way my father always had. He still does."

Kol's mother's voice rises as the words of the song plead with the Divine to show favor to the one who died, to give him a comfortable hut beside a hunting ground rich with game. The melody is so sad, I feel the weight of Mala's grief pressing down on my chest. My hands still.

The song ends, and Kol turns toward me. The light of the lamp catches in his eyes, but they stay dim and cold.

"But when my mother died," I say, swallowing hard, forcing myself to continue, "that was different. I felt like I'd died, too. I didn't feel sad. I felt empty. And I didn't want anyone to try to change that. I wanted the emptiness.

I cherished it like it was something solid. It was proof that she had been there. I wanted the pain so I wouldn't forget."

Another song begins, this one in unison like the first. "To your land, to your land," the chorus repeats. "Bring him safely to your land." I think I hear the voices of Chev and Seeri joining in.

Kol sits up and raises my hand to his lips. His fingers are still cold, but his mouth against my skin is warm. "I'm sorry for what happened to your mother—"

"That's not why I'm telling you this. I'm telling you this because I don't want you to do what I did. I shut everyone out after my mother died. Partly because I needed to be strong for my sisters. Partly because I didn't want to share even the smallest piece of my grief with anyone else—I wanted to keep it all to myself. But shutting all that pain inside let it eat away at me. It chewed at my heart until I felt like my heart was gone."

Kol raises his eyes to meet mine. "But your heart isn't gone."

My breath catches in my throat. "No, it's not. But it almost was. Don't let that happen to you. Don't hold yourself apart from the people who love you. The people you love."

There's an emptiness in Kol's eyes, and I know I'm right. I know he's trying to protect that emptiness. But then he lets his lids fall shut. When he opens them, the corners of his mouth curl up just a tiny bit. Not a smile, but acceptance. "You're right." He lies back down. "They need me, and I need them, too. Just for a little while tonight, I think I needed you more."

"I need you, too," I say. I bite back the words I want to say. Tonight is not the right night.

Later, with his wound dressed with moss and wrapped in another supple hide, hidden from his mother's view behind clean pants, Kol emerges from the hut and joins his clan. I hang back, aware that people might think the wrong thing if they were to see me come out with him. Everyone calls his name when he appears—offering him a place to sit near the fire, bringing him a mat of food—but no one asks why he stayed away. They are just happy to have him with them now.

"The High Elder's son," I hear a voice say.

"The future High Elder," another answers.

As these words repeat in my mind, the room grows suddenly smaller and darker. *The future High Elder.* I knew that, of course. I've always known that Kol would become the High Elder when his father died. But despite that knowledge, it hadn't entered my thoughts today.

Not until this moment.

I step out of Kol's family's hut. The fire has grown. Its light spreads to the edge of the meeting place, throwing tall shadows on the walls of the circled huts. Kol turns toward me, and his face is illuminated. He doesn't see me, though. He's accepting condolences from the members of his clan.

I watch him—Kol, my future betrothed. And I remind myself that I'm ready. I'm ready to be betrothed. Even to the new High Elder of the Manu.

I linger at the edge of the crowd, listening to song after song until the sun begins to rise, but then I say good night to Kol and his whole family and go to bed. The music continues, though, and I don't sleep well. When finally the light coming through the roof vent glows along the walls and I know the sun is well into the sky, I let myself get up.

I leave my brother and sisters asleep in the hut—they all came to bed after me—and step out into the cool morning quiet of Kol's camp. People will sleep late today. So many songs were sung, so many stories were told. Stories of Arem, and all he had done on behalf of the clan. Stories of his hunting skills. Stories of his talent for working stone into tools.

Stories of how he'd trained a fine son to take his place as High Elder.

This morning the camp is silent, except for the waves in the bay. Called by the sound of the sea rushing to the sand, I follow the trail from the ring of huts to the beach.

As I draw closer—the cold gray surface reflecting clouds of soft gold—I catch the sound of voices. At the water's edge, Mala's sister, Ama, and her sons are prepping the boats to fish. They see me. Their heads lift in turn. Someone has pointed me out.

"Mya!" Ama waves to me, and I find myself hurrying forward to greet her. She stands in ankle-deep water loading a boat, but she wades onto shore as I reach the sand. "You're up early," she says.

Kol's cousins wind rope and fold nets, stacking them onto the deck of a double kayak that floats in the shallow waves of low tide. Ama stands with a spear in her left hand and a pack propped against her knee. The hide of the pack is almost black from the many layers of oil rubbed in to protect it from water. Her tunic has the same dark sheen. "I came to help," I say, and the words surprise me more than they seem to surprise her.

Ama's eyes sweep over my clothing—I'm still dressed in my betrothal clothes, not really best for fishing—but still she smiles. "Have you ever hunted with these?" She unties something like a sash from around her waist—a strip of hide worked thin and supple, about as wide as her palm and about as long as her arm. She hands it to me, then stoops to pull large chunks of walrus ivory out of her pack.

"A sling?" I ask.

"Yes." She smiles like my mother used to when I correctly identified an edible plant. "So you've used one before?"

"I've used one, yes. But not exactly like this." I take the

strip of hide from her hand. It's soft and lightweight, like the hides used to wrap infants in summer. The ivory pieces are scuffed and marked—these have brought in their share of game. "I've used something similar," I say. "But the ones we use are woven from strips of sinew to make a sort of flexible basket with a long tail. We use them to hurl rocks, not chunks of ivory—"

"You use them on land?"

I nod. "To hunt grouse," I say.

"Ah, yes. We hunt grouse here, too. But these are for seabirds, so for these we use walrus ivory."

Of course, I think. *A weapon for the sea should come from the sea.* The Spirits know their own.

Ama nods at the sling in my hand. "But you've used this type of weapon to hunt birds?"

"I have—"

"Good. Then I have a hunting partner."

With a quick flash of a smile, she picks up the pack and moves to prep a second double kayak with the efficiency of someone who lives more on the sea than on the land. "Tie that sling around your own waist. I have another one for me." She turns away briefly to instruct her boys, but they move even before she speaks; they are so skilled at the task of launching out to fish.

"I know not to hunt out at sea alone," she says. "It's too dangerous without a partner, even for me, and I can't take

the boys away from their fishing. I would've asked someone, but . . . not today. Not on a day like today." Her voice
falters, and she presses her lips between her teeth. She turns
her shoulders away from me, letting her eyes trace the horizon, and when she turns back again, her composure has
returned. "You were sent by the Divine this morning, I
think," she says, forcing her mouth into a thin smile. "You
and I will bring in good food and good blessings to this clan
on this day. The Divine brought you here to help me."

Could this be true? I wonder. *Could it be the Divine's will
that I am here with Ama this morning, to bring some good to Kol's
clan?*

To the clan that will soon be my own clan?

I say nothing, but I follow Ama to the boat. She offers
me the rear seat. "We're heading out to a rocky island outside the mouth of the bay. A colony of black shags nests
there every summer—hundreds of them. Just to the south
beyond the point."

Once we are out on the water, my head clears of every
thought that doesn't concern action. I focus on the movement of my paddle. I look ahead to the hunt, rehearsing in
my mind the motion of my arm as I swing the sling, the feel
of my fingers as I release it at just the right moment.

Two long rocky ridges enclose the bay like two cupped
hands. As we paddle out we hug the ridge to our left—the
one that forms the southeast boundary. Beyond it lies the

open sea. I look up at the rocky cliff—gray stone worked smooth by the wind, crisscrossed by floes of ice—and I notice people walking high up along the crest. They carry tools—long poles and axes—tools for digging a grave. My eyes drift over the figures, and among them I recognize Kol's brothers Roon and Pek. At the front I see Kol, walking alongside Urar.

I think of the gashes across Kol's knee. I hope he showed them to Urar as he planned, and that the healer has treated them and offered chanted prayers.

The tide is coming back in, and the crash of the waves against this cliff creates a steady rhythm that ripples through me. My hair stirs on my shoulders. The wind swirls across the fur of my tunic.

Ama digs harder and faster at the water, and I match her strokes, pushing the kayak farther out to sea and leaving Kol behind.

For the first time since Arem died, I don't see his bleeding body when I let my eyes fall closed. Instead, I see a cloud of birds with broad black wings—the game I will help bring in for Kol's extended family. When I open my eyes again, Ama is slowing. We pull within sight of a flat, bare rock that wriggles with black shapes like a giant hill of ants. These are the birds we've come to hunt. Before we draw close enough for them to sense our presence, Ama twists in her seat, signaling me to stop.

"You've never hunted shags?" she asks.

I shake my head, squinting against the icy spray that pricks at my cheeks and eyes.

"They're nice big birds—lots of meat on each one—and this island is covered with them. Since they're nesting, we can bring the boat right up on the beach. They won't fly away. But many will take off and hover over our heads. Those will be our targets." She swivels in her seat and points with the paddle to the island's western shore, where the rocky surface crumbles into a pebbly beach. I follow her lead, paddling until the water beneath us is shallow enough to allow us to jump out. My sealskin boots keep my skin dry, but still, the cold cuts through to my feet and ankles. The bright knife it sends to my mind clears out all my lingering, murky thoughts, and I'm grateful for it. Dragging the kayak ashore, we gather up our supplies. Ama and I each untie the slings wrapped at our waists. She pulls six heavy chunks of ivory from her pack and hands me three.

Before us, dotting the ground from one edge of the island to the other, are rows and rows of birds squatting on mound-like nests. As we approach, they honk and squawk, and those closest to us take off. Just as Ama promised, though, they don't fly away; they won't desert their chicks.

They care for their offspring, and it will be their undoing.

I block these thoughts from my mind. To a hunter, these

birds are not individuals. They are game. Game that live in relationship with the clans, just as the Divine ordained it.

The game give their lives so that we can live. And in return for feeding our children, the Divine gives them food for their own children to eat. This is the relationship between the clans, the game, and the Divine. It has always been this way, since the Divine made the first woman, and told her to reach her hand into the sea for the first fish. And from the bones of the first fish, she made the first spear point to shoot the first deer as it grazed on the grass the Divine had given it. This was the plan of life the Divine gave to the first woman, and it has held the world in balance ever since.

Ama loads her sling as I stand back, studying her. "Watch me once first, all right?" she says, though she doesn't even turn toward me to check if I'm listening. All her attention is on the birds and on the weight of the chunk of ivory in her sling. Her wrist flexes, the sling bobs up and down, and then it's spinning over her head.

Above us, the shags fill the sky like a cloud of gnats over the grassland when the air first warms in the spring. They are so thick, their broad wings overlap like layers of clouds. Their black bodies block the glare of the sharply angled rays of the rising sun.

The sling whips at the end of Ama's arm, sailing over her head, whirring with a loud *whoosh . . . whoosh . . . whoosh . . .*

as it cuts through the air near my ear. Then her hand twists and she releases one end of the sling. The ivory stone flies.

The birds rise up, as if they float on an unseen wave of air. All but one. One bird falls, soundless except for the thud of his body on the ground. Ama hurries to him. With one jab of her spear through his neck, she is sure he is dead.

When she returns with the bird and the retrieved piece of ivory, a wide smile spreads across her face. "You are very good luck, I see. Now it's your turn."

I push down all the thoughts that try to float up—that I am not good luck, that her kill had nothing to do with luck at all, but only skill.

I take my turn, mirroring each of the steps—loading the sling, the spin, the release. I close my eyes and picture the ivory landing the strike I need. I open them just as Ama lets out a burst of sound—*Yes!*—and I hurry to her side. She stands over a huge bird, its wings spread wide across the beach, its skull broken. "Nice shot," says Ama. "Dead before he hit the ground."

A sudden rush of joy floats up and fills my head with heat.

But then Ama runs off to find the ivory, and I bend to scoop up the bird. A patch of feathers has been knocked from its head, and bright red blood oozes onto the sand. I turn my eyes away when I pick it up, keeping my gaze fixed on the surface of the sea. The sunlight swoops sideways on the waves—I'm dizzy. Vomit rises in my throat, but I swallow it back down.

The hunt continues, and though I occasionally miss, Ama lands almost every one of her throws. Retrieving the chunks of ivory proves to be the most challenging task of the morning, but by the time the net is full, we've brought down six birds. Together we lift the net and haul it to the deck of the kayak. The birds shift, a tangle of feathers, blood dripping as we carry the load across the beach. When a trickle flows out of the net and onto my hands, it brings me back to the mammoth hunt, to the sight of Kol cradling his father's bleeding head. As Ama balances the net across the kayak, satisfying herself that it won't tip into the sea, I squat at the edge of the water and wash the blood away. The sea is sharp and piercing with cold, but I hold my hands submerged until they go numb.

It's like this—with red fingers so cold they can hardly wrap around the shaft of the paddle—that I help Ama bring the boat back into shore. Kol's young cousins crowd around us. They wait patiently in the shallow water as I untie the sash of the kayak that wraps around my waist. Ama is already out of the boat, and the oldest of her sons helps her haul in the net full of birds as the younger two take my hands and help me onto shore. My legs shake beneath me and the youngest boy laughs. "That happens when you sit a long time on the cold sea." I smile, but I know better. It isn't cold or stiffness, but the memory of blood that makes it hard for me to stand.

"We'll bring in your birds with our catch," says the oldest, a boy made of long limbs and a toothy smile. He lifts his gaze from my face to the sky. "The morning meal is about to be served, and then it will be time to prepare. The burial will take place when the sun is at its peak, at the time of no shadows."

When the Divine is at the center of everything, I think. *When the Spirits of the dead rise right to her side.*

My eyes slide to the ridge that encloses the bay to the south—the place I'd seen Kol walking earlier with the tools to dig the grave. The ridge is bare now. The tide slaps a steady rhythm against the boats, like a heartbeat. A chill runs down my spine, and I hurry back up the trail alone, wondering if I might find Kol along the way.

FIVE

The scents of smoke and fish roll from the kitchen. I hear Mala's voice coming from inside, and I slow my steps, listening at the door for Kol, but I don't hear him. I don't see him in the meeting place, either, though many of the Manu have already gathered for the meal.

In my family's hut, I find Seeri alone. "There you are! They've called us to the meal. Chev and Lees are already outside." Seeri's eyes shift to the hem of my pants, dripping water onto the floor. "Were you wading?"

"I went out with Ama this morning. We brought in a kill of six seabirds."

Seeri's face pinches for a moment, like she's caught between laughing and crying. She runs her hand across her face and smiles—a slow, soft smile—and shakes her head. "You are already doing what's best for the Manu clan, already behaving like the betrothed of the clan's High Elder."

My stomach tightens at her words, and I fold myself onto the piled hides that form my bed. "Seeri," I start, my voice tentative. "Can I tell you a secret?"

She sits down across from me. The pinch returns to her face, but now it's changed. "You're my sister. You can always tell me your secrets." But her eyes are wary.

"For so long," I start, my voice carefully measured, "I couldn't forgive the Manu. I blamed them for our mother's death. I hated them. But then I met Kol and all that changed. My feelings for Kol softened my feelings for the Manu. I forgave them. I even decided I could become one of them. I could join their clan to be with Kol."

I watch Seeri stiffen at these words. We've talked this over many times in our hut back home—the way our betrothals will separate us. If I marry Kol, I will join his clan, since he will be the next High Elder of the Manu. But if I leave the Olen, then Seeri will be next in line to be High Elder, after our brother Chev. So if she marries Pek, he will have to join the Olen.

Seeri and I will separate, and so will Pek and Kol.

"But now I'm terrified. I was happy to become betrothed to Kol. I knew that one day he would be High Elder of the Manu. *One day*, but not *now*." I drop my head, and I feel the ivory beads in my hair shift. The beads Ela braided into my hair for my betrothal. "I know I'm ready to be betrothed to Kol," I say, "but I don't know if I'm ready to be betrothed to the Manu's *High Elder*. It's all happening so soon. I thought I would have lots of time before I had to be the spouse—the partner—of the leader of the clan that took our mother's life."

Someone shuffles by the door of the hut, and I worry that I can be heard outside. I feel like a traitor. For the longest time, I thought my feelings for Kol made me a traitor to the memory of my mother. Now I feel like a traitor to Kol. No matter where I place my loyalty, someone is betrayed.

I tip my head back, turning my face up to the vent overhead. The room feels small and airless.

"You have nothing to be ashamed of," Seeri says. "I'm sure I would feel the same way in your place. Pek probably feels the same about joining the Olen."

"I know, but . . . This is so hard for me to say."

"What is it?" Seeri's words are clipped. A dread has crept into her voice. "What is it you can't say? Have you changed your mind? Have you decided to refuse Kol?"

The door pulls back just a bit. A boy outside clears his throat. I jump up, hoping to see Kol, but it's Pek.

"Sorry. I don't mean to disturb you—"

"Is Kol with you?" I ask.

"He's across the bay. He went to the Bosha this morning. To give them the news and bring Kesh home."

Pek takes a step into the room, and my attention catches on the ways he's changed since yesterday. The hollows under his eyes and the sag in his shoulders. Seeri, too, even with Pek right beside her, seems dimmed by grief today. All but her eyes, which are burning with the fear that I've changed my mind about Kol.

"My mother asked me to call you to the meal," Pek says. "She won't start without you."

This courtesy of Mala's weighs on me like a heavy obligation. I'd love to stay in this hut—take my mat alone as I did the first night I visited the Manu—but that would be unacceptable. I mean something to the Manu now; I have a place in their clan, though that place is rough and unformed, like the blade of a new knife only half-carved from a piece of obsidian.

Once in the meeting place, Roon greets me with a mat of fish and arrow grass. The rich, oily scent of the fish reminds me how empty my stomach is. I haven't eaten since we arrived yesterday.

Chev, Lees, and Morsk—Chev's closest friend, who served as one of our party's rowers—are seated with Kol's mother and several other elders of his clan. When she sees me, Mala waves for me to come and sit beside her.

"I want to thank you for bringing in the game," she says as I take my place. "Ama was full of praise for you when she brought the birds to the kitchen." She reaches out her hand and places it on mine in a simple gesture of affection, but I snatch my hand away. Heat rushes up my neck. I instantly regret my reaction—it was thoughtless at best, an insult at worst—but Mala lets it go. She pats me on the shoulder. "I'm sorry. I didn't realize my hand was so cold."

"It's not. I—I was startled," I stammer. I know I should take her hand, return her gesture of friendship to make it right, but I can't. I can't let anyone mother me, not even Kol's mother.

Not yet.

As soon as the meal is over, Mala announces a meeting of the clans—all three clans—Manu, Olen, and Bosha. It's clear she's discussed this already with Chev. He's not surprised.

"Some clan business," Mala says, "that should be taken care of before the burial." I look at the sky. The sun is more than halfway up—the meeting must start soon. But then I hear voices coming from the shore. Boats have landed—Kol has returned. All at once I realize why Mala wants the clans to meet.

She wants to betroth her sons before she buries her husband.

I want to linger in the meeting place for Kol. I want to see him—I almost *need* to see him—to see that he's walking without a limp and know that his wounds are healing. But Seeri won't let me wait. The moment the mats are cleared, she's rushing me into our hut to primp.

"This meeting is not something you go to with your hair arranged by the sea breeze," Seeri says. "Sit. I'll fix it the best I can." I drop down onto my bed and she pulls out an ivory comb. She untangles a strand that hangs down my back and leans over to whisper in my ear.

"You haven't changed your mind about this betrothal, have you?" she asks.

"My feelings for Kol have not changed."

"Good," she murmurs. "Now hold still."

I hold my head upright, letting her redo a braid she's dissatisfied with. A shaft of sun pours in through the vent, and I watch motes of dust rise and fall with the small shifts in air caused by Seeri's quick fingers. It's peaceful, and my pounding heart begins to calm.

The motes of dust scatter as the hide that forms the door is swept aside and Chev strides in. For a moment, he stands in the doorway, studying me. Lees slides in so close behind him, she's in before the door can fall closed. "It's time," Chev says. There is something bubbling under his skin—a forcefulness he is struggling to keep in check. I'd like to think it's a sort of joy at the betrothal of his sisters that's stirring him up, but I can't help imagining that it's something else—a sense of what is about to happen—a sense of the expansion of the reach of his clan and his own power.

Maybe it's a bit of both.

"Bring your spear," he says, grabbing one of his own

from where it leans against a wide beam carved from the thighbone of a mammoth. "We'll be convening on the beach." He turns to look at Lees. "For privacy," he adds.

But Lees has always been stubborn. As Chev moves to the door, Lees tries to follow. "This is a private gathering of clan leaders," my brother says. "You are not invited."

"But if my sisters are to become betrothed—"

"You will be the first to hear all about it when they return." He strides out, followed by Seeri. I grab my own spear—ivory tipped, like Kol's—and absentmindedly reach for the beads in my hair. As I step through the door, I glance back over my shoulder. Lees is still on her feet. I have no doubt she intends to be at this gathering, even if she has to stay out of sight.

I walk alone to the beach—Chev and Seeri are already too far ahead for me to catch them—and I glance around, hoping to see Kol. The boats are back from the Bosha clan, but maybe he returned to his hut while I was in mine. When a male voice calls my name from over my shoulder I spin around, but it's not him. It's his brother Kesh. He walks with Shava, his betrothed from the Bosha clan.

"We're so glad you're all right," Kesh says, as Shava embraces me.

"Kol came this morning to the Bosha camp to bring us the news," Shava adds. Despite her training as a storyteller, she can't quiet the shake in her voice as she describes the moment when one brother told the other of the loss. I bite the inside of my cheek, hoping the pain will distract me from the picture her words create in my mind.

While we stand on the edge of the path, a woman with white hair pulled back in a long braid strides by. She is petite, but her head is held high. "Is that Dora?" I ask.

"She came from the Bosha camp with us," answers Shava. There's something in her tone—she speaks so low, it's almost a whisper, as if she is used to speaking about Dora in secret. "And the girl with her is Anki, her daughter."

I look up at their backs as they pass. I remember them, of course, from Lo's burial. But I also remember them from my childhood—from the days when I was a small girl and the Olen and Bosha lived as one clan. I remember Anki's envy of my closeness with Lo, and how she and her brother, Orn, seemed so pleased when our clan split and my family went away.

Now Orn lies in a grave beside Lo's—both victims of the attack they made on my family's clan—but I've been told Dora and Anki played no part in the attack. Still, as I watch them go—mother and daughter side by side—I can't control the flush of rage that rolls across my skin. Perhaps they didn't help with Lo and Orn's schemes, but they didn't stop them, either.

This is what I'm thinking about—my reluctance to forgive and to trust—when we reach the beach. Someone has brought pelts from camp and strewn them on the dark sand, and people sit between the dunes, well back from the water's edge. Three gray dire wolf hides lie on the higher ground, and I drop down onto one. Shava and Kesh sit beside me.

From this seat, I can survey the gathered crowd. Kol's clan is represented by his mother, his brothers Pek and Kesh, and their father's brother and his wife. From my clan I see Chev and Seeri sitting beside the two elders—husband and wife—who rowed my canoe to this camp yesterday, and my brother's longtime friend and Seeri's former betrothed, Morsk. He's one of my brother's closest advisors, so I'm not surprised he is here. The Bosha sit the farthest from me, on the part of the sand that begins to slope toward the shore. They huddle together like seals—Dora, her daughter, Anki, and two others I don't recognize.

"Who is that, seated with the others from your clan?" I ask Shava.

"Oh, they're both elders. The woman is a cousin of Lo's . . . or a cousin of her father, maybe. Definitely part of that family. And the man is her husband. They've been helping to lead while we have no High Elder."

I study their faces. I must know them—they would have been five years younger when the clan split and my family moved south. But I can't place them. Just as I lean over to ask Shava their names, two sounds distract me—a rustling in the dune grass, and shuffling footfalls on the path.

I do not need to look to know who is creeping through the dunes. It can only be my sister Lees. I knew she would come to listen in. But the footsteps turn me around.

Coming down the trail is a boy whose warm eyes are dimmed by loss. A boy whose soft mouth is pressed into a taut line.

Kol.

He arrives with Urar, leaning close to him and speaking low, and I notice that he is limping. Memories of last night flash through my mind—his pant leg torn at the knee, blood flowing down his shin. I see the way he winces each time he takes a step with his left leg. I see the way he uses his spear to support his weight.

I watch him closely, my pulse growing quicker as his eyes flit from face to face. They move to Shava, then Kesh. My palms press against the ground beneath me, my fingers digging into the cool sand. His eyes will move to me next. I watch him, unblinking, until his gaze meets mine.

A twitch at the corner of his lip . . . I think he is about to smile. Heat floods through my chest and rushes up my neck.

And then his mother says his name and he turns away. She is welcoming everyone on behalf of his father, and she is introducing Kol to the gathered crowd.

He walks to her side, and I notice the limp all but

disappears. He doesn't want her to know how badly he's hurt.

As he passes in front of me, he slows. His eyes touch mine again, and I am carried back to the moment when he saw me watching him in the canyon, when he first looked through my defenses and knew my purpose for coming here. For a brief instant he sees into me again, and then his eyes sweep back to his mother and he moves away.

My breath goes ragged. I listen to the beat of the waves, steady and constant, and try to draw that steadiness in. Memories flash through my mind like lightning—the flame illuminating Kol's skin, the heat of his lips against my hand, Seeri's question: *Have you decided to refuse Kol?*

"While my husband is still formally High Elder, I want to discuss some business between our clans that he felt was important. The Manu have ties . . . history . . . with both the Olen and the Bosha, and preserving those connections for the good of all was his constant thought and concern. So first, before business with the Olen, I wish to discuss the Bosha clan." With that, she presses her gaze—heavy with grief but also with the weight of her question—onto Dora and the other Bosha elders. "Who will be the Bosha's new High Elder?" She asks this question without a flinch of hesitation. There is nothing to indicate that she knows she is overstepping her rights. Perhaps she isn't. The Bosha's last High Elder, Lo, set fire to the Manu camp, putting all their lives at risk. Shouldn't the Manu have the right to ask who will take Lo's place?

The two elders who came with Dora and Anki glance at each other. Perhaps one of them is the new High Elder. I think I see a subtle nod from the woman. Her husband stands.

"We are happy to answer your questions. But first a confession, and a request for forgiveness. My name is Thern, and this is my wife, Pada. We are both elders of the Bosha clan. It is with shame that we admit that we were fooled by Lo. We failed as leaders, and our failure caused pain and damage."

I watch Dora as Thern speaks. Her eyes flit briefly to Anki's before returning to her hands, folded in her lap.

"This is why our answer to your question is that we have not chosen a new High Elder. Nor do we intend to. Instead, we hope to gain the forgiveness of the Olen clan, and ask them to allow us to rejoin them, reuniting the once-great Bosha clan." He turns to face my brother. "If you will accept us, we would have you, Chev, as our High Elder."

Though I didn't recognize either Thern or Pada at first—there is a lean hardness to both of them that wasn't there five years ago—I recognize their names, of course. Slowly, like seeing someone step out of a thick fog, their faces come back to me. I remember Pada especially, the second cousin of my best friend. She was older than us—beautiful and strong. I remember she kept her hair short to keep it out of her way in the hunt. My mother refused to cut mine to match, though I begged and begged. I wanted to be just like her, up until the day she chose to stay behind with Vosk.

She stood on the shore as I boarded the boat and Lo taunted me about my pendant. She was there when I crushed it under my boot against the rock. She called after us as we pulled away from shore, asking the Divine to forsake us and drown us in the sea.

I remember feeling so relieved that I still had my long hair—that I wasn't like her. I cannot forgive her. I cannot accept anyone who so strongly rejected my family.

But Chev is different. He can accept anything, as long as he thinks it will lead to a return to the days when our father was High Elder of the Bosha. He gets to his feet from where he sits beside Seeri and crosses to the center of the circle. Thern meets him there and the two men exchange humble nods. So forgiving, so kind. But I see the slight shift in Chev as he fills with the knowledge of his expanding power. No smile, but heat rises in his eyes.

Mala stands. "I want to thank the Bosha elders for their openness," she says. She steps forward, and Chev and Thern return to their seats. "I am certain that the Spirit of my husband is pleased to have this answer, as well."

Mala lets her eyes sweep over the circle, addressing the group as a whole again, letting us all know that she would like to now speak about the Olen.

The time has come to discuss the Manu's business with my clan.

Though I hear Kol's mother's voice, the sound stretches and bends into a low humming murmur, as if my head were underwater. I recognize the sound of my brother's name, and the words *thank you* and the name of our clan. The word *friendship* swims through the hum, and *willingness to help*. Then she asks the purpose of the visit. It's a formal question—part of custom. She can have no doubt what our purpose is. I saw it in her eyes the moment I stepped out of the boat and onto this shore.

The sound of the waves at the water's edge, the wind rustling in the sea grass, and the echo of my own name—these sounds break through and fill my head. My eyes flick to Chev as he gets to his feet.

"I speak of my sister Mya first, because Kol is the future of the Manu clan. The Manu is on the cusp of new leadership—a great honor and responsibility will be conferred upon Kol soon." Chev turns to face Kol, standing directly between us so that I cannot see his face. Something churns inside me like a catch of fish trying to escape the net. Every part of me twists and writhes. "The Manu have suffered a great loss, and we mourn that loss with you. But we also look forward to the future of the Manu. With that future in mind, Mala, I would like to betroth my sister Mya to your son Kol."

My eyes are on the sand at my brother's feet when he steps aside, opening the line of sight to the place where Kol sits. If I looked up, I could see his face. I could see what everyone else sees—his reaction to my brother's words.

They are all looking at Kol. They all know what I want to know. What I need to know. So reluctantly, haltingly, I raise my eyes.

And when I see Kol's face, his answer is there.

SIX

I see Kol's face, and a little part of me dies. I have seen his smile before. But this is not a smile.

This is more.

The twist in his lips, the quickness in his eyes . . . they speak to me in a language I don't completely understand. He opens his mouth and I think, *Yes, now I will know what the words are, all these unnamed feelings will have a name.*

"Mya," is all that he says.

But spoken by Kol, that one word is enough. Because tucked within that word—tucked within my own name—are all the things that have no names. The sound of my name from Kol's lips calls to me like the echo of a long-forgotten dream. He moves toward me, and all the coldness in me is replaced by the heat I see in his eyes. A heat that cancels out my fear of marrying the High Elder of the Manu.

At least for now.

"Mya," he repeats, but in my name there is something different—a secret tucked away. "I have something for you," he says.

He returns to the place where he sat beside his mother, and he picks up the pack he carried in with his spear. He brings it to the center of the circle and sets it at my feet. Everyone watches him. Every move he makes seems infused with meaning. He flips the pack open and takes from it something small.

A waterskin. A small waterskin that might belong to a child.

But then I recognize it. I've seen it before. It's the pouch of honey—the very same pouch of honey I rejected when Kol tried to give it to me on the first day we met.

"I wanted you to have this once before as a gift from me, but you wouldn't accept it. I wonder if you would accept it now, as a token of this day." He lifts my hand and places the pouch in my palm. The honey inside feels warm from the heat of the sun. "Mya, will you honor me by being my wife?"

And at that moment I know what Kol has done. Yes, he's found a way to take away the horror we've all felt since last night. He's given us something to look forward to for tomorrow, after his father is buried today. And he's done it all with this simple gift, something he brought with him here, to prove to me and everyone else that he hasn't been backed into this betrothal, but came seeking it.

"Yes," I say, and I bring the pouch of honey to my lips, bringing Kol's hand with it. I press a kiss to the inside of his wrist, holding it there long enough to drink in the scent of his skin mixed with the salt breeze and the sweet honey.

Behind our backs, people stomp their feet and cheer. A ripple of words passes around—congratulations to our families. Kol just keeps that smile on his lips and that fire in his eyes, and I realize it might truly be possible for me to love the future High Elder of the Manu.

Kol tips his head close to my ear. "You are so beautiful. You are the only reason my heart is not consumed by sorrow today."

I pull back and look at him, at the muted glow in his eyes. The muted smile on his lips. I nod, and walk with Kol back to his place in the circle, where I sit down beside him on a wide bearskin pelt.

Out of the corner of my eye, I see something stir the dune grass that spreads toward the path. Something is there. If the circumstances were different, I wouldn't even notice it, or maybe I'd assume it was a bird or a vole.

But I know that it's not. I know it is my sister Lees, staying hidden, listening. I can only imagine how much she will have to say to me in the hut tonight.

My brother, who had been hovering just at the edge of

the circle, returns to its center. His eyes are a bit puffy and his cheeks slightly flushed.

"I would like to speak now about my younger sister Seeri and the second son of Arem and Mala, Pek." My brother hesitates, raising a large hand to his face and covering his eyes. He draws in a long, slow breath. Could it be that he's overcome with emotion? He'd wanted Seeri to marry his friend Morsk. She and Pek had fought him—had worked to change his mind. Could he have found their love so moving?

"Chev." Kol's mother leaps to her feet like a rabbit escaping a snare. "If Seeri is interested in a betrothal to Pek, such a betrothal would honor and please our family, as well. My husband and I have always wanted a union between Seeri and Pek. If that is what she wants."

"It is," Seeri starts, climbing to her feet as quickly as Mala had. She is so lovely. There is a vulnerability in the way she stands—her hands floating at her sides, all her weight tilting forward as if she is about to unfurl wings and fly. "It is what I want, as long as it is still what Pek wants."

With all eyes on him, Pek's chest gives a single heave, and he raises his face. Wordlessly, he gets to his feet and moves to Seeri, who takes his hand.

They worked to be together, I think. *They suffered through uncertainty and worked to change Chev's mind, and now they have a future.* My thoughts are distracted by the sound of cheers.

Pek holds Seeri out at the end of his arm, as if presenting her to the gathered clan leaders, and she blushes. But I don't see even a hint of embarrassment on Pek's face, damp with tears. I stamp my own feet in approval.

"I know Arem would be filled with happiness at these betrothals," Mala says, emotion breaking through her voice for the first time today. "Even though we will lose Pek to the Olen, we know that he will not really be gone to us, as the Manu look forward to a strong alliance with the Olen. In fact, I think it won't be long until we will have a third betrothal, between our youngest, Roon, and your sister Lees."

My brother, still standing, takes a step back from Mala. He drops his eyes, clears his throat, shakes his head. "I'm sorry," he says, "but that betrothal won't be possible."

Up until these words from Chev, I've been slumped contentedly against Kol's shoulder. But now I sit upright. I must have misunderstood him. But I see the look of confusion on Mala's face, and I know I heard him correctly.

"The Olen are in a difficult situation, despite these advantageous betrothals today. Pek will be a great gain for our clan, and I'm happy to have him as a brother. But his marriage to Seeri creates a problem for the Olen. I am the clan's High Elder, but I am childless. That will not change. The Divine knows the next High Elder will not be my child. So the Divine looks to my sisters. The oldest, Mya, will be the wife of the High Elder of the Manu. Seeri, the next, has also chosen to marry a Manu, and despite Pek's many strengths, he would not be the ideal father to the child who would grow to lead the Olen clan."

A hole opens inside me, rippling wider, as if this proclamation of Chev's is a stone dropped into a dark lake. Without knowing what I intend to say, I climb to my feet. "But Pek is an excellent hunter. He's skilled at boat-making and hut-building—he and Kol built the hut we sleep in—"

"All this is true. If those were all the things necessary to father a strong High Elder, I would happily relent." He pauses, and looking around seems to notice for the first time that every person gathered here is watching him, waiting for this explanation. He closes his eyes and rubs his fingers across his brow. "Let me tell you a story," he continues.

"There was a High Elder who needed to take a warrior with him to face an enemy clan. He could take with him his son or his son-in-law. His son-in-law was the better fighter, but he had been born into the enemy clan. So the High Elder took his own son as his companion on the journey. He was the better choice, because he would have unshakable loyalty.

"If Seeri marries Pek and he joins the Olen, where will their child's loyalty be? To the clan of her mother or her father? How can their child be the next High Elder if that question can't be answered?"

"But," Mala says, "Mya will be the mother of the next Manu High Elder, and she wasn't born into the Manu clan. Yet I have no doubts about her loyalty."

"Because you have no choice," my brother answers. "There are no young women in this clan. But there is a young man in the Olen, one who could marry Lees and be the father of the next High Elder." He turns in place until his gaze falls directly on Morsk, who climbs to his feet. A murmur ripples through the gathered crowd.

"Why didn't the High Elder in your story take his daughter on the journey, instead of his son or his son-in-law?" I ask. Chev doesn't turn toward me to answer. To do so would be to acknowledge this challenge I'm making to his authority.

"Because she was already dead," he says.

I watch him warily. "You're imagining problems that don't exist," I say. "Seeri's child with Pek will make an excellent choice for the next Olen High Elder."

Finally Chev turns, and when his eyes meet mine, they are heavy and dark with sorrow. Or perhaps regret. "That's easy for you to argue," he says, his voice diminished—almost resigned—under the burden of my gaze. "You're not the High Elder. Your only concern is for your family. But I have to give the good of the clan equal weight to the good of my family. Perhaps even more weight. You'll never really understand that, because now that you're betrothed to Kol, you'll never be the Olen High Elder."

A noise distracts me—a scuttling across the ground behind me. I look back and catch sight of Lees, dirty from crawling in the damp grass, scrambling to her feet. Before I have the chance to move, she takes off running up the path toward camp.

I swing my head around, and I see that Chev's gaze rests on the place where Lees just disappeared from view.

There is no use trying to reason with Chev here. In private it would be difficult. With this audience, it would be impossible.

Kol squeezes my hand, and I can see by the concern in his eyes that he saw Lees, too. "I'm sorry," I say. "I have to go after her." I slip my hand out of Kol's grip and hurry away.

The path to camp is empty. I walk all the way to the ring of huts alone. Lees must have moved fast. I creep along the outside edge of the huts, crouching low in what little shade they throw. I know the Manu must suspect that betrothals are being discussed today, and I don't want to raise any questions by being seen alone. So I stay out of sight and consider where I might find my sister.

I head first to the hut of Kol's family, but the door hangs still and everything's silent. Standing outside my own hut— the hut Kol and Pek built on our family's first visit so we would always feel welcome in this camp—I hear the shuffle of feet from inside. I slide through the door, expecting to find my sister and Roon.

Instead, I find myself face-to-face with Morsk. He must have followed right behind me when I left the beach. And like me, he took care not to be seen.

There's something disconcerting about his uninvited presence here in this private space, but I refuse to let him see my unease. "I don't know what you're doing here, but if you're looking for Lees, I'm quite sure she doesn't want to see you."

Morsk replies with a quizzical smirk. He runs a hand through his hair in a disarmingly shy way. Under different circumstances, I might concede that Morsk is handsome, but as my brother's conspirator in a plot to control my sister's life, I see nothing attractive about him at all. Any charms he might possess are as alluring as venom.

"I'm not looking for your little sister," he says. "I'm looking for you."

"Me?" I take a step back. Morsk is broad across the shoulders, and all at once he seems to fill the room. "Why are you looking for me?"

"I have a proposition for you."

I take another step back, but Morsk takes two steps closer, coming within arm's reach. I draw in a deep breath and remind myself that he's close enough to kick in the groin. "Which is?"

"I know you don't want Lees to be forced to marry me. And I don't either, actually. I'd much rather have you."

Sometimes when I'm startled, my head fills with a buzzing sound that drowns out the world. But not now, not this time. Instead, a stark silence stretches between me and Morsk, a silence wide and glaring like a field of deep snow. The only sound that breaks through is the sound of Morsk's exhaled breath as he takes a half step toward me.

I let the point of the spear I hold at my side angle toward his chest, not as a threat, but as a reminder to myself that I am safe. He can't control me. Not Morsk, not even my brother. Thoughts tumble and fall in disorder in my mind. "I thought you didn't like me," I say.

He smiles, but his smile is for himself, not me. "I didn't think I did. But when we crossed paths with the Manu again, I changed my mind about you. I realized I didn't want a girl like Seeri after all—a girl who would fall right into the open arms of a Manu boy. I wanted someone with enough nerve to resist the clan that killed her mother. I saw the way you rejected Kol, the way you refused to accept a man who I myself find quite unacceptable. I saw the way you fought to protect your people when Lo and her clan attacked.

"Your brother wants one of his sisters to carry on the Olen High Elder line, but it doesn't have to be Lees. Lees is safe—you can make sure of it. With one word, you can save Lees from her betrothal to me. All you have to do is take her place."

SEVEN

"**B**ut I'm already betrothed," I say, planting my spear in the space between me and Morsk so that the point hovers right in front of his face.

"Betrothals can be broken."

He's right, of course. "Yes. They can, and yours to Lees will be broken. But mine to Kol will not. You and my brother may think that you can manipulate my life and the lives of my sisters, but you will learn that you are wrong."

I don't wait for Morsk's reaction, but I think I see a hint of self-doubt in his eye as I jostle past him and push my way through the door. My pulse pounds so hard in my ears my steps fall out of rhythm as I turn and hurry back down the trail to the beach.

Halfway there, at a spot where the trees grow crowded together thick enough to create some patchy shade, I hear something moving. I slow my steps, and from the corner of my eyes I see a shadow slide between darker shadows. Someone steps out onto the trail right in front of me. My pulse quickens even more, and I flinch back.

But it's Kol.

He smiles. "Did I scare you? I'm sorry."

"You scared me on purpose," I say, but my tone comes out teasing. He can't tell that the tremor in my voice is left over from my encounter with Morsk.

For a moment, I consider telling Kol what happened. After all, it concerns our betrothal, so it concerns us both. But then I bite my lip and keep the words inside. I don't want to talk about Morsk right now.

Kol looks down, his dark hair sweeps forward like the door of a hut, and I can no longer see his eyes. "You're right," he says, still keeping his gaze on the ground. "I shouldn't play like that with you, at least not right now. I know you're upset about Lees."

He looks up, flipping the hair from his eyes, and one corner of his mouth hitches up. "I was just happy to have one brief moment with you alone, I guess—"

"We were alone last night—"

"That's true, but it's different now." Kol steps closer to me—close enough that I feel his breath on my ear when he speaks. "Now we're *betrothed*." Kol lets this last word roll on his tongue, as if he's tasting it. A shiver runs down my spine, and I want to pull him into my arms. "But this isn't a time for play," he continues, taking a half step back. "Did you find her? Is she okay?"

The memory of Morsk's smirk presses on my chest like a weight. His words—*All you have to do is take her place*—tumble inside me like falling rocks, hammering it down. The weight is so heavy I feel like I can barely breathe—like my lungs can't lift to fill—and I marvel that Kol can't see how I'm struggling.

But he does see. He just misunderstands. "Mya, what is it? What's wrong with Lees?"

"I couldn't find her," I say. "I'm sure she's found Roon. At least for now, I'm sure she's fine."

This thought of Lees and Roon together is so airy and light, it sweeps some of the heaviness from my chest. My hand moves to the pattern on my tunic, and I feel it rise and fall with my breath.

Kol's gaze moves to my hand. A question lights in his eyes for just a moment, and then he reaches for me.

He catches my right hand in his own and pulls me toward him, turning me so that my back presses tight against his chest. I had forgotten the feeling of his body against mine, though I had tried to keep the memories alive. They all come flooding back now—memories of his arms wrapped around me as we stretched out on the ground. The cool touch of his hands on the warm skin of my back.

His nose traces a line down my neck, and his breath stirs

my hair. "My betrothed," he whispers, just before he presses his lips into the space beneath my ear. Heat runs across my scalp and down the length of my body, melting everything in its path. Every tense memory, every nagging fear melts away.

I sigh and turn to face him.

Kol's lips touch my cheekbone, skim across the bridge of my nose, and come to rest lightly on the corner of my brow. Tipping my head back, I take him in.

As I study his face, I can't deny that there are many different Kols. The one who raised his spear to me. The one who couldn't accept that Lo would plot to attack the Olen. And the one who came to my camp in the midst of a deadly storm. The one who risked his life to warn us, and then helped us defend the camp.

And then there is the Kol who looks back at me now from behind warm, dark eyes. There is something about this Kol that I've never seen before. There is a quiet strength in this Kol—a calm assurance. This Kol trusts himself. He makes me want him to trust me, too.

I scan his face for more clues to the person he really is, when he draws closer to me and my eyes fall shut. His mouth covers mine, and if Kol's face holds unfamiliar mysteries, his kiss does not. It takes me and carries me, up to the cliff above the crashing sea, where we sat together in the rain outside the cave. The very first time his lips sought mine. Only this time, I won't pull away.

His arms enclose me as I draw him closer. He is everywhere, and yet I can't pull him close enough. At the edge of my mind, something scratches, the sound of something trying to break through, but I turn away from the intrusion. What could matter when Kol's lips are fluttering against the curve of my cheek, tracing my brow, pressing lightly on my eye? Behind my lids all the colors of the sunset burn.

The sound comes again—a scratchy digging in dirt— and I am forced to pull back. My eyes open to reveal my brother, Chev, just over Kol's shoulder. He clears his throat. "I don't mean to . . . I wanted to ask Mya about Lees."

Kol pulls away reluctantly. His eyes remain closed even as he tips his head toward the sound of Chev's voice. An impatient sigh escapes his throat as his lids finally flick open and his lips press into a thin line.

This is yet another version of Kol. Someone who loses patience with my brother. Someone who might let Chev interrupt a kiss, but will make sure he knows he isn't pleased.

Could this be the new Kol, the Kol who will soon be High Elder?

"What about Lees?" I ask. I realize that down the path, the meeting of elders is still going on. I hear Kol's mother's voice.

Chev steps forward, silently asserting his authority. "I saw you follow her. Is she okay? She should not have been listening—"

"You knew she was there—"

"I suspected—"

"Well, it doesn't matter. I couldn't find her."

Chev looks from me to Kol, and back to me again. "I should have guessed. I had expected to find you consoling her. . . ." His gaze floats back to Kol, sweeping from his head to his feet. "I didn't expect to find you here . . . like this. . . ."

Heat spreads up my neck. My ears and scalp burn.

"Don't lecture me," I say in a hoarse whisper. "Don't deflect from what you've done. You didn't even warn her, let alone give her a choice! But you gave Morsk plenty of choices. He was offered a betrothal to me, then Seeri, now Lees. You've honored Morsk's wishes, but you won't honor your own sister's—"

"Because one of my sisters must marry a member of the Olen." I can almost see Chev's anger flow into his hands, balled into tight fists at his sides. "No one else can be trusted to be the father of the next High Elder—"

"If you're so concerned about the next High Elder, why don't *you* make the sacrifice? Why don't you give up Yano, marry an Olen woman, and father the next High Elder yourself?"

As soon as the words are out of my mouth, I regret them. I love Yano and know that Chev could never be with anyone else. Beside me, I feel Kol stiffen. He knows that I have said the most hurtful thing I could say, just for that purpose—to hurt. "I'm sorry," I say. "I never . . . I don't mean that. I never should have said it. Yano—"

"I know you didn't mean it. I know you love Yano."

"I do," I say, and my brother blurs around the edges as my eyes sting with tears. "But you see the hidden truth there? We all agree you should have a choice. Morsk should have a choice. So why can't you see that Lees should have one too?"

Chev shakes his head. "It's not that easy." He drops a hand on Kol's shoulder. "You'll understand soon. The burden of making decisions for a whole clan is a heavy one." With that he turns and walks back to the meeting, uninterested in hearing any more of my arguments.

We wait, listening to the sound of gravel crunching beneath his boots, until it fades when he reaches the sand. He addresses the crowd again. Words like *Bosha* and *future* and *alliance* rise and break apart on the wind.

"Should we go look for Lees together?" Kol asks. "She is surely with Roon—"

I am ready to say I'll look alone. That Kol needs to go back, to return to his mother's side. I look out at the ridge where I'd seen Kol and his brothers walking this morning—the ridge where they were digging a grave.

But I don't see a bare ridge of rock and ice. Someone is there. Two figures, each burdened by a large pack, carrying a kayak between them. "What? They can't. . . ."

Kol turns and looks in the direction of my gaze. Any hope I have that it is just a trick of the light abandons me when Kol speaks his brother's name under his breath. "Roon." Thoughts shift behind his eyes as he runs through the same possibilities I do, reaching the same conclusions.

"They must've stolen down to the water the long way . . . pulled a boat from the bay out of everyone's sight. . . ."

"And looped back around to the ridge. No one will see them put the boat in the water. . . ."

Even as I speak, the two figures drop down on the far side of the ridge, the boat no longer visible. Just their heads and shoulders stand out like silhouettes against the bright surface of the sea beyond them.

Voices grow in volume. People are on their feet on the beach. The meeting is coming to an end. Soon everyone will be preparing for the burial.

"Come with me," I say, grabbing Kol's hand. "We need to stop them."

And then we are running, heading for the spot where Lees and Roon just set a boat into the sea.

EIGHT

By the time we reach the far side of the ridge, they've loaded the boat and pushed it out from shore. Roon stands in the surf, holding the kayak steady while my sister ties herself into the front seat.

If I'd hoped I was wrong about what they were doing, it can't be denied once Roon sees us coming. He yells to Lees to hurry as he pushes the double kayak out into deeper water. Waves crash, swallowing his voice. Lees is still tying the sash at her waist when he hops onto the deck and slides his feet into the rear seat.

"Roon, stop!" Kol's voice bursts from his throat as he hobbles up behind me. But Roon turns away from his brother, moving faster.

"You can't make us stay," he calls.

But Kol can. He has already clambered down the face of the ridge to the water's edge and is splashing into the sea.

And though Kol is clearly limping on his left leg, he hardly slows. The pain in his knee must be terrible, but the threat of his brother getting away is even worse.

"Stop now!" he yells. One final warning.

Then he is there, right beside Roon, grabbing him by the shoulders and pulling him from the boat. Kol's knee buckles, but he rights himself before he falls. Roon pushes hard against Kol, but it's futile. Despite his injury, despite his pain, Kol is determined to stop his brother. I watch as Roon slides from the kayak and tumbles headfirst into the sea.

The boat rocks hard. Lees shrieks. Sun glints off the paddle in her hand, its wood bleached white from wear.

Roon rights himself, whipping his wet hair from his face, spraying Kol with icy water. For a moment, as he stands facing his brother in the shallows, his fists balled, I wonder if he will try to strike him. If he's thinking of it, Kol doesn't wait for him to act. He grabs the kayak and walks away, pulling it to the base of the ridge, my sister still sitting in the front seat.

Scrambling down the rock face, I reach the spot where the boat bobs in the waves. Lees defiantly remains in the seat—still tied in—with no apparent plan to move. Roon, drenched through and shivering, stands in the water at her side. He glares at Kol as my sister glares at me—as if they hate us.

"You fools," are the first words I say.

"Save yourself the trouble," Lees says. "We don't want your counsel. We won't stay. You cannot force us—"

"It isn't just me you're defying—"

"I don't care about Chev—"

"Do you care about the Divine? Check the position of the sun. It's almost time for Arem's funeral. The Manu will pass along this ridge in just a little while, carrying their High Elder to his grave."

I notice Roon flinch, just a small buckle of the knees. Maybe it's a reaction to what I said. Maybe it's the icy water dripping from his hair, running down his neck and under the collar of his parka.

"How do you think the Divine would respond if Roon did not attend his father's burial?" I continue. "How do you think she would reward such disrespect? Do you think she would bless the Manu—or the Olen either—if you two ran away at the time Roon should be the most faithful to his family and clan?"

Lees stares right through me, her eyes filling with rage, until the rage melts into tears. The back of a damp hand— bright red with cold—sweeps across her face, and sobs roll out of her. "I won't stay. Let the Divine destroy me. I won't stay to marry Morsk."

Roon, still standing in ankle-deep surf, slides an arm around her shoulders and pulls her against him, and she drops her head to his chest. Her words are muffled by his parka as she chokes and coughs, "I won't stay. I won't stay."

As angry as I am, I'm not immune to Lees's tears. With each sob, my resolve weakens.

I want to tell her she won't have to marry Morsk. I want to tell her we'll change Chev's mind, but I can't promise that. My head echoes with Morsk's words to me as he stood too close in the hut—*with one word, you can save Lees.* My eyes move to Kol but he is turned away.

"Roon," I say, my tone changed—anger replaced by concern. "You should get up on land before you freeze."

When he doesn't move, doesn't even shift his weight, Lees pulls away from him and starts to untie the sash. "She's right," she says, her voice steadying. She knows there is nothing to be gained with sobs. She wipes her eyes and unceremoniously climbs from the kayak, tugging Roon behind her when she scrambles onto the rocks.

The four of us sit looking out to sea, and no one speaks for a long time. I begin to worry about what might be happening back at camp. Urar will be preparing Arem's body, rubbing it with red ocher. A stretcher would have already been fashioned of long shafts of bone or ivory, draped with a mammoth pelt to carry the body. People will be looking for Kol and Roon soon.

"Where were you running to?" I finally ask.

"I won't say," Lees answers. She tilts her chin up but

keeps her eyes focused on the sea. "When we get our next chance, we'll go, and I don't want you to know where to look." Her voice remains even and calm, but her words cut me like claws.

"You can't do that," I say. "You can't . . ." My voice trails off. She can do whatever she wants, and I know I'm powerless to stop her.

"Don't worry. We're prepared."

A wave comes in hard, jostling the kayak and freeing it from the rocks. The receding water pulls the boat out, and Kol splashes in and catches it before it can wash farther out to sea.

He reaches a hand into the front seat and pulls a pack out from beneath the deck. The size of it brushes me back—the size of a pack you might take on an extended hunting trip. "How long were you planning to stay away?" I ask, fear hushing my voice to a murmur.

"Forever," Lees answers, and with that one word the fear flares and knocks the breath from me.

"You took everything you would need to survive?" Kol asks, his tone incredulous.

"We did—"

"Tools, pelts, weapons?"

"Yes—"

"Food?"

"Everything," Roon says. "The pack on Lees's back is full of food. Enough to hold us until we could hunt."

"But where did you get it all?" I ask. I turn to my sister, looking at her with a new understanding. I have been underestimating her.

"Roon helps in the kitchen. He's been stashing away whatever he can—"

"Before today? Before Chev's announcement?"

"We had a plan." She turns to me now, a hard edge of determination darkening her eyes, stealing their warmth. "I didn't know what Chev would do when he found out about us, but I knew it wouldn't be good."

My thoughts snag on Lees's words like a toe catching on a hidden root—I'm so taken by surprise I've no chance to keep myself from tumbling. I clutch at fragments of memories of Chev, grasping for something that will right me and set me back on my feet, but every thought that comes to mind sends me spiraling farther. He has never been particularly hard on Lees—no harder than he is on any of us—but she knows his priorities. What reason has he ever given her to trust that he would let her interests come before the clan's?

But then, isn't that what it means to be a strong High Elder? To put the interests of the clan first, no matter the sacrifice? I can't say that Lees's charge against Chev is wrong. But I can't say that Chev is acting outside the code he's set for himself.

But what is right? As Kol sets the pack of supplies at my feet, I turn that question in my mind. But I find no answer.

As we sit, I watch a group of gulls circle a rocky island far out in the water. I remember the shags I hunted this morning, the way they wouldn't leave their young. How this instinct to protect was a weakness instead of a strength.

Images rise and fade in my mind—the rocky island, the swarm of birds, the broken skull, the blood dripping from the net. Instinct isn't always best. Am I protecting Lees by forcing her to stay in camp, I wonder, or is this instinct a weakness in me, too?

I stare hard at the pack of supplies, imagining Roon readying everything he and Lees would need. They will run again. She said so herself. And when they do, they will be sure they can't be found. I will lose my sister forever.

My eyes move from the pack to the boat to the paddles. I turn to Kol, who casts no shadow. The sun is directly overhead. It's time for the burial of his father. There's no more time to think, only time to act.

"I have an idea," I say. "A way to keep Lees safe from Chev's plans."

NINE

smile, and I see Roon smile too. He leans toward me. "You're going to let her go, aren't you? You're going to let us run away."

"No, I'm not," I answer. I feel Kol's gaze. "My plan is not to let *you* and Lees run away. . . ." I say.

I turn to Kol just in time to see his eyes flash with surprise. "So *you*, then? You will go with Lees?"

"Yes. And you and Roon will stay."

Kol stands. For a moment he seems caught between turning away and coming to my side. He looks down at his shuffling boots before crossing to me, taking my hands, and pulling me to my feet. His lips lower to my ear. "You would run away—*today*—the day we became betrothed? You would leave before my father is buried—"

"We can't wait," Lees interrupts. Despite the fact that Kol is clearly speaking just to me, my sister feels she can answer. "It will take until nightfall to get there."

"To get *where*?" Kol turns to her, all patience gone. His tone is no longer tender. Instead, his voice is like a fire starter, relentlessly drilling down. "Where are you going that is so far away, it will take until nightfall to arrive?"

"I don't know," Lees say. "Only Roon knows the place."

Kol whirls on his brother. He doesn't ask. He doesn't have to.

"I won't say until I know this is not just a trick. I need Mya to promise to go with Lees. If she'll promise to go, I'll tell."

Kol swallows hard. He drops his gaze to the ground. "It's too dangerous. Mya, I know you want to protect your sister. I can't blame you, but I can't stand the thought of the two of you running away alone. Please say you won't go."

There is a stretch of silence, tight like a rope binding my heart to Kol's.

"I can't promise that," I say. My voice is so small, these words so hard to say. "But I can't promise to go, either. Not until I know where I'm going."

Roon looks at me with the eyes of prey that's been cornered. He glances at Lees. She smiles and nods and he takes a deep breath. "To an island north and west of here." His words come out like a confession—once the first have broken through, the rest come tumbling in a torrent. "I found it while exploring the coast, searching for another clan. It's big. It has game—even fresh water. It's perfect."

Kol shakes his head. "We know all the islands northwest of here—"

"Not this one. It's too far offshore to see—beyond the horizon."

Kol eyes his brother as if he's weighing every word he says. "Why have you kept this to yourself? And how do you know about an island beyond the horizon?"

"It wasn't a secret, I swear. I hadn't even met Lees yet, so it was never part of a plan or scheme or anything. I found it by chance. I got washed out by a storm—I couldn't paddle hard enough to get back to shore—so I came upon it completely by accident. But I knew if Mother or Father ever found out—about the storm, about an island beyond the horizon—that would be the end of my explorations. So I kept it to myself."

I shiver at the thought of Roon dragged out to sea in a small kayak, beyond the view of land. Nothing but danger lies beyond the horizon—that wisdom has been handed down for generations. Some say it's the hunting ground of huge predators that crest the waves to swallow boats whole. Some say a great waterfall drops into a deep abyss. But everyone knows it's forbidden.

"It's far too great a chance to take," Kol says. "Surely you see that."

I cannot meet Kol's gaze. If I look into his eyes—if I

remember his lips pressed against my throat—I won't be able to carry out this plan and paddle out to sea, leaving him behind. "You need to stay," I finally say. "Both of you need to bury your father. But I can go ahead with Lees. We can show Chev how far we're willing to go to resist his plan."

"But why not just stay and confront him? Tell him what you are willing to do—"

"Chev doesn't work like that. I have to leave," Lees says. She's up on her feet, standing right in front of Kol. He may not want to look her in the eye, but she is going to force him to. "Words aren't enough to change his mind—"

"This time they will be—"

"But why? What would be different? By staying, I'm proving he has power over me. What motive does he have to seek out any other option?"

Lees's words explode on my ears. I think of the offer Morsk made me. *You could give Lees her freedom.*

Does Chev know about Morsk's offer? Have he and Morsk conspired together? Is this Chev's way of getting what he wants while making sure it looks like I was given a choice, rather than forced against my will?

Lees still stands in front of Kol, still confronts him with her questions. "What other option does he have?"

Me, I think. *I am his other option.*

I shake the words from my head and grab Kol by the arm. "Would you walk with me for a bit?" I ask.

Both Kol and Lees glance around, clearly noticing the short stretch of ground we can safely walk at the base of this cliff. There's really nowhere to walk to.

There's only somewhere to walk away from. Or some*one* to walk away from. It's clear I want to talk to Kol out of Lees and Roon's hearing.

I'm sure Lees doesn't care. She seems pleased to have a reason to drop back down on the ground beside Roon, who's been silently staring out to sea. He's probably planning their next move if Kol succeeds at convincing me to stay.

I lead Kol as far out on the point as we can safely go, until we are surrounded on all sides by the sea. I shudder a bit at all the water. At how far it stretches. My stomach lurches and I turn away, back toward Kol.

But even looking into his eyes, I feel something vast and wide opening up in front of me. I want to close that distance—to draw closer to him, but I fear that telling him the truth about Morsk's proposal might only push him away.

I tell him anyway.

As the story unfolds, I watch his face. I study his reaction. In some ways his eyes are indeed like a vast sea. Calm. Placid. But changeable.

As I tell Kol my story of looking for Lees and finding Morsk—of the way he'd come too close to me, the way he'd insulted him—his eyes change. Like the sea when a dark cloud rolls in and whips the wind into a storm.

"Does your brother know about this proposal?" he asks.

"I don't know. But I would think he might. . . ." I hesitate, but I need to tell Kol everything, even if it's a truth I'm ashamed to admit. I think of my fear that Chev would welcome this proposal of Morsk's. "It may even have been his idea," I say.

The line of Kol's jaw hardens, braced against the winds that stir in his eyes. "Then we are not allies," he says. "How can we be, if Chev cannot be trusted? If he says one thing to my face and another behind my back?"

"If he would trade your future—our future—for his own?"

"He won't—he can't. I won't let him. Because I'm going to show him that he doesn't control us. I have the power to leave him, and so does Lees. And we'll do it. We'll show him that we can leave, because we will leave."

I'm not sure what I thought of this scheme as I formed it, but as I say these words out loud, I realize that this is the strongest move I can make. I know Kol's angry. I know he wants to confront my brother. But I'm angry too.

So we will both confront him.

Kol will confront him with words, and I will confront him with action.

"I *do* want to speak with Chev myself—to reason with him—but he needs to come to us. If he does, I will know he really intends to listen." I imagine for a moment my brother's face, the look of anger in his eyes, when he learns Lees and I are gone. "I'm sorry I'm forcing you to speak for me—to account for me," I say.

Kol runs his fingers down my arms, curls them around my hands. "Your hands are cold," he says.

"I'm nervous. Not for me, but for you. My brother will not take this well. I wish I weren't putting you in this position—"

"You're not." Kol lifts my fingers to his mouth and breathes on them to warm them. "I'm your betrothed. Our interests are one now. Our actions are one. I'm happy you would trust me to speak for you." Kol bends his head, his lips hovering above mine, when I hear Lees's voice. Then Roon's.

It's time to go.

It doesn't take long to go over the details. Roon describes all the landmarks that will help us find the island. The mouth of a river. The point that is crowned by a double peak like two fingers pointing to the sky. Small islands that form a line out to the horizon in the west. "A dozen of them, strung in a line like ivory beads on a cord. Except the last. The last will loom dark in the distance, a single bead of obsidian. Unlike the others of bare rock, the last one swarms with black shags.

"Follow the line of those islands and you will come right to it," he says.

Lees climbs into the front seat of the kayak, just as she

had before. As Roon stands out in the water holding the boat steady, I get one last moment alone with Kol. He winds his arms around my waist and pulls me against him, but I don't wait for him to kiss me. I don't have time, and I feel greedy, knowing that I won't kiss him again until he brings Chev to the island. I lean into him and press my mouth against his.

Kol's lips are cool and taste like the sea, but a warmth spreads through me the sea could never give. His hands run up the back of my neck and I feel his fingers lightly thread through my hair. I imagine a net winding around me, a net of Kol's love, and I feel safe. I drink it in—the feeling of security his hands give me. I'm not sure when I will feel so safe again.

Despite the fact his family is almost certainly searching for him and Roon, they refuse to leave until Lees and I are on our way, and we can't delay any longer.

Once we are on the water, I look back only once. Kol and Roon stand side by side, waving good-bye.

We paddle north, following the coast, never drifting too far from shore. Maybe this is because we both know that in time we'll need to let the land disappear completely behind us as we head out beyond the horizon.

My arms tire as the sun moves out into the western sky, but my thoughts never slow. I think of Kol and of his brothers. All of them standing over the grave. I think of Mala. What will she think when she notices I am not at the burial? What will she say when Kol tells her the reason why? Will she blame me? But she was at the clan meeting—she even suggested there might soon be a betrothal between Lees and Roon. I remember the look of surprise on her face when Chev refused. She wants the best for Roon and Lees, so I can only hope she agrees with what I've done.

As we move farther and farther north the coast becomes less varied. Vegetation thins. Eventually the shore is made up of one long line of rocky beach backed by a high cliff that stretches as far as I can see.

Lees and I don't speak again until we've been paddling so long I begin to fear we will never see a landmark. Then my fear only worsens when we finally do. It stands out from far away—a point crowned by two peaks that stretch into the sky. By this time the sun has sunk so low the sea has turned the color of flint. No light penetrates the gray sheen—the rays are too shallow. Instead they collect like puddles of violet and red, floating on the surface until an oar scatters them on the waves.

Just south of the double peak I spot another of Roon's landmarks—the rocky shore is split in two by a wide river with high banks. On the north bank of the river, not far upstream from the place where it empties into the sea, I notice a camp. Smoke rises from fires, twisting skyward in the slanting rays of evening sun.

I call over my shoulder to Lees, alerting her to the clan. Roon made no mention of them, so I assume they haven't been camped here for long. Though I have no reason to believe they're not friendly, I have no reason to believe they are, so I direct Lees to paddle farther out from the land. Paddling toward the setting sun, my eyes tire and confuse. I think I see a shadow on the horizon, and I turn to check if the shore is still within view.

When I turn, I see something I hadn't expected. A man in a kayak is following us out, paddling hard. His arms beat the waves with determination and speed.

He is not following—he is chasing.

Lees notices him, and when she turns back to me, fear replaces the exhaustion in her eyes. "Who is that?"

"I don't know," I call. Panic and fatigue snarl my thoughts. He must be from the clan on the river. Is he trying to drive us away? Or to stop us from paddling too far out? "I don't know, and I don't want to know. We have to stay ahead of him."

Even after being at sea since midday, fear motivates us. Once we agree to outrun the stranger, our combined efforts are too much for him. He drops back. I see him raise his paddle and lay it across the deck of his boat. He's given up.

When I see him turn back toward shore, I let myself

slow. I glance at Lees, but she is no longer looking back at me. She is staring straight ahead.

I look past her shoulder—to gaze once again into the immense and limitless sea—and I see what has caught Lees's attention. Not far away the shore of a rocky island looms up and out of the dark water. Another rises right behind it, and behind that one, another.

We have reached the string of islands and they are just as Roon described—like beads strung on a cord, pointing us out to sea. Lees and I slow and then wordlessly steer the kayak beyond one island, and then the next, fighting against all instinct, pushing farther out to sea as the night comes down.

The sky is impossibly pale, as if covered by a coating of snow. It's so pale—so washed in the long summer twilight—the starlight can't break through. If only I could see the stars—the campfires of those who inhabit the Land Above the Sky—I could follow their pathways and stay on a westward course.

I wish I had a truly black sky—an obsidian sky—so I could clearly see the trails of light. I think of Kol and the burial ceremony for his father that took place today. Somewhere in tonight's sky a new star will shine, when Kol's father builds his first campfire among the dead.

Lees and I turn and look over our shoulders more and more frequently the farther west we move. Our eyes squint into the distance as we both watch the edge of the last island disappear.

"We should be there soon!" Lees calls, her voice fired with anticipation. This is her way—to make the best of the worst. To choose excitement when she could choose dread.

I'm so glad she's here to balance out the darker voice in my head.

We paddle hard, watching the horizon, my eyes sweeping south to account for the northward drift of the waves, until at last I glimpse a shadow on the water.

The eastern edge of an island.

I flick a look at Lees. A fire lights in each of her eyes as a smile as warm as a roaring hearth breaks across her face.

Our oars stab the water in unison, turning the kayak slightly south, as the shadow on the water grows bigger and darker. The silhouette takes shape—trees and ledges and outcroppings of rock gain clarity as we pull closer.

We have lost almost all light, but all my fear is gone.

By the time we pull the kayak onto the beach, the sun will finally disappear for its brief rest, and the stars will shine at last. I'll be able to lie on my back on the beach and look up and see their light, like a sign from the Divine. I'm so full of hope for this, I almost don't notice the change in the sea.

At first, I think it's only me—that my exhausted arms are not responding to me as I think they should. I stroke the water on the left side of the kayak, but the kayak still veers left. I push harder, dig faster, and I see that Lees does, too. But still the kayak pushes south.

Until all at once a wave picks us up and turns us, dropping us so hard, water splashes across my face. This boat suddenly feels much smaller than it did a few moments ago.

Like this—fighting against a suddenly stormy sea—a stormy sea despite a clear, windless night—we fight our way to shore.

At last, with legs wobbling like stalks of kelp, Lees and I tumble out of the kayak into the shallow water and haul it up onto shore. The grade is steep, and we just manage to get it out of the sea and up onto solid ground, when the ground goes out from under us.

I find myself beside Lees, both of us on our hands and knees, as the island shakes beneath us.

TEN

My mind goes back, reeling to the moment in the canyon, as the mammoth herd thundered by. My cheek braces against the cold sand, and I bite the inside of my lip. My mouth fills with the taste of bile and blood.

Then everything stills. Just as I begin to believe the foot of the Divine will appear on the sand in front of my eyes, the shaking stops.

The stillness stretches. Could the feet of the Divine have passed over these islands like stepping-stones? Could this be our punishment for having traveled beyond the horizon?

If so, she has moved on, at least for now.

I find the strength to lift my head, and my eyes meet Lees's.

Her gaping gaze darts from my face to the ground to the sea and back again. Her hands, clutched to her chest, shake as if the ground were still moving. "Do you think that's my fault?" she asks. "Because Roon and I angered the Divine?"

Her sweet self-reproach overcomes my anxiety, and I sit up. "No," I say. "I don't think anything you've ever done could anger the Divine that much."

"But you said—"

"I said if you and *Roon* ran away and he didn't attend his father's burial—"

"Then what? What could have brought that on?"

"I don't know," I say. "It's stopped for now. Whatever brought it on, let's hope it's over."

We pull the boat far enough up away from the water that we are sure high tide won't reach it, but I tell Lees to leave it right there—right in the wide-open space, away from trees and cliffs. The sky is finally black, the stars finally shining. I don't dare trek back under cover. Not after that quake. Instead I ask Lees to dig out something for us to eat while I spread the mammoth hide across the cold ground.

"We'll sleep right here," I say. Even though I know it's the only choice, the chilled air that swept in with the dark sky sends a shiver through me. "It won't be cozy, but at least nothing will fall on us."

Lees spreads out a piece of caribou hide and places on it a full skin of water and two piles of dried mammoth meat and berries. It's nothing grand, but it fills our stomachs. Fear had soaked into every bone of my body during the quake, but it finally drains away, replaced by a deep ache.

Dragging ourselves despite our fatigue, Lees and I stash the packs of food and other supplies beneath the overturned kayak. When we're done, we wrap ourselves between the folded halves of the mammoth hide. Before I can say a single word to Lees, she drops her head against my shoulder. "In the morning, we'll scout around to find a better site," I say, but her body has already gone heavy and still with sleep.

I lie awake a long time, listening as the waves lap the shore to my right and the wind stirs the dune grass to my left. I feel like I will never relax enough to drop off, but I must. I wake with a start as something thuds against the ground.

Lees is curled away from me. Her long hair, all loose from her braid, covers her face. She is definitely asleep. I sit up and run my hands through the sand—cold and damp with morning mist.

I swivel in place, sweeping my eyes across the tops of the dunes. Nothing stirs. My gaze scans the horizon, but nothing breaks the line of the sea except for an occasional gull diving for its morning meal. But then I notice faint footprints that mark the surface of the sand. Human footprints. Two lines overlapping—one leading to the overturned kayak, one leading back toward the dunes. My eyes trace the tracks back toward the tall grass and this time I notice movement. A figure—a person hunched over and moving fast—disappears up the trail toward the cliffs.

I jostle Lees's shoulder until she opens her eyes. "Someone's here. Someone was near the boat."

Lees sheds her sleepiness as soon as she understands the threat. "Did they get anything?" she asks.

If we lose our food, we won't have a thing to eat until we've successfully hunted. And if we lose our food and our weapons, what will we do then? Without a means of bringing in game, we'd almost certainly have to go home. Even the best toolmaker—even Kol's father—would struggle to make proper hunting tools from the limited resources on this island. Though I hope it will be only days until Chev relents and sends for us, I can't be certain we won't be here long enough for the food we've brought to run out.

"I don't know. I couldn't see if she carried anything—"

"She?"

"It might've been a girl. The person was moving fast and I only saw her back, but something made me think of a girl."

While Lees checks on the supplies, I run through the possibilities of who might be on this island. Could a clan have landed here after having become lost? We're so far from shore, I can't imagine anyone landing here without being lost.

"They got just one thing," Lees says. I turn to her, hopeful, ready to calm down and understand that this is not a tragedy. We are not in danger. But then I see her teeth pressing into her bottom lip. "They got the pack of food."

We have no choice but to go after it. We can hunt, but we don't know what game we'll find. Even fishing—usually the shortest path to food—is harder when you don't know the waters.

Lees and I drag the kayak and the rest of the supplies to the tallest grasses and try to stash it all out of sight. Before we hike away, I grab the most valuable items—the water-skin, a net, the atlatls, the darts. I toss it all into a pack that I sling over my shoulder, grab my spear, and lead Lees up the path to the cliffs.

We stay low, hiding behind the tall grass. The dunes rise to the base of a towering wall of rock—the cliffs we saw from the sea. From a gap in the dunes, I notice the mouth of a cave, partially blocked by large boulders that must have fallen during last night's quake. A woman lies beside the rocks, so close I worry she might be pinned. My eyes scan the area around her. She's alone. Whatever I hoped to gain by staying out of sight, I throw it away when I rush to the woman's side. Lees calls my name as I dart into the open.

"Stay there," I say. "Stay out of sight. I just want to see if I can help."

From up close, I can see that the woman's arm isn't pinned under the rock she lies beside, as I'd feared. Instead, it's propped against it to elevate a bloody wound on her wrist that's bound and wrapped with leaves of a plant I don't recognize. These unfamiliar leaves lie across the woman's face and neck, blood caking where it seeped around the edges. I lean over her chest, watching for any indication of the rise and fall of breath.

As my hand hovers over her, a stone cracks against my wrist. It bounces away, but before I can look up to see where it came from, another lands hard against my head, just above my left ear. White light sears across my vision and I drop to one knee, slumped over the woman on the ground.

"Don't touch her!" The voice is young and female, and comes from a ledge partway up the cliff. I look up and see the girl—small and skinny—and I think it must be the same person I saw running away with our food. Her eyes wide like a startled deer, she picks up another sharp rock and cocks her arm back. I jump to my feet. I don't know what she thinks I will do—what she hopes I will do. Whatever it is, she doesn't expect me to pull the sling from around my waist and load it with the rock she just threw at me.

She doesn't wait for me to take the shot. Before I can rotate the sling even once around my head, the girl is racing toward me, tackling me to the ground.

"Stay away from my mother!" She scratches and snarls at me, pulling my hair and slamming my head against the ground, but she's small and I easily throw her from my chest.

Before I can get to my feet, though, Lees has emerged. She grabs my spear from the spot where I dropped it and points it at the girl on the ground.

"It's all right," I say, thinking the spear might terrorize this child—she can't be older than Lees and Roon—but she ignores it. Instead she scrambles over the ground to the woman's side.

"Don't worry," she whispers. "I have more for you." Her hands clutch at something on the ground around her— more leaves, apparently dropped when she fell. She scoops them up and presses them to the woman's face. Folding the woman's limp arms across her chest, she drapes the leaves on the woman's hands and adds more to her wrist. The leaves are dry and wilted, and when an arm slides to the woman's side, they float up on a current of air before wafting back down to the ground. "Mother," the girl mutters, clutching at the leaves. "Hold still. You have to let me help you."

I'm not sure what's worse. That the girl's mother has died, or that the girl stubbornly refuses to let it be so. I watch her working, peeling back a blood-soaked leaf from the woman's face and smoothing another in its place.

I come up behind her and set a hand on the girl's shoulder. I notice her knee protruding through a tear in her pants. An angry abrasion covers the bottom of her exposed thigh. She must have been with her mother when the cave collapsed. I wonder how bad her own injuries are.

"It's too late," I say. But she tugs her shoulder from my grasp.

"It's not. I can save her. I can save her. . . ." Slumped over the body of her mother, her voice becomes a jumble of murmured words of comfort for the dead woman on the ground.

"It is," I say again. "There's nothing more that can be done."

The child never looks up, so dedicated is she to her work. I watch her, and an unbidden memory comes to me like something long forgotten rising from the bottom of a dark lake.

I see a girl, climbing from a kayak steered by her brother as it docks on a strange beach. The boy calls to the girl, but she won't listen. Instead, she runs headlong into the water toward a kayak that is coming in behind them from the sea. Other boats are there—her clan climbs to the shore, shaking with exhaustion, but she notices no one. Her eyes are on one boat—one double kayak—where her mother lies in the rear seat as if she's sleeping.

The girl reaches her mother's side. She runs a cold wet hand across the woman's cold wet face. A sudden flash of fear burns through her as someone lifts her from behind.

Her brother carries her, kicking and flailing, to land. He drops her on the sand and orders her not to move. "Watch your sisters," he says. "I'll take care of the rest."

The rest . . . That's what Chev had called her. But I knew what he meant. He meant our mother. He meant he would take care of our mother, because she was dead.

The girl still crouches in front of me, but her edges smear as my vision blurs. Hot tears run down my face.

An arm drapes around my shoulder. Lees tugs me to her side. "She's dead," I say. The words come out in a shudder of pain that's been held like a clenched fist for too long.

"I know." I'm not sure, but I think Lees knows I'm not talking about the woman on the ground.

I don't notice at first, but at some point the little girl stops leaning over her mother and turns her attention to me. She begins to say something, but her voice cuts off. A sound comes from the cave—rock falling, and after, a faint sound like an animal in pain.

Lees looks up—she's heard it too—and she hurries to the mouth of the cave. The girl is right behind her.

"What are you doing?" I call. "You can't go in there!" I jump to my feet, hurrying to grab them and hold them both back. Lees turns her ear to the cave and closes her eyes, listening.

"Did you hear that? Someone's alive in there. We need to—"

But before Lees can say what we need to do, the quiet of the clearing is split in two by the long, high howl of a wolf. The howl of a wolf coming from inside the cave.

"It's Black Dog!"

The girl turns her dirt-smeared face toward me, her tired, red-rimmed eyes wide and bright again. "Black Dog is alive!"

Before I can reach out to stop her, the girl scrambles over the rocks that fill the opening of the cave and disappears from view.

ELEVEN

She's gone before I can catch her by the arm. Right behind her, Lees runs to the mouth of the cave and climbs up on a boulder that partially blocks the way.

"Lees, stop! You can't go in there—"

"She could need help—"

"She's not your responsibility." My eyes brush over the body of the dead woman. I don't mean to abandon her daughter, but I can't let my own sister run headlong into danger to help someone who isn't even of our clan.

"But the dog—"

"What could you possibly know about dogs?" I ask. Lees has never seen a dog in her life. Neither have I.

"Father used to tell me stories about them," she says. "Before he died."

This stops me short. I wouldn't have guessed Lees remembered any stories from our father at all. She was only six when he died. "He told you about dogs?"

"About how long ago our clan kept dogs. How they were like wolves, but tame, and helped the people with their work."

I know these stories too. Stories of the days many generations ago, before a storm took the lives of half the clan. All the dogs were lost in that storm, and our clan has never kept dogs since.

Maybe dogs remind Lees of our father. Maybe the thought of seeing one feels like reaching back to him, to the stories he told in the past. Before I can ask, Lees is beyond my grasp, climbing through the mouth of the cave. I call her name but she never turns back.

Lees's willingness to help a person who is not clan is beyond my understanding. She hasn't been groomed for clan leadership. She hasn't been taught to never let anyone or anything come before the clan. She's fortunate—in so many ways, she's the most free of the three of us—because the least is expected of her.

At least until now.

I call her name twice after she drops down into the cave, but I get no response. I have no choice but to follow.

Inside the cave I find two boulders as high as my shoulders. Above my head, light pours in—these rocks must have formed part of the ceiling before the quake loosened them and let them fall. A sound—part howl, part cry—comes from beyond the place where Lees and the other girl stand. They have gone far back into the cave. Sweeping my eyes over the space beyond the girls, I see nothing.

The sound comes again and Lees drops to a crouch. "There!"

The other girl straightens and slides farther into the dark, skirting the edge of a huge trench that splits the floor in two. "Be careful!" I imagine this girl falling into the trench, and my stomach drops. As I get closer, I see how deep it is—at least as deep as the height of three men—with sides too steep to climb. She would be lost to us if she fell in.

I think of this as I move closer to Lees, reaching for her hand. I edge forward, peering into the hole. It's narrower at the bottom than at the top, with straight, smooth walls. And at the very bottom, tucked so far into the rock that his voice is muffled, stands an animal that looks like a wolf with a black coat. If I saw him in the wild, I would think *wolf.* I would think *run.*

He sees the girl, and he howls again. His front paws claw at the steep ledge of rock that separates the two of them as if he intends to climb straight up to her, but his feet skid back down. He tries again, manages by force of will to climb a bit, but then tumbles to the bottom once more. He lets out a yelp as he twists from his back onto his feet. The sound bounces from the walls, mingling with the skittering of pebbles.

This dog confounds me. Everything about him tells me he's a predator—everything except his behavior. He whimpers, and I suspect he's no danger at all.

I *suspect*, but I can't be sure.

"Don't cry, Black Dog," the girl says. "We'll get you out. We'll find a way."

"Don't tell him that," I say. The dog whimpers again, and the sound claws at my heart the way his feet clawed at the rock. "We can't help him. We can't reach him, and there's no way to lift him out."

"Yes, there is," says Lees. I turn toward her, to ask her what she has in mind. But before I can get out a single word, she is far below me, clambering down into the trench.

"Lees!" I don't think; I don't wait for her to turn. Instead I scramble out to the rim of the pit and start to climb right after her. There is only a small incline at the top edge where the rock slopes. Then it drops off sharply—too sharp to climb up or down. All I can think of is getting my hands on her and pulling her back out while I still can.

"Don't follow me," Lees says, as she crawls to the lip of the rock that plunges straight down to the floor of the pit. Without a look back at me, or even a glance at the girl, she swings her legs out and drops to the small circle of ground beside the dog.

My legs convulse so hard, I drop onto the slanted rock where I stand. I almost can't look down. When I force myself, the world around me spins. A loud sound echoes though the cave—the sound of my voice as I scream my sister's name. My ears ring with her name, mixed with a buzz like a thousand honeybee wings. I tremble so hard, I almost lose my balance and join her at the bottom of the pit.

But I can't fall to pieces. I need to stay calm. I look around, searching for tools that could help us. The two girls are calling to each other, Lees shrieking with delight that the dog is being friendly to her. The other girl sobbing that Lees is with the dog and she is not. My eyes move from rock to rock—there's nothing here. The net outside isn't strong enough for Lees to climb. It would never hold her weight. Would my spear be long enough to reach her, if I lay across the ground and dangled it over the wall of the pit? Could she use it to pull herself up, or would she just slide back down again?

Far below, I hear her, struggling to find footholds. "I didn't expect this to be ꜱo hard," she says, breathless with effort. The other girl shouts instructions to her, but I know it's no use. Even before Lees climbed down, I knew there was no climbing up those straight walls. If I'd thought it were possible, I'd have climbed down myself.

My eyes search the cave, but I find nothing long enough to reach her, nothing strong enough to pull her up. All I see are rocks—small rocks, big rocks, boulders.

"Wait," I say. It comes out as a whisper, a word spoken

more to myself than to the girls. But they both hear and they both listen.

I look across the wide mouth of the trench at the girl. This girl who is not even clan. This stranger for whom my sister is risking her life. "What's your name?" I call.

"What's yours?" There's a clear note of distrust in her voice.

"I'm called Mya," I say. "And that's my sister Lees, putting herself in danger to rescue your dog."

"My name is Noni," the girl says.

"Well, Noni, you and I have a big job to do."

Together, Noni and I gather the largest boulders that we can lift and bring them to the rim of the trench. There are others bigger and heavier—those we would have to roll—but I don't dare use those.

After the boulders, we collect the bigger rocks. These we stack separately, off to the side.

I stand back and study the shape of the trench—the way the walls slope down from the front edge, but drop almost straight down from the edge that faces the back of the cave. Even the sloping side drops over a ledge a few paces down, right where Lees climbed over. Though the trench is wide at the top, it narrows as it deepens, so that the space where Lees and the dog stand is a circular spot of ground only about twelve paces wide.

With Noni's help, I carry one of the largest boulders to

the rim of the trench and look in. "Stay as tight against the back wall as you can," I tell Lees. The dog, sensing that something is about to happen, huddles against her. "Lees, you need to stay out of the way. I'm going to let it roll down. If it comes close to you . . ." I trail off. What can she do if it comes close to her?

"If it comes close, I'll jump," she says. "Don't worry."

I do worry, of course. But with Noni's help, I slide the boulder forward until it rolls into the trench.

It tumbles quickly, crushing chunks of rock as it slides down the slope and over the overhang to crash into the bottom of the pit. Lees jumps back, and the dog yelps and dives behind her legs. The boulder rocks forward, coming to a rest in almost the center of the space.

"All right," I say. "That's the first one."

In this manner—Noni and I dropping one boulder after the other into the pit—the pit gradually fills. Lees builds a small wall to stand behind and keeps the dog out of the way of the falling rocks.

Boulder after boulder falls, each making the trench a little shallower.

After the sixth boulder and a pile of the bigger rocks, Lees can reach my outstretched arms when she climbs to the top of the mound. Still, the dog is skittish and won't follow.

Noni takes my place, leaning over into the trench and calling, "Black Dog!" At the sound of her voice, the dog bounds up the rocks. He comes partway and begins to slide back down, but Lees grabs him by the scruff of fur behind his neck. My breath stills, my heart freezing from the sudden chill that runs through my blood at the sight of my sister so close to the jaws of a wolf. *But it's not a wolf. . . . It's not a wolf. . . .* I whisper this to myself as she hauls him up, dragging him until he finds footing on the sloping edge of the trench. Noni leans over and grabs him by the front legs and he is out.

Once Noni pulls Black Dog out of the way, I lie down on my stomach again and reach for Lees. Each heavy thump of my heart lifts my chest from the ground. Exhaustion swamps me, but I cannot slow my effort. She is not out yet. My fingers wrap around her thin, cold wrists. She seems frail, like the little girl she was just a few years ago. Rocks fall and echo, tumbling out from under Lees's feet as she scrambles up and drops onto the ground beside me.

All that I plan to say—all the anger and scolding—fades from my mind when Lees's arm drapes across my back. I sit up. Black Dog jumps up against Noni as she bends to pet his fur. He runs a circle around her and licks her face. I've never seen anything like this—a tame predator, not only showing no threat but showing a kind of affection I would never have thought possible. "Look," Lees says. "He loves her."

I almost object. As I get to my feet, I almost say that a predator can't love its prey. But I don't let the words out, because watching the reunion between this girl and this dog, I think maybe I am completely wrong.

What enchantment does this island hold, I wonder, if this is possible?

The dog runs a circle around us, even pausing to jump up against my own legs. I leap back, startled, wondering if he meant to dig his teeth into my throat.

"You don't have to be afraid," Noni says. "You can stroke his back. Go ahead. Lean over him and stroke him."

He runs away from me, and I let out a deep breath. I do not want to touch this animal. I do not want to get near his teeth. But when the dog runs away, retreating behind Noni, I bend at the waist, making a show of my willingness to try.

From the blackness at the back of the cave comes the sound of falling rock. The dog lets out a howl, and I flinch. "We need to get out in the open," I say. "It's too dangerous in here."

I let the girls go first, and the dog follows right behind them. I climb out last. There are so many things I want to ask Noni about—how she and her mother got here, and where they came from—but before I can speak, she is screaming, grabbing at the dog and pulling him away from her mother. "Stop! Black Dog, stop!" Looking, I see the dog licking blood from the woman's face. "Get away," she says. The dog leaps over the woman's body and lies down, curled against her legs. "He's so hungry," she says. "He doesn't know better." Her voice is composed, but tears spill from the corners of her eyes.

I think of the food—the food Noni stole. "Well, give us back our food," I say, "and we can all have something to eat. Even Black Dog. That's first. But then we need to work hard, setting up a camp and digging a grave. It's too late in the morning to prepare for a burial by midday, so it will have to be done tomorrow."

I think of Kol, far to the south in his camp. I imagine him standing beside his father's grave. I hear the echo of the drum. "We'll dig the grave after we eat, and tomorrow at midday, we'll bury her."

"No! I won't let you—"

"Noni, there's no hope for her. She's dead, and we need to treat her body with respect—"

"Then we can't bury her. That's what my father's clan, the Tama, do. But my mother was born into another clan— the Pavu clan—and they don't bury their dead."

"Then what—"

"They burn them."

TWELVE

Noni returns the pack of food she stole, but she offers no apology. I don't ask for one either. I think of her mother, dead or maybe dying, when Noni dared sneak up on two sleeping strangers. I think of the fact that she took only food—she left knives, an ax, atlatls, and darts. I think of how long she may have gone without food while she tried to save her mother.

And I decide there's nothing to discuss. She did what she had to do to survive and to help a person she loved. Isn't that what we all do every day?

We don't eat much, and what we do eat gets consumed in a hurry, sitting on the dunes facing the water, like we're on a break during a long journey and don't have time for a real meal. Noni gulps down pieces of dried fish and clover roots like she thinks I might change my mind and take it away from her. Even so, she shares what she has with Black Dog. I scoop out some extra fish for her, since she gave him almost half of what she had.

Noni eats with her head down, concentrating only on her food, but when she finishes she finally looks up at me and Lees. Something in her gaze says she's trying to decide if we fit into her dreams or her nightmares.

"So, Noni," I start, "are there other people from your clan here?"

"No," she says.

I wait, giving her a chance to offer more of an explanation of her presence on the island. But that one word is all I get. "So you came here with only your mother?"

"We ran away," she says.

"Were you running away from a betrothal?" Lees asks. Her voice is excited, as if she's forgotten what it means to run away. The gravity of leaving your home behind.

"No. We were running from my father."

Lees goes quiet. So does Noni. The only sound comes from the dog, as he sniffs the ground for dropped scraps.

"You paddled out to sea to escape your father?" I ask. "How did you know you would find land?"

"We didn't." Noni scoops the final bite of clover root into her mouth. "But my father's reach has no boundaries but the sea. Everywhere else, he's found us. So the sea was the only choice left." She scrapes the last of her fish to the ground, and the dog snaps them up. "I was wondering the same thing about you. I wondered why two girls would be all the way out on the sea. And why they would arrive right when the ground stopped shaking—"

"Right when it *stopped* shaking? Did it shake for long?"

"All day," she says. "The first tremor came at first light. They stopped and started, over and over, until you landed on the shore after dark." She keeps the same reluctant tone—like I'm a child tugging on her pant leg, begging her to tell me a story.

"And when did you—"

"I don't think I want to answer any more questions," she says. "I think I want to ask questions now."

She asks us where we came from, and we tell her the truth. She asks us how we knew about this island, and we tell her the truth.

"So why, then?" she asks. "Why did you come? You must have been running from something."

"Our brother is the High Elder," Lees says, "and he wants to make me marry a man I don't love."

"My father is the High Elder, too. The High Elder of the Tama."

"Is that the clan camped at the river? Straight into shore from here?" I remember the man who pursued us out to sea when Lees and I paddled past, but I keep this thought to myself.

"Yes," Noni says. She glances up at me, then just as quickly slides her gaze away.

"And you and your mother left when your father did something bad?"

Noni sighs. She is not eager to tell this story—no spark of anticipation lights her eyes. Instead, they darken with resolve.

"My father is a hard man. Hard and violent. All my life he's been violent toward my mother. Sometimes he was worse than others. Sometimes . . . he was much worse." Noni pauses. She takes a drink from her waterskin. "We've tried to run away before, but he has always found us. And every time he's dragged us back, he's punished her worse for leaving. Finally, she stopped trying. I think she would have never left again if he had never . . ." Noni stops. Some subtle change ripples across her, and I'm carried back to the canyon where Kol's father died, to the moment right before the mammoths began to run. "The day before we left, she caught him with me, and she swore he would never touch me again." Noni's hands fly to her face, muffling her last words.

"Your father beat you too?" Lees asks, her eyes wide.

"He did. . . ." Noni's voice drops so low, I almost can't hear her. "Since last summer, my father has beaten me even worse than he's beaten my mother," she whispers. "It was as if he wanted to find a new way to hurt her."

Lees touches her arm, but she flinches back.

"I'm all right," she says. "I know it wasn't my fault. He's a selfish man. A man who does whatever he chooses, and hurts—even kills—people who try to stop him. He chose to beat me, and when my mother tried to stop him, he killed her."

"He killed her?" I ask. "I thought she died from the quake—"

"No. She was so badly hurt. He meant to kill her. I'm sure that was what he wanted."

The tide is coming in. As Noni speaks, the urgency of the waves seems to grow. A vague fear stirs in me. I look out over the sea, almost expecting to see a boat on the horizon, but the water is smooth and clear in every direction. I force myself to draw a deep breath.

"He let her go to the healer, but what can a healer do with a body so broken? Nothing but chant and pray. Her injuries—on her face and her arms—those were the ones you could see. But she had injuries you couldn't see. Blood came up her throat. . . ." Her voice snags on the words. She climbs to her feet and the dog reacts, pacing a circle around her. She looks back toward the cave, and I know she is thinking of her mother's body, lying in the open. She shuffles restlessly, and I'm about to get to my feet and suggest we return to the cave, when she sits back down. The dog lets out a low whine and settles down beside her again.

"She fell asleep in the healer's hut that evening, so I slept in our hut with my father. But in the darkest part of the night, she woke me. She was taking me away.

"It wasn't sensible—no one so hurt should try to travel—but she wouldn't be deterred. Black Dog would not leave my side, so she let him come. We took a boat from the river. This time we had to go to a place where no one had ever gone before, so we headed for the horizon.

"The Tama never go far from shore. We had no idea what we would find, but we knew whatever it was, it couldn't be worse. My mother prayed to the Divine that she would provide a camp for us. And she did.

"She led us to this island—a place full of game and freshwater. My mother was so happy, she thanked the Divine over and over. I think she knew she would die, and she wanted me to be safe."

Noni is interrupted by a loud howl. Not Black Dog this time. This time, it's a wolf. Then a second voice joins the first.

My mind turns to my own home—to my clan and family far away—and I can't help but feel grateful that no matter how bad our problems with Chev might be, he cares for us. He is nothing like the evil High Elder Noni's father is. I might question his decisions, but I know he would never willingly put us in danger.

Another howl cuts through my thoughts, and I realize

the wolves can smell the scent of human remains. "Noni," I say. "I think we need to move your mother's body."

"You're right."

We head back to the cave without talking. Even Lees stays quiet, despite her habit of speaking to fill up the silences.

When we reach the cave—when I see her mother's body in need of burial—I realize there is one thing I must say to Noni, though I hate to. I don't tell her about the man who pursued us from the shore of the Tama's camp. But I do tell her something that may upset her just as much.

"Noni, we can't burn your mother's body."

"But—"

"The column of smoke would be so thick, it would be visible from shore. From your father's camp. He'd know you were here."

Noni shakes her head. She kneels beside her mother's shoulder and picks up her hand as if she were trying to comfort her. "We can't bury her. She wouldn't want that."

"What if we moved her into the cave?" Lees asks. She kneels down beside Noni on the ground. "We don't have to bury her, but maybe we could *cover* her. We could collect rocks—just a thin layer would deter predators, but she wouldn't truly be buried."

Noni stills, staring at her mother's hand in hers. "Yes," she finally says.

We work quickly, the three of us gathering all the small

stones from the floor of the cave. Noni works as hard as Lees and I, despite the purpose of our task.

When it comes time to move her mother, though, Noni breaks. The face she kept frozen even as she told her story finally melts when she bends down and brushes back her mother's hair. Tears stream from her eyes, but she doesn't bother to wipe them away. She lets them drip from her chin, dropping onto her mother's cheek. "I'm sorry," she whispers. "I'm so sorry."

"Noni," I say, "it's not your fault. You couldn't have protected her from your father—"

"That's not what I mean," she says. "It's my fault I couldn't save her."

My eyes trace over the dead woman's face—the leaves are still draped across her cheekbones. My eyes flit to her wrist. The leaf wrapping still covers her wound there.

"The feverweed. I did my best. . . ."

"I've never seen this plant before." I pick up a leaf that lies on the ground, one of many that fell or blew away as Noni struggled to treat her mother's wounds. "What does it do? How does it help?"

Noni draws a deep breath and lifts up the bottom edge of her parka. On her abdomen, just below her navel, a long gash is packed with feverweed. I gasp.

"My father's work," she says. "When I tried to help my mother." Dried blood stains her skin, but the wound is healing. "The plant stops the flow of blood. It takes away pain if you chew it, and it will bring down a fever. My mother always used it with me when I got hurt. She was always able to heal me."

But I couldn't heal her. She doesn't say it. She doesn't have to.

"Some injuries can't be healed," I say. It's not much, but it's the truth. Right now, I can't think of anything I can give Noni but the truth.

Later, we make camp right on the beach. Lees finds three long branches to use as tent poles, and we wrap the mammoth hide around them to form the outer wall. We eat more of the dried meat and roots. Lees begins to talk about hunting together. Black Dog plays in the surf, but he looks around restlessly. He's ready to hunt, too.

"Tomorrow," I tell him when he jumps against my legs and splashes seawater over my boots. "Tomorrow we will be ready to hunt."

Though I don't say the words aloud, to myself I wonder if tomorrow we may even be on our way home. Kol and Chev would have certainly spoken by now. Could it be possible that Chev has already changed his mind and Kol will soon be on his way?

When we climb into the tent to sleep, the room falls quiet almost as soon as the hide drapes shut. But although fatigue tugs at my limbs and my eyes grow heavy, I don't sleep. I lie awake and think of Noni's father and the violence that drove his family from him. What would he do if he knew that his wife had died? If he knew that Noni was here, would he come for her?

Would I try to protect her? She is not of our clan, and clan must come first. Defending Noni could put Lees at risk. But how could I let Noni's father take her, now that I know her story?

The sound of the girls' rhythmic breathing soothes me, and my eyes grow heavy. I let my lids fall shut, and I think of Kol sleeping in his own hut—the hut where we shared that cup of honey I brought to him, hoping to make peace.

Soon we will have our own hut that we share. A bed that we share. And I'll never have to sleep away from Kol again.

I fall asleep, warmed by the thought of my body stretched out in a bed beside his. I drift off, willing him to visit me in my dreams.

Until I wake with a start, as the ground beneath me shakes.

THIRTEEN

I sit up.

It's morning. By the shade of light streaming from the gap in the hide overhead, I can tell it's very early—not long past first light.

The quake felt so real, but the longer I'm awake, the more I wonder. I reach back into the murky gloom of sleep, to the moment right before the ground beneath me shook. . . .

I was dreaming of Kol.

He was beside me. . . . We were in the cave high in the cliff near my camp, lying together beneath the mammoth hide I'd wrapped him in when the cold sea had almost frozen the life out of him. My skin was pressed to his skin, but the cold was gone, replaced by a searing warmth. Kol leaned over me, and the shadow of his face fell over mine. . . .

And then the ground shook. And I sat up.

Nothing in our makeshift tent is out of place. The pack

of food still hangs from the notch where it was suspended to keep it off the ground. Even the waterskin loosely looped over the pack hasn't fallen.

Just a dream, I tell myself. But I shiver as the memory of Kol's warmth slips away.

I slide out of bed, careful not to disturb Noni or Lees, and slip on my boots and my parka. Grabbing my spear, I step out of the warm stillness of the tent and into the chilly breeze of the beach.

The stillness falls away—the world outside is active with momentum. My heart's rhythm falls in time with the rush of the waves, the whisper of the wind in the trees that cling to the ledges behind me. My head swivels on my shoulders, and there, high up on the cliff, something moves. Something big.

The sun is rising on the other side of the island, and the western shore is still shadowed. Yet I know I saw movement.

My hand flinches on the shaft of my spear. My eyes search the stirring leaves, hoping to see it again. An elk? It must have been an elk. The quick glimpse of a broad brown back passing between trees, so far out on the edge of the cliff so early in the day. Only an elk would trust its footing on those steep ledges above the sea.

Lees and Noni will sleep a long time yet. I could be back before they wake, dragging a kill behind me.

It isn't long before I've packed supplies and gathered up weapons. Along with my spear, I take an atlatl and darts. I wrap the sling Ama gave me around my waist again today and drop some palm-sized rocks into my pack. I slide my waterskin over my shoulder.

The trail from the beach winds up the cliff wall, climbing and switching back a few times, splitting off at different ledges that overlook the beach before breaking into smaller paths. Some head back to the shoreline at the foot of the cliff. Others wind down the gentle slope that descends from the cliff's southern face, where trees spring up, protected by the steep rock from the north wind. I stay on the main trail, following it all the way to the top of the cliff, to an overhanging rock that gives a startling view out over the water in every direction. It's beautiful, but there's something lonely about the vast stretch of unbroken sea, and I don't linger.

From here, the trail winds around the peak and drops slowly down into trees, toward lower cliffs that border the western shore. With each step the light dims and the shade deepens, as the trail becomes a broken pattern of shadow and sun. The shade pushes in so close, I can feel it on my skin like the cool mist that rises off the water early in the morning. I peer through the growth that borders the trail, looking for both predators and prey. Dense swaths of trees alternate with open clearings, and at intervals light pours through gaps, filling me with a sense of something peering back at me—something unseen.

Still, when I stop and search the brush, I find no sign of the elk I saw earlier.

I begin to think of turning back when I hear the laughing sound of running water—the spring must not be far. Noni told us that a creek runs from one of the highest points on the western edge of the island, filling a lake in the woods south of the cliffs. Though she'd been on the island only a few days before we arrived, she'd explored, searching out sources of water and feverweed. Noni loves the lake—she said it lies so still and wide it reflects the clouds. I tell myself I will hike there when the girls wake, after we've had a morning meal of fish and cleaned the elk I'll be bringing back to camp soon. I tell myself all these things to quiet the voice of doubt that whispers in my thoughts—doubt that an elk was ever there at all.

Then something moves in the corner of my sight. Something beyond the trail, beyond the trees that edge the path. Something is coming.

I hear it moving off to my right—the side of the trail that skirts the cliffs. A dark shape like a living shadow slides between the trees, bending back branches that snap as it passes. Spots of pale sunlight catch in its fur, fewer than twenty paces from where I stand. A smooth, brown coat covers a wide, high back.

The elk. It must be the elk. As it moves behind me, gravel and twigs crunch under its feet. I stop.

Peering into the space where the animal passed, I notice a wide swath of flattened underbrush. The thought of bringing in a kill of such size thrills me, but I hesitate. The wind blows in off the water, and something like dread crawls across my skin.

Another twig snaps, and I realize my prey is getting away. I practically run back up the trail, watching for movement through the trees. About halfway back toward the overhanging rock, I finally catch up to it.

I can't quite see its edges. It's hidden by thick shade, but now and then it presses against branches and moves under the light. At a small opening in the trees that allows a circle of sun to reach the ground, I see the height of its back.

That's when I know it's not an elk. It's far too big. The peak of its back is far too high from the ground.

I continue to follow it, as the mistake I've made sinks in. Not an elk. Not a deer. Much bigger. My fear sharpens as the dark shape moves into a clearing at the end of the path, right at the overhanging rock.

It's a short-faced bear. His shoulder is as tall as the top of my head.

Terror stills my feet. I'm certain that he will soon smell

my scent and turn on me. I draw a deep breath and prepare to run.

But then I see what the bear sees, and I know he won't turn around. He is pursuing other prey. Right in front of him, at the end of the trail, a man stands with his back against the ledge of rock.

Kol.

He doesn't see me. The bear is too big—so big he blocks Kol's view, so big he blocks his escape.

The rock ledge pins him from behind—the drop over its side is too long and steep—and the path to his right is blocked by the bear. But there is another path to his left—a trail that follows the ledge of the rock wall. I see him throw a quick glance down that path before turning his full attention back to the bear.

He takes a slight step to the side, keeping the bear in front of him, but positioning himself so he has a route behind him. I watch him—his eyes darting from the bear to the trail and back again. My breath comes so quick, I feel as if I'm struggling not to drown. My heart kicks like legs treading water.

The wind blows in, and on the air is the scent of the bear and something else. Something like cold blood. The blood of all the prey the bear has killed. Though the wind is cold, sweat beads on my lip and my brow.

Kol's back leans against the ledge, and he bends out as far as he can. His arm extends over his shoulder—the arm that holds his spear.

One spear. It looks so small beside the huge bear—too small to stop him, or even to make a difference. But what options does he have? He cocks his arm, bringing his hand behind his ear, and fires his spear into the bear's side.

The bear's growl is sharp and clear and cuts through all other sound. But he doesn't drop. He doesn't even sag. Kol's spear sticks out from his side, a deep gash torn through him, but still he has strength. Sound pours from his open jaws. The sound itself seems to push me back. I dig my heels into the dirt beneath my feet, refusing to be moved. My spear slides in my hand as I ready my shot.

And then the bear rears.

All his weight moves, and the sight of him—dark, rippling with power—reminds me of the sound of thunder. His huge back legs straighten, and he lifts his massive frame upward. He teeters, the only sign that a spear has been planted in his flesh, and brings a huge paw forward, landing a blow to Kol's head. Kol ducks, but the bear's claws scrape across the back of his scalp.

He falls, landing at the bear's feet, but he doesn't stay down. He isn't giving up. He crawls away, trying to reach the path behind him.

I focus on the hole in the bear's side, torn open by Kol's

spear. I have just one shot. Then we will both be unarmed. I need to make this strike count.

But before I can throw the spear, Kol pulls himself up. Blood leaks from the gashes in his scalp and runs down his hair, beading and dripping onto his shoulders. He moves so slowly, like a small child putting weight on his feet for the first time, unsure if he can trust his legs to hold him. But they do hold him, and as I watch, he turns his back to the bear and stumbles forward, almost falling.

But he doesn't fall. He catches himself. And then he runs.

The path behind him hugs the cliff as it descends, and he stumbles more than runs, falling forward with every step. The bear stays right behind him, not giving up.

But I won't give up either.

I follow, hoping for the trail to open on the perfect vantage point—for the Divine to reveal to me the perfect chance to take the perfect shot. Only the perfect shot could bring him down. I hurry to stay close, but then Kol stops in the middle of the trail.

In front of him and to his right, a face of smooth rock rises straight and unbroken, towering over his head. To his left, the path drops off to the ground below, too high a drop to jump. Kol reaches up, feeling for a ledge. From where I stand, slightly uphill of him, I see that just above his hands, the rock levels off. A flat terrace, wide and grass covered, is only a small space above the reach of his searching hands.

The bear growls again, a guttural sound full of fatigue and pain. The wound Kol gave him is taking a toll, yet he doesn't withdraw. He doesn't turn and look back the way he came, wondering if there might be an easier way to feed himself today. Maybe he knows his wound is bad—maybe he knows he's dying. Whatever his reasons, his focus stays on Kol. Still, the bear doesn't move in. Not yet. He's waiting, gathering his remaining strength for a final assault.

My choices are few. I could strike with my spear, or I could try to get above Kol—to the terrace that's just beyond his reach—to try to pull him up. My eyes scan the deep gash under the bear's ribs. Blood pools in his coat. Could I land a second strike in the same place? Would it be enough to drop him? If not, what will he do? Will he kill Kol before I can move to help him?

I can't be sure, but I also can't stand to wait and do nothing any longer. I creep as close to the bear as I can and throw my spear.

It pierces the bear's hide, lodging no more than the width of a hand below Kol's. The bear turns and looks back in my direction. His head dips but he does not fall. Instead, he swings back around to face Kol.

I have to climb. I have to try to pull Kol up.

I shrug off my pack and run my hands over the cliff wall. It's steep, its surface pitted and ridged, and my fingers dig into narrow crevices above my head. With this tenuous grip, I pull one foot up—one small step—and wedge my toes in place. Then another step—just as small, just as difficult.

Still, little by little, I rise.

Hand over hand, foot over foot. My fingers dig so deep into the cracks within the stone, my skin tears and blood coats my hands. I hardly notice. It doesn't matter. All my focus is on my toe pressing into the rock, finding a foothold. Then another. The climbing gets easier. I pull in a breath, and a hint of hope expands inside me.

When I can see over the top of the wall—when I can feel grass under my reaching hand—I let that hope take hold. I scramble up the last few steps until I'm standing, looking down on Kol and the bear.

From here, I can see the size of him. He is tall enough to look Kol in the eye, and he is almost as wide as Kol's arm span. Even the spears protruding from his side look small and inconsequential from here.

I move quickly, scooping up three big stones from the ground. Breathless and shaking, I fling the first one at the path behind the bear. It lands hard, and I throw the second from behind him, hitting him squarely in the back. He swings his head around. The last rock lands against his rear leg, and the bear lets out a growl of warning as he shifts his feet, lumbering in a circle toward the unseen aggressor that would dare attack him a second time from behind.

With the bear distracted, I turn my attention to Kol. I watch him sweep his eyes over the ledge until he sees me. Relief flashes across his face. I want to shout his name, but I don't dare make a sound. Instead I silently drop to the ground and reach for him.

Flat on my stomach, I extend my arms. Kol takes my hands.

The ground, cold and hard, digs into the skin of my hips. Kol's arms interlace with mine and I shift all my weight back, pushing hard into the ground beneath my knees.

My blood-slick hands slide along the inside of Kol's sleeves, and a sticky red trail coats the sealskin. Kol slips away, slithering out of my grip.

I lunge forward, grabbing his hands, and one foot catches under him. His weight shifts. He pushes off that foot, and he moves closer to me. My hands clutch the hide of his parka, and he springs upward. All at once, his chest rises over the edge of the rock. One leg swings over. Then the other.

With one final grunt, he flips his body onto the ground beside me.

For a moment I hover over him. Relief crowds out every thought, and I forget to speak. I forget to cry. All I do is drop to the dirt beside him and pull him into my arms.

I would stay like this if I could. I wouldn't need to ask him how he came here or why. I wouldn't need to ask him anything at all. If I could simply lie on the ground here and hold on to him, knowing he is safe.

But he won't lie still. He sits up, and before I can stop him he is climbing to his feet, running a hand over his hair.

It comes away coated in blood.

For a moment, he stares wide-eyed at his hand. "I think," he starts, but he doesn't finish. His left leg buckles beneath him, and he drops down hard onto his knee. "Still a little weak, I guess," he says. I remember the night of the stampede. The deep cuts in his knee.

I crouch down in front of him. "How bad are you? Can you walk?"

He slumps forward and blood runs across his forehead and down his cheek. I think of Noni and her feverweed—the claims she made that it could stop the flow of blood. Would I know the plant if I saw it? My eyes sweep the sparse shrubs and vines that grow between the rock face and the trees.

Before he gives me his answer, a twig snaps.

Then another.

The sound comes from the shade of the woods, just about fifteen paces from the ledge . . . just ten paces from where we sit.

I look at Kol, and I realize what a grave mistake I've made. To climb the rock to get above him, I was forced to drop my pack and leave it behind. My pack with the atlatl and darts.

And our spears are in the bear.

I reach for my knife—the small thin blade of flint tucked into Ama's sling that is tied at my waist, and I know that this weapon will be useless against a short-faced bear. Or a wolf. Or any other predator that might step out of the shade and into the sunlight.

I glance back at the way we just came, wondering if it would be possible for us to flee by going down the rock face. I could retrieve my pack. But would we be putting ourselves back in the path of a wounded bear?

Could Kol even make that jump, I wonder, as he swipes more blood away from his eyes.

One more snap of a twig—this one louder than the others before it, and I prepare to scramble down. I'll help him. . . . I'll ease him over the ledge.

But then I hear my name, and I turn back.

At the edge of the clearing, just this side of the trees, stands Chev.

FOURTEEN

Framed by the branches that edge the woods, my brother's face peers at me like the face of a ghost. My thoughts reel, fighting and thrashing at the end of an unseen cord like a harpooned seal fighting against the rope.

Chev couldn't have known where to find us without Kol. Kol must have brought him here. Because here he is, not surprised to see me, but surprised to see Kol on the ground, blood flowing down his face.

"What happened?" Chev asks, as he rushes to Kol and drops to his knees. He takes his head in his hands, tilting it to look at his wound.

Watching him, I want to shout for him to back away. I want to scream that he is not needed to tend to Kol's injuries. But I know it won't help Kol if I fight with my brother now. Instead, I speak in a voice just loud enough to be heard. "I can take care of him. There's a plant on this island that slows the flow of blood. I'll find some. We can use it to treat his wounds."

My words rattle in the air. Despite my calm tone, inside my gut something kicks and writhes, like a beetle on its back that can't right itself.

"It was a bear," Kol says. "I guess it got the best of me." Kol says this as if it's a joke—as if we are meant to laugh. But Chev's frown deepens.

And my anger soars.

"I can take care of Kol," I say. "There's a girl on this island who will know how to treat his wounds. I'll take him to her."

"What girl? Do you mean Lees? Because I know you brought her here." Chev gets to his feet and slides an arm around Kol's back, under his arms. He draws him to his feet.

Bile rises in my throat as I form the words I want to spit at him—that it is his fault Kol is here in the first place . . . that if he hadn't meddled in his sisters' lives, none of this would be happening. But then Kol shrugs off Chev's arm and stands on his own.

"I'm fine," he says. "It's a head wound. Head wounds bleed, but I swear I'm fine." Kol turns to me. Blood still trickles along his forehead, but it does seem to be slowing. A smile spreads across his face like the sun on a cloudless day. It's a smile that could melt me. It always does. "I'm here with you. I'm all right."

And though the anger still burns in my throat, though I still taste it on my tongue, I force myself to let it go. Kol's eyes glow with the warmth of the meadow, and I let my anger float away on the breeze, as insubstantial as smoke.

Kol is here. He is right in front of me. What use do I have for anger now? If he brought Chev here, there must be a reason. And the light in his eyes tells me the reason must be something good. As my anger abates, curiosity takes its place.

"Why—" I start, but my question is interrupted by the sound of feet on the trail below. Before I can look down over the ledge, I hear a voice.

Seeri's voice.

She calls and waves two spears—both bloody—Kol's and mine. "I found these spears in a bear!" Before I can grab hold of his arm to help, Kol is sliding over the ledge and scrambling down the face of the cliff to join her. She tosses him his spear as if she's playing with him—as if she is challenging him to a throwing contest—but I notice her disheveled braid, the hem of her tunic, her own spear—all stained red with blood.

Chev and I follow Kol over the ledge, dropping down onto the trail beside him. Though my palms scrape a bit on the rock, sliding down is much easier than climbing up. Seeri is waiting for me on the path. She hands me my spear.

"I'd embrace you," she says, "but I should wait until I'm a little less bloody."

"You've killed it then?" Kol asks Seeri. It seems so obvious, so simple, as if he were saying, "You've gathered the roots," or "You've filled the waterskins."

"She didn't do it alone." A voice—a boy's voice—calls from farther back on the trail. Pek comes around a turn and Kol smiles.

"Then why is your spear the only one still clean?" he asks.

"Someone had to lure the bear to Seeri—"

"And then run away," she adds.

"I wasn't running away. I was getting clear so you could take the shot." His tone is light, with only a touch of defensiveness or maybe wounded feelings running along the edge of his words. But then Seeri laughs and it's clear she's just teasing him. Pek laughs, too, and all at once I feel the relief of knowing that the bear cannot threaten us anymore. My family is safe. There may be other bears on this island, of course, but the one that injured Kol will not be a danger to him anymore.

Not Kol. Not Seeri. Not Lees or Noni.

"The girls," I say. "Lees and Noni—"

"Noni?" Chev asks, raising an eyebrow at me.

"I left them sleeping—"

"We saw your camp on the beach," Kol says. "But we

saw you heading up the trail to the cliff. We assumed you and Lees were together, so we followed."

"When we couldn't find you right away, we split up," says Seeri. "Kol was lucky enough to find you—and the bear—before the rest of us."

I want to scold Seeri for making light of the bear attack, but Kol smiles. "Seeri and Pek are not leaving me alone again," he teases. "I'll take them with me to check on the girls. You take a little time to talk to your brother."

Kol says these words in the same offhand way he spoke of the dead bear. But I know these words are bigger than that. Kol can play down the significance of what I need to talk to my brother about, but it doesn't change anything. This conversation will have an impact on the future of both clans. We all know that.

I walk to Kol's side, brushing his hair from his forehead, looking for the wound he got from the bear. He steps back, out of my reach, and smooths his hair back down. "It's healing," he says, but I notice my hand is smeared with blood where I touched him. I show the red streaks to Kol. "Head wounds bleed, Mya. I feel fine." He winks, as if that proves something.

"When you get to Lees, show that wound to Noni, the girl who's with her. She'll know how to dress it."

One corner of Kol's mouth curls up. "Don't worry about me—"

"Promise you'll show her—"

"All right. I promise."

So I let them go. Dread flickers through me as Kol's face turns away . . . as his head swivels toward the path behind him . . . but still, I let him go. It's strange how the separation of just a few days has taught my heart what matters. Has taught me what to fear. But I know he won't be far, and he won't be away from me long.

My brother calls after them, "Keep an eye out for bears," and I think this might be a moment of levity from Chev, as close to teasing as he comes.

"And you keep an eye out for Morsk," Kol calls back over his shoulder. Before I can ask what he means, Kol, Seeri, and Pek disappear around the curve of the path.

"Morsk?" I say, tilting my head to look at my brother.

"Noni?" he says in reply.

I study my brother's expression—his hard mouth and set jaw, but also his sunken cheeks and tired eyes—and I see that there is more here than his stubborn refusal to answer me before I answer him. There is also the reluctance to admit that I don't have to answer him. That he can't force me to answer.

"Noni is a girl we met on the island," I finally say. "She came here with her mother, but her mother died." Chev's eyes widen. I want to tell him about Noni's father, to ask if he saw the clan on the shore, but I don't. There are other things to talk about first. More important things. "And what about Morsk?" I ask, my thoughts turning to his proposition in my family's hut. The memory of the way he stood too close, the way he blocked my path to the door, sends a flush of anger across my skin.

My brother shakes his head. "Come sit with me. I have something to say." He leads me back up the path to the overhanging rock, but he doesn't stop to look over the water. He slips under the cover of shade, steps off the path, and drops down onto the forest floor. The sun, much higher in the sky now than when I passed through here this morning, paints splashes of gold in a pattern on the ground. Chev sits in a circle of light and I sit opposite him, in shadow.

"It's a bold act, to leave your clan. It's a bold act that sends a bold message."

"I know."

"But what you did was even more than that, Mya. You didn't just leave your clan and your High Elder. You left your family and your brother. I understand you were angry at the decision I made, but you left without even speaking to me about it. I had to hear about it from your betrothed. I wanted to talk to you—to talk to Lees—but you were already gone."

"But Chev," I start, my voice a bit too high and a bit too loud, "talking doesn't always work with you. Sometimes only action is effective in getting you to listen."

Chev takes out his knife and digs a circle in the dirt. "And you thought this action—leaving your clan and family, even your betrothed—would be effective at changing your High Elder's mind?"

"I'd hoped," I say. "But it wasn't just that." I don't want Chev to see my actions as nothing more than manipulation. To see Lees's actions as nothing more than running away. "We were prepared to do whatever it took to give Lees her own choice. Even if it meant never going back."

Chev raises his eyes at these words. "Would you have done that? Stayed away for good?"

And with these words, I know we've won. He doesn't ask if we will do this. He asks if we would have. If we'd had to. If he hadn't changed his mind.

"Never mind. Don't answer. I know you would have. I guess that's why I'm here."

Sitting here in this broken, fragmented light, I feel the history of my life with my brother—the broken, fragmented life I've spent beside him—wrap around us in the same gold warmth. Patches of warmth. Memories in pieces. Warm, but broken. If we try to hold them and make them whole, they flicker and stir like the light on these leaves.

"So . . . Morsk?" I ask when the silence stretches too long. "Kol said to keep an eye?"

"He followed us here." At these words, I rise up on one knee and my head turns back toward the path. "Don't worry. There's no threat—nothing to be concerned about. But I told him. I said that Lees would not be marrying him. And he became . . . upset." Chev pauses for a moment. "I told him you wouldn't be marrying him either."

At this, I sit back down, giving him my full attention again. "So you knew—"

"No. I swear I didn't know he was thinking about you at all. I certainly didn't know he had talked to you. But Kol told me. He was furious. . . ."

I can't help but allow myself one small moment to think of this—to imagine Kol, *my betrothed*, confronting Chev on my behalf. I imagine his anger. I hear his words, telling him he will not honor an alliance with a clan whose High Elder goes back on his word.

"So Morsk followed you here?" I ask, forcing my thoughts back to the present.

"We were followed. The canoe stayed too far back to see clearly, but it could only have been Morsk. He's the only one we spoke to about where we were going."

I pick up my spear from the spot where I dropped it on the ground, but my brother shakes his head. "I'm not expecting trouble from him, though I can't help but wonder why he came. I know he isn't pleased to lose. He thinks I'm making a mistake—weakening the clan by forging ties with the Manu. He may have followed to confront me. To try to change my mind before I can make an announcement to the clan."

"Or else to confront *me*," I say. "To change my mind about his proposition."

Chev doesn't reply, and I go quiet, too, letting his words echo inside my head. *Weakening the clan.* "You don't believe that, do you? That an alliance with the Manu will make us weak? It can only make us stronger—"

"Be patient with Morsk, Mya," Chev says. "He only wants what's best. And he thinks the Manu may gain too much influence over the Olen, if so many sisters of the High Elder are married to sons of the Manu High Elder—"

"But we won't be married to the High Elder's sons. Kol is the High Elder now—"

"You know what I mean. But I understand you, as well. And I agree with you, mostly. I think the alliance with the Manu will strengthen us, as long as we are vigilant about our independence. We wouldn't want to let ourselves be absorbed into another clan. There's too much at stake—our history, our stories, our customs could all be lost.

"More even than that, it would go against the will of the Divine. Don't ever forget who created the clans, Mya. The Divine established the Bosha and chose who would lead them. She did the same for the Manu. The will of the Divine must be respected. Look what happened when Vosk and Lo went against her will. When they tried to lead a clan they were never called to lead."

These words stir up memories in me that flash across

my mind, ending with the image of Lo's lifeless body at the bottom of her grave. "Is that why you came for us? Because our family was chosen? Were you worried Lees and I would anger the Divine?"

"The Bosha and the Olen will rejoin, Mya, and our family is called by the Divine to lead that clan. That's true, and it's important, but that's not the reason I came for you and Lees."

All this Chev says while looking at the dirt, watching the lines his knife traces on the ground. But even though he won't look at me—even though he won't say the words—I know that he loves me. I know that he loves Lees. Only love would have moved my stubborn brother to leave our camp and come to us. Only love and the need to be sure he doesn't lose us.

I realize, as I watch the twists and turns traced by his knife, that I must have known this in my heart all along. It was this truth that prompted me to take the action I did.

The truth that Chev would never let us go.

"You asked before if I would have stayed away," I say. Chev's hand slows. Is he nervous about what I might say? "The truth is I don't know what I'd have done." I pause until my brother's hand stills and his eyes meet mine. Something in his gaze reminds me of the past, when we were still children. "I never really thought I would have to decide. I think I always knew you'd come."

"How could you have known that? I didn't even know what I would do—"

"Because you were called by the Divine to lead. That's always been clear to me. I guess I knew you would do the right thing."

My words are broken off by a sound—a sound of something moving. A swish of a step. The brush of a branch.

I hear it from the left, and Chev does too. I rise up on one knee, my spear ready, when another sound comes from the right.

Chev has his spear in hand so quickly, I never see him reach for it. The knife stays ready in the other hand.

I nod toward the left. I will walk that way. He rises to his feet without a sound and glances right.

With my back almost touching my brother's, I turn my head slowly, sweeping my eyes from the highest branches to the underbrush. "Bears, wolves . . . Morsk," I say. "It could be any of those." His only answer is to prop the shaft of his spear onto his shoulder. I do the same, and we each take one step into the shadows. The shade deepens, then thins, as I reach the path. I stare down into a denser stand of trees, but nothing stirs.

On the other side of the path, I find tracks. Squatting down, I see that they were made by a wolf. I pivot in place, sweeping my eyes across the dark brush, searching for movement, when I hear a voice.

Chev's voice. A quick short cry—*my name?* Then silence.

I start toward the place where I left him. I try to run. *He needs you*, I tell myself. *He called your name. He needs help.*

My legs move. My eyes search. But at the center of my being, I know that I will not be able to help. I know that the cry I heard was not a cry for help at all. It was a different sort of cry.

A warning.

I crash over the trail and into the shade, my feet stuttering to a stop when I reach the place where Chev and I sat together just a few moments ago. The grooves his knife carved into the ground leap out at me. They point in a line, and I follow the direction they point as I creep farther into the trees.

I don't have to walk far. Only ten paces. That's where I find him. He lies on his back, his throat slashed, his blood pooling in the open hood of his parka.

His knife is gone. His spear is gone. "No no no . . ." I hear myself speaking, muttering, as I drop to my knees and press my hands to his cold, still throat.

"No, no, no," I say again, but this time it isn't muttered. This time it rolls out as long hard sobs. Not a wolf. Not a bear. Not an animal at all. An animal doesn't disarm its prey.

Only a human predator will do that.

I touch Chev's cheek. His skin is cool. I bend over and

press my lips to his forehead. "I love you. I love you," I whisper. I had the chance to say it just a few moments ago. I should have said it. I say it now, over and over, hoping that somehow Chev's Spirit still lingers and he hears me. "Don't go," I sob. "Don't leave me. Don't leave *us*."

A sound comes from behind me, beyond the trail. I spring to my feet, my spear in hand. "Who's there?" Another sound—the clear snap of a twig. "Come out!"

I don't hesitate. I don't expect an answer, and I don't wait for one. I hurry into the trees toward the sound, as farther away, farther down the trail toward the center of the island, I think I catch the rhythmic sound of running feet.

I turn in place, and behind me, near the spot where my brother fell, I hear a voice. The muted voice of a man, whispering to the Divine. "Don't let this be. Don't let this be."

I hurry back, feet flying over the ground—no fear, no hesitation. I plunge into the darkest shade, right up to my dead brother's side. There I find a man—a man kneeling beside him, a spear in his hand.

Morsk.

FIFTEEN

I raise my spear, training it on the middle of his back. "Get up," I say, knowing that when he turns—when he rises to his feet to face me—my spear will be pointed right at his heart. "Leave your weapon on the ground and get up!"

He glances over his shoulder and sees me standing over him, and I know he knows. I have the shot. I have the opportunity. I can and will make him pay for what he did to my brother.

My brother who called him a friend, who trusted him. Tears fill my eyes, but I still see clearly enough to kill my brother's traitor.

He gets to his feet slowly, his arms extended at his sides, his eyes wide. I know he feels the fear—I imagine the pounding heart in his chest, the throbbing pulse in his temples, the numbness that runs up his arms as his blood chills—and I drink it in. I revel in the thought that my brother's killer knows that I am about to kill him.

"He trusted you." I don't know why I say this. To shame him? "But I knew it was a mistake. I knew you were an enemy from the moment you backed me into a corner in my own hut—"

"Mya—"

"Don't even say my name—"

"Fine. But please listen. I'm not an enemy—not to *you*, not to *Chev*—"

"Don't say my brother's name either," I spit. "How can you stand there and lie? He told me you followed him to this island. It isn't hard to figure out what happened—"

"I heard him call your name! I was looking for him—for you—to warn you both!"

There's something in his voice, like the wind bringing a storm. Something urgent is at its core, and it makes me listen. I don't want to. . . . I want to believe that he is Chev's killer, because it would be so easy to kill him.

I don't lower my spear. I keep it aimed right at his chest. I remember the fear I felt, however fleeting, when Kol flinched toward me with his spear raised on that first hunt together. That is the fear I wish for Morsk to feel, even as I give him a chance to speak. "Warn us of what? You were *seen*, Morsk. You were seen by Chev and by Kol. They saw a canoe follow them. They knew you were pursuing them—"

"Why would I come in a canoe? One man alone in a canoe? Think about it—"

"And yet you're here! You expect me to believe that you found us without following—"

"No, I *did* follow. But I didn't follow your brother." His eyes drop—his gaze sweeps over Chev's body on the ground—and I can't help but look, too. My heart chokes in my chest as if a fist is closing around it. When I meet Morsk's eyes again, I see my own pain reflected there, and for the first time since I found him over Chev's body, I feel a flicker of doubt that he killed my brother.

A sound starts in the back of my mind. A quiet buzz. It grows and stretches, filling the empty spaces between my thoughts, becoming a roar. In my mind's eye I see two double kayaks—Kol and Chev, Pek and Seeri—all rowing hard, pushing north toward this island.

And behind them I see another boat. A canoe, pursuing the people who matter to me most to an isolated place where they are unseen and unprotected.

I think I know the answer even before I ask the question. "So who were you following? Who was following Chev?"

I drop my spear to my side as Morsk answers, as he names the paddlers I see in my mind's eye. "The Bosha. Dora and her daughter, Anki. And the elders who spoke at Mala's meeting. Thern and Pada."

I knew. Somehow I knew not to trust them. When I saw

them in Kol's camp, something cold and dark seemed to cling to them. Now I know what that something was.

Revenge.

Morsk's gaze sweeps down the length of my arm to my lowered spear, then springs back to my face. "So you believe me?"

I don't answer. I can see that Morsk is suffering, and I know that if I said I believed him, it might lessen his pain. But I don't want to lessen Morsk's pain. Not yet. I'm still not sure if I trust him.

"Then where are they?" I ask. "If *you* didn't kill Chev, where are the people who did? Why didn't they kill me too?"

"I think they saw me. Maybe they thought they were outnumbered or had lost the chance to surprise you. I didn't see them, but I heard them running away."

I think back to the moment I heard Chev call my name. Hadn't I heard footsteps, too? If Morsk is telling the truth, could his presence have actually protected me from Chev's killers?

I drop onto my knees beside my brother's body. I tighten the laces of his parka, tugging the collar up and over the gash that circles his throat. His blood has a thick, dark scent, like damp clay. His skin is cool, though it still holds a hint of warmth. I could almost fool myself into believing he's still alive, if his eyes weren't open in a lifeless stare.

I can't help but wonder what they saw last—Dora standing over him? Or her daughter, Anki? Did the person who cut his throat do it with his own knife? Did she gloat when she killed him? Did she mention Lo or Orn?

I drop my head to Chev's chest, my body shuddering with sobs. I don't know what to do now, and I don't care. I can't imagine a world without my brother in it. I don't want to know that world. I want to stay here by his side. "I love you," I whisper again. "For all the times I didn't say it, I hope you knew it to be true. I love you."

I kneel like this for a long time, until finally my sobs slow. Morsk doesn't speak, though I know he is still there. I hear his feet crunching over the leaf litter on the ground, pacing in an ever-widening circle. Finally, I sit up. I look down on Chev's face—his eyes still wide, his tan skin dulling to gray. I touch his left eye and then the right, pressing his lids shut. "I love you," I say one more time, knowing I can never say it enough. Then I look around for downed limbs that might be nearby, anything usable for lashing together a travois.

"Do you have twine?" I say, not even looking up at Morsk.

"Mya . . ." My hand falls on a long branch, and I lift it to check its length. One end is rotted, and I let it fall. "Mya, we can't take the body with us."

I let these words wash over me, still reaching around the underbrush. "If you don't have twine, we may be able to find vines. Otherwise we'll need to carry him—"

"No. Mya, we can't." And there it is in his voice again—the urgency of the oncoming storm. "The people who did this to Chev—they have other targets. They didn't come here just to kill your brother. You're also a target. You need to move—to find your sisters and warn them. You need to help the living—"

"But if we leave him . . ." I break off. I can't say it. *If we leave him, his body could be eaten by scavengers. Dire wolves. Even buzzards.* "I can't leave my brother behind," I say, but even as the words pass my lips, as quiet as a whisper, I know it's what I have to do.

Because Morsk is right. I have to help the living. My sisters. Any of us could be the next victim. Even Kol. I have to warn them. That's what my brother would want me to do.

"Not out in the open. He deserves better than that," I say. I think of Noni's mother, covered in small stones. It felt almost like decoration as we placed them on her body. "We need to cover him. I want to feel like we've done a sort of burial. Something . . ." My voice breaks, and I go quiet. I don't want Morsk to try to comfort me.

I get up from the ground and begin to walk farther into the trees, off the trail, until I find a depression in the ground—a place where the terrain naturally dips. I hear Morsk walk up behind me. All at once I realize that I may not be safe with him, and I turn, my heart beating in my chest like waves crashing in a stormy sea.

Morsk returns my gaze. His spear is at his side. His cheeks are stained by tears.

A flicker of understanding lights his eyes. "I'm not creeping up on you," he spits. For the first time since I found Chev, I see anger in Morsk. "I only came to offer help."

"Thank you," I say, a note of reconciliation in my voice. "Could you help me move Chev here? I think if we lay him where the ground naturally drops down, we could cover him with branches."

Together, Morsk and I lift Chev from the ground. I try, but fail, to look away from the pool of blood where he fell. Anger rises in me and burns my throat. I taste it in my mouth. Not just anger, but more than that. A longing for revenge.

Morsk helps me gather branches, twigs, and leaves, to camouflage my brother as best we can. It won't make much of a difference—we can't camouflage the scent. But it makes me feel a little better to give him some sort of burial. Each twig, each leaf, each handful of grass is another silent good-bye.

We leave his face uncovered until the end. Morsk steps away to give me some privacy, and I'm grateful. I want to make my brother one last promise before I walk away. As I drape each eye in pale green leaves, as I cover his face in moss, I whisper to him. "I will make you proud of me," I say. "The Olen clan will not weaken. We will thrive. And you will always be remembered."

The first few steps down the path to the beach are terrible. The next few are even worse. I force myself to keep moving, but the lack of Chev follows me like a shadow that has weight. Like a burden too heavy to carry.

It's strange to travel over this trail with Morsk—this same trail that I traveled over alone this morning, when I was still excited about the island and the elk I thought I was tracking. We are almost to the spot where I first realized that what I thought was an elk was not an elk at all, when something—or someone—rustles in the woods to our right.

We stop, ducking into the shade of the trees that edge the path. We're closing in on the ledges above the beach, and the breeze has picked up. It churns the leaves, masking all other sound. But there is sound within the sound—measured and even steps within the random and swirling wind.

Someone is walking nearby.

The steps grow louder, closer. I drop onto one knee, my spear shouldered, my head swiveling in every direction, waiting to see that flash of Dora's white hair. Shadows weave between shadows, and finally I see a figure.

I loosen my grip on the spear. It's not Dora. Not Anki. Not Thern or Pada. The girl moving toward me wears a betrothal tunic, and the sight of her face floods me with relief.

Seeri.

She walks side by side with Pek. Kol walks behind them, his steps a bit too uneven, every second step a shuffle as his left leg drags along the ground. His wounded knee. It must be causing him pain.

Seeri runs toward us, expecting to see Chev. When she notices Morsk with me instead, her steps slow. Her eyes widen as her gaze sweeps the path. "Where's Chev?"

She drops Pek's hand and steps toward me. I know she will see the answer on my face, so I fold my arms around her and hide my face against her shoulder. Behind her back, Kol's eyes meet mine, and I can see that he knows why Chev isn't here. A hollowness opens in his eyes—the same hollowness I saw there when his father died.

When I see that look in his eyes, the tears come. I sob against Seeri's neck, but I still don't answer her question. I don't know if I can say the words.

"What happened?" It's Kol, his voice. I open my eyes, but he isn't asking me. He's asking Morsk.

"We found him. It was already too late—"

"Too late?" Seeri asks. "You mean he's dead? But how?" Her voice is soft—a mere whisper—but then she swallows a sob and her voice is almost a scream. "Who did it? How? Did you see? Did you see anyone?" Seeri raises her tear-soaked face and drags the backs of both hands across her eyes. "Because we did. . . . We saw two people. . . ." Her words get caught in her throat, garbled by tears.

Pek wraps an arm around her. "We saw two people who shouldn't be here," he says. "We went to the camp on the beach—"

"Wait." I swing around to stare into Pek's face, afraid of what he might be about to say. But I have to hear it. I have to know. "Who did you see?" Fear falls down on me like cold rain. It soaks into me, chilling me to the bone. "Dora?" I ask. "Anki?"

"No." Kol answers. His eyes are still trained on Morsk, like a hunter's eyes trained on his prey. His voice holds a question. No, not a question . . . an accusation. "We saw the other Bosha elders. Thern and Pada."

He steps forward, and I notice the limp even more. Morsk seems to notice it too—his eyes drop to the ground near Kol's feet, then flick back to his face. Morsk's weight slides away, a subtle step backward. He is afraid of Kol. I can feel his fear. The ground crunches beneath his foot. His heel is coming down on the path.

"Don't," I say, more to Morsk, but in truth the word is meant for both of them. "Don't step into the open—"

"Are you hoping to be seen?" Kol asks. His spear flicks up from the ground as he flexes his wrist. The point comes so close to Morsk's cheek, it's a wonder it doesn't cut him. Morsk flinches, but he does as I say—he doesn't take another step away. "Are you hoping to signal your partners? Did you lead them all here? You knew that they would find Chev here—you were the only one he told. The only one he trusted."

Kol swallows, and I see pain in him. Not just physical pain, though that is clearly part of it. But it's more than that. He thinks Morsk killed Chev. He thinks the man my brother trusted most betrayed him.

"And not only Chev, but all his sisters are here, too. Even Seeri, since she came with us. Did you plan with the Bosha elders to turn the Olen leaders over to them? What are you getting in return?"

"I did not lead them here! I followed! I followed so I could help. So I could warn Chev and Mya—even *you*. I swear it—I did not bring anyone here. Why would I—"

"Because Chev told you that you had lost, that he'd changed his mind. That you would not be betrothed to Lees . . ."

Kol takes another sliding step forward, and though his presence is threatening—the raised spear just an inch from Morsk's ear—I see the sweat on his brow. His hair sticks to his skin at the temples and a heavy bead runs down the side of his neck below his ear. His teeth are clenched in pain.

"Stop," I say. I want to say that I know his wound from the bear and the lacerations across his knee need attention. I want to tell him to sit down and rest. But I don't. His expression is as hard as stone and just as shut off. He would not listen to me. So instead, I ask about the only other thing that matters at this moment. "You say you saw Thern and Pada in the camp. But did you see Lees? Or Noni?"

"No," says Seeri. She looks at me, her eyes a pale gold, as if they drained of color when she learned of Chev's death. Her face is pink from the sting of the cold breeze against her wet cheeks. "The way Thern and Pada moved in and out of the tent—it was clear no one else was there." Seeri casts a sideways look at both Kol and Morsk. "We've got to get moving, looking for them. If Dora and Anki killed Chev—"

"If . . . ," Kol says. He turns to me, and I realize that this is the first time since he found me with Morsk that he has looked me in the eye. "You didn't see them, Mya?"

"No." I know what's coming next before he says it.

"And you didn't see Morsk before you found Chev dead?"

"No," I say. For just a moment, the world around us dims. A cloud must be passing in front of the sun. And at that moment, I feel Kol draw closer to me. The stark outlines and bright contrasts fade. Light softens on his face. I hold his gaze as I shake my head. "I didn't see him, but I believe him. I believe he came to warn us." Kol flinches, and I remember my own sense of disappointment when I realized Morsk wasn't my brother's killer. The disappointment of not being able to avenge Chev so easily.

Yet Kol doesn't drop his spear.

"Don't you trust her?" Morsk asks. I notice his weight shift again. He leans in toward Kol—toward me—ever so slightly. "Because her judgment is the only one that matters to me. She is my High Elder now."

She is my High Elder now.

These words roll through my mind like an echo as the cloud rolls away from the sun. Stark white light reflects from every surface. The words roll outward, then back in. But it's not Morsk's voice I hear, or Kol's, or even Chev's. It's the voice of my father, as if he stands behind me at this very moment, one hand on my shoulder, whispering in my ear. *She is my High Elder now.*

The sensation of my father's presence is so strong, I reach up and touch my shoulder, expecting to lay my hand on his. My fingers brush across my tunic—it's warm from the heat of the sun.

Seeri's right. We've been standing here too long.

"I trust that Morsk has come to help us," I say. "And now we need to do all we can to find Lees and Noni before anyone else does."

Seeri strides forward, her shoulders swinging as she steps around Kol and Morsk. She may have been patient during their standoff, but she is ready to move. Pek, always aware of her needs, stays close by her side. "Where do we go from here?" he asks.

"Noni—the girl we found here—told us of a lake to the south of the cliffs. She was anxious to take Lees there."

And so we cross the path and step into the woods—woods that grow thicker and darker on the southern slopes of the cliffs, protected from the north wind. We cannot trust the trails. We need to stay out of sight.

The farther we travel under the trees, the more the island seems to belong to the Spirits—a place where they dwell between the shadows and sunlight, rustling in the canopy with the wind. We hurry along a swath of brush that's been laid flat, maybe even by the bear we faced earlier.

If I'm leading, Seeri is just beyond my shoulder. I can feel her presence, hear her strides in time with my own. It's a comfort to me to know she's there. Because in this moment, Morsk's words still ringing in my ears, I feel strangely alone. Kol chooses to stay behind—to let me take the lead—and I want to look back, but decide not to. Not yet.

Maybe it's best if for a little while, we are both alone with our thoughts.

How could this have happened? How could Kol and I have both become High Elders so soon after becoming betrothed? And how can I marry the High Elder of the Manu and still lead the Olen? This was never meant to happen—Chev was to lead the Olen. It was never to pass to me.

But now that it has, can I step aside? Can I let the role

of High Elder pass to Seeri or to Lees? The forest shivers with each step I take, as if a crowd is parting. I feel a crowd of Spirits pressing around me—Spirits of all the living things within this forest, but also the Spirits of the dead—my father, my mother, my brother. I feel them gathering around me now, watching me, coaxing me to act.

But what would they have me do?

I know what Chev would have me do, and I feel the weight of the responsibility that he must have felt himself, responsibility to ensure the future of the clan. I know that my father would remind me that I owe loyalty to my family. But what about the loyalty I owe to Kol, my betrothed?

This thought of Kol slows my steps, forcing me to turn around. Seeri and Pek are over my right shoulder. Morsk is close on my left. But Kol is far behind, his movements labored.

I realize, all at once, that it was more than the need for solitude or the desire to give me time with my own thoughts that has kept him hanging back from me. And it was more than anger on his face when he confronted Morsk. It was even more than pain.

It was illness.

The clenched jaw, the sweat on his forehead, the limp in his gait. He is ill, and I failed to see it. I was too caught up in my loss of Chev and my fear of the Bosha to notice how much he needed help.

As soon as I see him—struggling over the brush-covered ground, laboring to lift his left leg high enough to clear the undergrowth—I hurry back to him.

But as I rush back the way I just came, Kol motions to me. He raises a hand—he's warning me to stop.

I slow, turning to follow the line of his gaze out of the trees, over the trail that leads farther downhill toward the lake. Voices float toward us, weaving through the woods. Someone is approaching.

I signal Seeri, Pek, and Morsk, who seem to have heard the voices too. I wave a hand away toward the deeper shade, motioning for us all to move farther from the trail.

Then I turn back to Kol. Our eyes meet just before his lids fall shut. He drops his spear, his knees buckle, and he collapses to the ground.

SIXTEEN

A hum fills my ears, drowning out the footsteps, the birdsong, the sound of Seeri, Pek, and Morsk moving under the trees. My gaze sweeps the ground all the way back to the spot where we entered the woods. The shaft of light that fell across Kol's face now shines empty, illuminating nothing but a crumpled shadow on the ground.

I stiffen. For just a moment I hesitate, questioning my eyes.

Then I am running toward him.

If the others see me, they pay no attention. They keep one eye on the trail while fading farther into the dense growth, sliding between the lower branches of trees so thick with dark leaves, they block out the sky. Only thin threads of light filter through to the ground.

I reach Kol. He lies on his back, his eyes staring up at the treetops overhead, as if he's not quite sure what just happened. The skin of his face, dripping with sweat just a little while ago, is now dry and hot to the touch. I drop to one knee and wind an arm around his waist. His eyes shift to me and he mutters one word. . . .

"Mya."

Pulling him toward me, his weight slouching against my shoulder, I stumble after the others, who are already hidden from view.

We follow them to a jumble of boulders that spring from the ground near the edge of the woods, right before it drops over a lower ledge of the cliffs, straight down to the sea. The whisper of waves mixes with the breeze in the trees, and the scent of salt filters into the thick fragrance of evergreen and dead leaves crushed under our boots. We duck behind a rock the size and shape of a sleeping mammoth. Not far away, just a few paces deeper into the trees, I see three shadows—Seeri, Pek, and Morsk—as they flatten to the ground behind another large rock.

My gaze traces the trail that cuts through the trees less than twenty paces away. My ears filter out the layered noises around me—the waves below, the wind, the flutter of wings—listening for the unmistakable sound of footfalls.

And then I hear it, distinct and clear.

Something moves through the splashes of light that dot the path. We all hold still, soundless, as it draws closer, stepping into view.

Not an elk. Not a bear.

A woman. Two women, side by side. One with dark hair, one with white.

Dora and Anki, spears at the ready, are moving along the path. They are moving away from the center of the island—away from the lake—the place where we hope to find Lees and Noni.

We will be fine. This is what I tell myself as I watch them. *We are covered in the thickest of shade. We are motionless, as if the Divine has turned us to the same stone we crouch beside.*

It won't be long. It won't be long. . . . They will pass us. They will continue back the way we came, moving farther and farther away.

But then a sound comes from deep within the woods. A howl. Something bounds toward us through the trees. Toward me.

Dora and Anki stop. They turn and look as Black Dog comes hurtling out of the deep woods behind them. They watch as he stops, howling, just five paces from the place I hide.

They each raise their spears above their shoulders. They each train their eyes on the dog.

And they each take a step off the trail—a step toward the five of us.

But Black Dog sees them, and he knows. His instincts tell him that they are a threat. One long, final howl pours from his throat and he turns and flees back the way he came.

The women slow. Like me, they must be wondering the meaning of what just happened. *Why would a wolf run right to this spot to howl? Was it a warning? And if so, who was it meant to warn?*

I watch the two of them as the wind stirs the leaves, swirling the light that splatters the ground like the liquid surface of the sea. For just a moment, light washes over my shoulder, Kol's back. We are exposed. Their eyes slide over the ground, searching, their focus shifting with the light.

Dora takes a single step toward the place where we hide, and my heart stops.

She takes a second, tentative step, and my heart restarts, pounding like a drum.

Her eyes sweep over the ferns and thickets, but they don't quite reach the rocks. Instead, she stays closer to the place where Black Dog stopped, sifting through the undergrowth with the sharpened flint point of her spear, as if she expects to find some hidden object. She lifts her eyes once, letting her gaze alight on first one tree, then another, searching the branches overhead.

The longer she stands under these trees, the more her eyes will adjust to the lack of light. If she were to flick her gaze over us now, she might see us, covered as we are by mere shadows and a thin layer of spindly branches.

We crouch shoulder to shoulder, and I slide my hand into

Kol's. His fingers are cold, and I want to lift them to my lips, but of course I don't dare move. I want to speak to him, to tell him I'm sorry I didn't see how sick he is, but I don't dare even breathe his name.

All I can do is swivel my head to search his face, to gauge his condition.

His eyes are on Dora and Anki, but his gaze is clouded. Still, as Anki strides closer, his eyes narrow. His attention sharpens. I turn my attention to Anki, too, and I see the thing that has Kol riveted.

I see the knife in Anki's hand.

My brother Chev's knife. The one with the obsidian blade. The one that was taken from his body when he died.

She swings the knife as she walks, twirling it in front of her . . . she is playing with it like a child. She takes another stride and tosses it into the air. It flips once and she catches it by the handle. Like this is all a game.

The sight of Chev's knife—this perfect confirmation that she is the one who killed my brother—reignites my rage. It's as if a coal had burned down to a smoldering ember, but now the sight of the knife in Anki's hand is like breath on that ember, flaring it back to life.

She takes another step, tosses the knife even higher, watches it flip once . . . twice . . . then snatches the handle out of the air.

My eyes flick to the shadows where I know Seeri hides.

I cannot distinguish even her outline. *Does she see this? I wonder. Does this rage burn in her, too?*

Then the Spirit of my brother puts an end to Anki's brazen game. She tosses the knife up, letting it tumble end over end, and reaches out to catch its bone handle. But something slows her hand, and the blade flips around and slices her palm. She cries out—a sharp gasp of pain—as it slips from her grasp and drops into a tangle of briars and shade.

I bite my lip, holding back the taunts that fill my mouth.

But then she drops to the ground, crawling on her hands and knees just a few paces away, searching for the knife. She is so close, I fear she will hear Kol's ragged breaths, but she is consumed by her need to find the knife.

She is completely unaware of our presence, I think. *She is completely unaware of how easy it would be for me to kill her.*

I watch her, and the fingers of my right hand—the hand that holds the shaft of my spear against the ground—begin to tingle. My eyes move to Dora. She is watching Anki, too.

In my mind, I take the shot. I plant my spear in Anki's back.

But then what? How long would it take her mother to retaliate? If Kol were well, I could count on him to take down Dora, but he's far too weak. And the others are too far away for me to signal.

No. This is not the right time. My fingers relax on my spear.

"Give up. It's lost," Dora calls. I watch her. Her interest

in the mystery of the wolf that stopped to howl has faded. She's ready to move on. "You know not to steal from the dead—even from Chev. You're lucky all you got was a cut on the hand."

Anki stands, dragging her cut palm across the front of her tunic, leaving a red smear. She sweeps her eyes across the ground at her feet one final time before running off in the direction of her mother, back toward the path.

As their rustling steps fade, I let out a long, silent exhale.

But before they are out of range, Seeri springs up from her hiding place. She stands at her full height, her spear over her shoulder, ready to throw. She takes a few sliding steps and I think she will do it. She is about to release the spear and let it fly into Anki's back.

But just as quickly, Morsk is on his feet, lunging toward her. In just three steps he is beside her, wrapping his arms around her shoulders and tackling her to the ground.

The women look back—they were not so far away that they couldn't hear them fall. We all hold still, hidden only by the low growth and the deepening shade, Morsk's huge hand cupped over Seeri's mouth. Dora and Anki stand and stare over their shoulders, searching for the source of the sound. Finally, when nothing stirs, they turn away.

We watch them recede, picking their way back to the trail, disappearing into the trees. No one moves until their footsteps can no longer be heard.

⌖

Then Seeri shoves Morsk away, kicking at him as she climbs to her feet. Pek rushes to her side, his hands on Morsk's chest, pushing him away from her.

"Why?" she spits. "Why wouldn't you let me kill her? She admitted to killing Chev—"

"Because he was protecting them," Kol says, his voice so thin I wonder if I'm the only one who hears it.

But no. Morsk hears. He turns on Kol. He dares to speak in a voice above a whisper.

"I wasn't protecting *them*. I was protecting *Seeri*. Seeri, Mya, your brother, even *you*."

"We don't need your protection." Pek spits the words, backing Morsk so far away from Seeri, I wonder if he intends to push him off the cliff. But then, with a final shove against his shoulders, Pek leaves him and turns back to Seeri, who is brushing broken bits of needles from the front of her tunic and the knees of her pants.

"If she'd taken the shot—then what?" Morsk asks. "Dora turns and fires her spear. Maybe she hits Seeri. Maybe she misses and hits Mya or you or me. But she would have hit one of us. And that's assuming Seeri didn't miss—"

"I never miss," Seeri snaps.

"It doesn't matter. It wasn't the best plan," Morsk says. He walks back to where he'd dropped his own spear on the ground. As he picks it up, Kol begins to rise to his feet beside me, and Seeri pushes the tension a bit further.

"I don't care what you think," she says. She walks to me and extends her hand to pull me to my feet. "I only care what my High Elder thinks. Mya?"

As I grip my sister's hand, I struggle with how to answer. I see the pain in her eyes, the reflection of the pain I feel, too. The urge she'd felt to strike Anki down . . . I'd felt it, too.

And yet, like Morsk, I'd judged it to be the wrong time to attack.

"Just like you, I want revenge," I start, letting Seeri haul me up. "Whether that was our best opportunity or not, I can't say. But I promise it won't be our last."

There's more I want to say—to Seeri and to Kol, too. But before I can form the words, a long howl comes from deep within the heart of the island—Black Dog. My eyes meet Kol's, and I can see he feels the same urgency I feel.

"That's Noni's dog," I say. "He belongs to the girl I left with Lees. We need to go find him."

Seeri nods, but her eyes slide to Morsk as she shoulders her spear. It's clear she trusts him no more than Kol does. With Pek in solidarity with his betrothed and his brother, Morsk is without an ally.

Unless *I* am his ally. Right now, I'm not sure how I feel.

Before Kol walks away, he squats down in front of a thicket of thorns. At first I worry he is getting sick—his skin is still gray, his eyes still dull—but when he straightens,

Chev's knife is in his hand. Relief washes over me at the sight of it. Though it may have been used to kill him, it is still his knife—the work of his own hands—and I would've hated to have left it behind.

Kol hands it to Seeri. "Hold on to it," he says, glancing at Morsk. "You may get a chance to use it."

For just a moment, anger flares in me, though I'm not sure why. Is it because Kol refuses to trust Morsk, or because he chose to give the knife to Seeri instead of me? It doesn't matter. I shove the anger down. This is not the time for emotional reactions. I can't be selfish now. I need to stay focused on our task.

I need to think like a High Elder.

As we move downhill toward the sound of Black Dog's howls, I notice changes all around us. Off to our left, the chime of water spilling over rocks comes from the stream that feeds the lake. The trees begin to thin, even as the underbrush thickens. A cold breeze whistles past my ears, chilling them. Overhead, a circle of blue appears—the open sky above the lake—ringed by dark green treetops.

And straight through the shade, running straight toward me, is Black Dog.

He jumps against my leg, runs a few paces back the way he came, then circles around and jumps against me again. He wants me to follow.

We move closer to the edge of the trees, and I notice the

scent of algae mixing with evergreen, and a sound I had not expected. The roar of falling water.

Sun hits my face as we step out from beneath the trees. Finally Black Dog stops. He runs out ahead of us and looks up, letting out another piercing howl.

Right in front of us lies the lake—an oval stretch of water that reflects the blue and white of the sky. A sharp cliff of black rock rises behind it, and tumbling from its top ledge is a spray of water and light—the waterfall.

Black Dog howls again, and I scan the ridge at the top of the falls and spot two figures seated on the highest ledge. Two figures under the broad sweep of the sun, waving at me.

Lees and Noni.

SEVENTEEN

Lees raises her hands above her head and calls out. "Mya Mya Mya!" Her voice rolls like a wave, a ripple of sound expanding over the trees. "You found us!"

And though relief washes over me at the sight of her, my stomach twists into knots at the sound of her voice. She is loud and she is high in the air, her voice carrying on the breeze, uninterrupted by the trees below.

It's likely that the sound of my name has been carried far enough to reach Dora and Anki. Maybe far enough to reach Thern and Pada, too. A shiver runs over me as I realize I have no idea where those two are. Perhaps they are quite close, and will emerge from the trees at any moment.

"And look who you've brought with you," Lees continues, her hand sweeping toward Morsk. "My future betrothed." Though Lees's words are mocking, there's a quaver in her voice. She had expected me to be alone, but here I am with this group of four. I'm sure she's surprised to see anyone with me at all, but to see Morsk must be particularly alarming to her. "Have you come with my brother to try to drag me back? Or has Chev sent you to say that he has changed his mind?"

These last words—so innocent and terrible—tear a hole in my heart.

I will have to tell her. I will have to be the one who tells her that her brother came here to give her whatever she wanted, as long as she came home to him and to her clan. And then I will have to tell her that he is dead.

"You need to come down," I call, yelling to be heard over the waterfall. I stride toward her, skirting the edge of the lake, trying to get closer so our words are more private. The others follow. I almost tell them to stay under the cover of the trees, but I think better of it. It makes more sense for us all to stay together. "There are things happening. Things I need to tell you—"

"But I want you to come up here!"

"We need to go!"

I watch her as she begins to scramble down, though Noni stays right where she is. The rock is steep, but handholds and ledges are plentiful, and she makes the climb appear easy. Still, the sight of her clinging to such a sheer face makes it hard for me to breathe. She stops about halfway up from the bottom and calls out again.

"You should climb up! There's a cavern at the top that leads to a passageway through the rock. I want to show you!"

A passageway through the rock . . . Could it lead to the other side of these cliffs—the side that faces the sea? Could it lead us closer to our camp on the beach?

"What kind of passageway? Where does it go?"

"I'm not sure—we didn't crawl the whole way through. But light comes in from the other side."

Climbing might be our best option, I realize, because of the need to get out of sight before one of the Bosha follows Lees's voice to the lake. Even if we couldn't use the passage as a path back to the beach, a cave at the top of these cliffs would hide us, at least for now.

I look at Kol. He leans on his spear, taking his weight off his wounded leg. "Could you make it up?" I ask.

"Of course," he says, so self-assured I know he is trying to be funny. "I'll carry the dog."

"Stop it," I say. "Don't tease me right now. I need to know if you think you could climb."

He lifts his drooping head and smiles at me. His smile is still warm, though the usual fire in his eyes has almost gone out. The corners of his lips turn down, despite the smile.

"You're in pain," I say.

"I can climb." And with those three words Kol walks to

the foot of the cliff and searches for the first handhold.

Pek bends down and holds a hand out to the dog, who stops howling long enough to sniff him. "I think he's crying because he can't get to the girls," he says. Lifting Black Dog and laying him across his shoulders so he is propped on the pack he carries on his back, Pek follows Seeri and Morsk to the foot of the rock. Seeri starts to climb beside Kol, and Morsk starts up behind her. "I'm not sure I can handle hand-over-hand and carry the dog, too," Pek says. "But I can try."

"Be careful!" Seeri calls. I watch as Pek holds the dog's feet against his chest with one arm and grabs hold of the rock with the other. He digs in a toe and takes his first step up the rock. He rises, establishing a good grip with his one hand before searching for overhangs for his feet. It's slow going but he makes progress, and seeing that Kol is also managing, I begin to hope we will all make the top. Seeri's feet are already off the ground the height of two men, though she still has the same distance to go above her.

Kol has managed to pull himself to a spot above my head when I begin to climb behind him. I gain on him quickly, though, and when I perch on a ledge beside him, I stop.

He is seated on a narrow sill of rock, his feet firmly on a wider ledge beneath him. His hands are pulled up into the sleeves of his tunic. "Just resting," he says. "And trying to warm my hands."

I can't blame him. Wind is blowing over the rock, gusting straight down the face. A thin film of water slicks the rock from the spray of the falls, and spots in the shade are so cold it feels as if we're climbing ice. My chilled fingers sting, and I prop myself opposite Kol. Checking my balance, positioning myself so that my legs hold my weight evenly, I slowly let go and rub my hands together.

"How are the others doing?" Kol asks. "Is Seeri to the top?"

Looking up, I am encouraged to see how far the others have gone. "She's just about to reach Lees now," I say. As I watch, she steadies her first knee on the shelf of rock beside the place Noni sits. Pek, even with the added challenge of carrying the dog, is not far behind. "I don't think Pek wanted to let Morsk get too far away from him," I say, only half-teasing. Pek is strong and clearly an experienced climber, but even the best climber would struggle to carry both a pack and a dog. "The extra motivation apparently helped. He's made the top. Seeri's taking the dog from him now."

I wait, still looking up at them, willing them each to make the summit safely. When Pek pulls in his feet and disappears from view, I turn back to Kol, expecting a smile or maybe a smart comment about Morsk.

But instead, I find him slumped sideways, his head leaning against the rock, his eyelids lolling shut. "Kol!" His name flies from my lips as I reach to grab his shoulder. But before I can touch him, he slides forward. The front of his tunic grazes my outstretched hands as he slips from the ledge.

I throw off all my cautious thoughts of balance and lunge toward him, grabbing his collar, the laces threading through my fingers and winding around my hand. The hairs of the elk hide dig into the skin under my nails. His weight tugs at my clutching hands, but the Divine holds me balanced, and I hold Kol.

His head jerks up and he snaps awake. As he realizes where he is—as he comes to know that he is about to fall—he grabs the rock with both hands and pulls himself back up.

It happens so quickly, yet I feel every moment, see every detail as if time doesn't pass at all. I notice the chill of his skin when the backs of my fingers graze his neck. I notice the shifting of his weight, leaning away and then toward me, as his foot underneath him finds a hold again.

And I notice the relief—the ripple of release that rolls from Kol to me and back again like a shared sigh. I notice the breeze that shimmers up from the ground, as if the whole island were sighing in relief along with us.

And I notice the quickness with which the relief we share is snatched away.

My fingers, numb from holding so long on to the cold

stone, have slowly lost their grip, even as I stared at Kol and hoped for him to hold on. I look down into the oval surface of the lake straight below, and I see the reflection of two figures—a boy and a girl, clinging to a ledge, white wisps of clouds sweeping across the sky above them. For a long moment only the clouds move, but then my hands are sliding along the rock and I am falling.

And then the surface shatters all around us, and I lose him in the lake's blackness.

The lake is a world of liquid cold that sinks down into my bones. My eyes open and I see shafts of sunlight stabbing through the surface, illuminating curious fish, a swirl of bubbles, and a figure floating through the water, lying on his back, arms spreading wide as he moves away from me.

Kol.

Swim, I tell myself. *Swim to his side and pull him out before he drowns.* But as I stretch out an arm, pushing through the long fronds of sea grass that grow up from the bottom, threatening to wrap around him like the limbs of some mysterious Spirit that lives in the lake, the water clouds with silt and debris that filters down from the surface—bits of rock and pebbles knocked free by our bodies as we fell.

I kick hard toward the place I just saw him—through the dark smear that has gobbled up the light—and one of my searching hands finds something soft, warm, and alive. My fingers trace over his face. I kick once more and I am beside him, wrapping an arm around his waist and pulling him up.

We break the surface, pushing into the cold bright air. I tread water. My eyes search the bank. I spot Seeri near the base of the cliff, hurrying down to help.

I swim as hard as I can, but I'm not Pek. Carrying extra weight slows me down. By the time I reach the shallow water at the edge of the rocky shore, Seeri is wading in. She grabs Kol by the collar and pulls him away from me. Morsk appears behind her, and before I can tell him I am fine— before I can tell him to attend to Kol—he scoops me up into his arms and carries me onto the bank.

"I'm fine," I say, but even as I say it, I hear the croak in my own voice. I hear the rattle of cold in my own breath.

"You need to get into the sun," he says, carrying me to a spot where a wide circle of light falls on a patch of grass beyond the rocks.

I get to my feet, icy water dripping down from my hair, running down my chest beneath my tunic. My feet are unsteady, cold water swishing inside my boots, and I sit down on the trunk of a fallen tree and pull off one boot and then the other, shaking out the water while scanning the bank for Kol and Seeri.

I find them close to the water's edge, as if she didn't dare move Kol far. Tugging my wet boots back onto my feet, I hurry to them. I reach Kol just as he sits up and gags, lake water pouring out of his mouth.

I drop down beside him. I want to wrap him in my arms, but before I can reach for him, he pulls away. He stretches out onto his side and his eyes flutter shut. I'm not sure he even knows that I'm here. A low moan rattles from his throat.

"Kol?" I say, pushing back the wet hair that covers his eyes, and I notice the heat in his cheek.

I need to get Kol into the sun. This is what I'm thinking as I turn to look back to the clearing where Morsk carried me. *I need to get Kol warm.*

Leaning forward, bringing my face against his, I let my lips press against his forehead. His fever fills them with heat. His eyes flutter open, and he says my name.

"Mya."

"You need to stay still now. You're sick."

Kol's lips twist into a lopsided smile. "I know."

Morsk comes up behind us and scoops Kol up to carry him to the sun. "You both need to try to get warm," he says. "I'm going to go search for an easier route up the cliff."

Seeri follows us to the patch of sun. She looks after Morsk as I kneel down beside Kol.

"I'll go help him," she says, "though I'll keep my distance. I still don't trust him, but you deserve some privacy."

When she walks away, I can't help but wonder if she thinks I need to say good-bye to Kol. Does she think he is dying? He can't be. He's sick with an infection, but he can't be dying.

He can't be.

"Kol?" I whisper. He turns his face toward my voice, and for a moment I'm hopeful he will open his eyes, but they stay closed.

Hope. I feel it draining from me like mead from a cracked cup.

I find myself whispering a prayer to the Divine, which is not something I have a habit of doing. I pray only when I'm desperate, when I know I need her the most, and I know that in a way, that is worse than never praying at all. It shows I believe, but not enough to do anything about it. I know the Divine can help me, but I also know I can do most things myself. I don't know. I suppose I don't want to admit when I need help.

But right now, I admit it. Right now, I need the help of the Divine and anyone else who will give it. "Help me help Kol," I whisper. "Help me get him to the top of this cliff and out of danger."

"Was that a *prayer*? A prayer *for me*?" It's Kol. He stirs and opens his eyes.

"It might have been," I say. "I'm just happy you're well enough to hear me."

"I once prayed for help when I was being chased by a saber-tooth. The Divine sent me you."

His voice is so weak, I lean over him to hear. His face is so close. His eyes cut into me, opening a place I've been trying to hold shut.

"I'm hardly the answer to a prayer," I say.

He coughs, turns to spit out another mouthful of the lake, and then pulls in a long, deep breath. As he lets it out—part breath, part groan—he curls onto his side and his eyes fall shut again.

I slide my fingers across his forehead. Though his hair lies damp and cold against his face, his skin still burns.

I look up to see Morsk and Seeri hurrying toward us. "We found a route that looks a little easier," Seeri says. Without speaking a word, Morsk scoops Kol from the ground and drapes him across his shoulders, not unlike the way Pek carried the dog. Kol groans, but that's all. He must be out. If he were conscious, he would object to being carried, especially by Morsk.

The route Morsk and Seeri found is longer to the top but much less steep a climb. As I follow Morsk up, using my hands only at intervals, I think how much Pek would've preferred this way up with the dog. Maybe Kol could have made it up without falling.

I push that thought from my mind. I can't look back. Only ahead.

At the top Lees runs to us, but Noni shrinks back, standing against a wall of rock that pushes even higher above our heads. She eyes Morsk. "Who are these people?" she asks me.

Certainly Pek has spoken to her since he reached the top

with Black Dog. Certainly Lees has told her she can trust each of us.

Or maybe not. Maybe she told her to trust all but one.

"It's all right," I say. "They came to help us." I feel Seeri and Pek beside me—I feel them flinch as I say that Noni can trust even Morsk.

And something about their reactions makes me flinch, too. I don't want to admit it, but their doubts are making me doubt, too. Could they be right? Could it be that I've been foolish to trust Morsk, just because my brother did?

But if Morsk was hoping to help the Bosha find us, why would he have carried Kol to the top of this cliff?

"You can trust all of them to help you," I say, trying to believe my own words.

"And what about them?" Noni asks. She lifts her hand to point to the other end of the lake.

I don't need to turn my head to know who's there. I knew they would come. As soon as Lees let out her cry, I knew.

I turn, and there they are. Dora and Anki. Standing in the very place I stood when Lees called out my name.

EIGHTEEN

I usher everyone back from the ledge, hoping we haven't been spotted yet.

"Why are they here?" Lees asks, her hand rising to her mouth. The look of fear on her face tells me she already knows.

"We need to stay ahead of them." I don't offer any more of an answer, and Lees doesn't ask. "Where's the cave you're so excited about?"

Standing here on this shelf of rock—a flat plateau that stretches only twenty paces before a higher cliff springs up behind it—I see no openings in the walls. Rivulets of water crisscross the stone—offshoots of the stream that feeds the falls—but these all meander through grooves they've dug in the rock, dropping over the edge or snaking into crags. But nowhere do I see an opening we could walk through.

Then Lees sits down on the stone we all stand on, and

slides her feet into what I thought was a depression in the rock.

And disappears.

Running to the place she just stood, I see what I couldn't see before. What I'd thought was a depression is actually the entrance to an underground cavern. Looking through the opening, I can see Lees standing on the floor of the cave below.

"How big is it in there?" I ask. "Will we all fit?"

"Twice as many would fit," Lees calls back. She climbs halfway out again, clinging to a few protruding nobs of stone that serve as toeholds, lifting her head and shoulders out of the hole. Her smile beams.

"Good work," I say. "We're coming down."

The opening is narrow, requiring some twisting and turning, but Seeri and Noni get through with little trouble. Morsk and Pek still stand over Kol, who is stretched out on the stone in the exact place Morsk set him down. I squat beside him. His eyes are closed as if he's sleeping. He doesn't stir. My heart sinks in my chest.

"What if I lifted his feet and Morsk lifted his shoulders?" I say. "Pek, you could go down first. Maybe you and Seeri could help take his weight from us—together we should be able to set him on the floor of the cave without letting him fall."

Pek's eyes scan Morsk's face. Distrust hardens his mouth

and jaw, but he nods. "Be careful with him, Mya," he says. At first I think he means Kol—be careful lifting him—but then I realize he means Morsk. As he drops down into the hole in the rock, he throws one more watchful glance back at him.

"Don't worry," Morsk says, "I won't let him fall."

Kol never opens his eyes as we transfer him through the opening into the cave. I'm the last to go through after Morsk, climbing down out of a windy world bright with sun, into a still, dim space.

I don't know what I had imagined, but I never imagined this. I stand in a small room with curved walls of rounded rock, as if it had been carved to serve as a drinking cup for the Divine. The ceiling is high enough that we can all stand at our full heights—even Morsk. The floor is pitted and pocked, carved by water that runs down the walls and trickles into several small waterways that flow farther underground, disappearing into the dark. It's cold down here. On the surface, I'd thought my clothes were nearly dry. The hides had shed most of the water, and they'd warmed so much in the sun. But here, in this damp, dark place, my clothes feel chilled and wet against my skin.

"Well, we're hidden. That's certain," I say. My voice, not even a whisper, but a breath of a whisper, fills the room and reverberates around me. I take a tentative step downhill, following the flow of water deeper into the ground. "How far have you followed it?" I ask Noni and Lees. "Do you know where it goes?"

"Not to the end. It narrows into a passageway you have to crawl through. Lees and I went all the way down to a tight corner, and even followed it around the turn. It leads to another space a lot like this one—one lit by a sinkhole that opens to the surface. As you crawl along you can hear water, like the creek might be running right overhead," Noni says.

I take this in. I remember hearing the creek right before I first saw the bear this morning. I wasn't far in from the cliffs that overlook the sea. If we could crawl that far through the dark—all the way back to the cliffs above the sea—we might be able to get back to the beach and to the boats without being seen by Dora and Anki, or Thern and Pada, or whoever else might be out there stalking us.

But before we try crawling that far, we have other things to worry about. I crouch beside Kol where Pek and Seeri placed him on the floor of the cave, and his eyes flip open.

"That was a terrifying trip to the top." A twitch flickers across his lips—an attempt at a smile? If it is, the attempt fails, as his lips twist into a grimace.

"You were awake?" I glance up at Morsk, who looks away. "I thought you were out. I thought maybe—"

"No, I was all too aware," he says. "I'm still alert. Just terrible at walking. Even worse at climbing."

He laughs a bit at his own words, but no one else makes a sound. Noni drops down beside him across from me. "If you could let me go outside, there's feverweed near the lake. I saw a whole patch of it. If he chewed it—"

"No," I say. Kol's eyelids, which had already dropped shut, flip open again. I touch his hand. It's scalding and dry. His eyes are clouded with fever. "Not yet," I say, squeezing Kol's hand. "Once we know we're safe—that they didn't follow—then I'll let you go."

But even as I say these words, I don't know that I could really ever take that chance. Could I risk the welfare of the whole group to get a plant I hope will help Kol? Maybe if they all pressed on, if they all got through to the beach, maybe I could get to the lake and gather some feverweed myself? "Noni, is there feverweed near the beach?"

"On the cliffs there's lots of it . . . more than here."

"And can we all get through the opening—the space we need to crawl through?" I stare into the dark, imagining the trickle of water I hear running into another tall, well-lit room. Still, I hear nothing but the echo of close rock and I see nothing but blackness.

"It's tight, but I don't think it's any tighter than the hole we just came through."

I lean close to Kol. A salty scent rises from his skin. I run my fingertips across his brow, and I notice his temples are damp. Could his fever be breaking?

"We're going to have to try to crawl through these caves to the beach," I whisper to him, though I know all the others can hear. Every small noise reverberates. But I don't care. Let them listen. They all know how I feel about Kol. I suppose this isn't the best time to concern myself with our privacy. "Do you think you can do it? Can you crawl?"

I think of his leg—his left knee that he's favored all day.

"Whatever we have to do, I'll do it. Roon will never forgive me if it's my fault Lees doesn't get back to him soon." From behind me, I hear Lees suck in a quick breath at the mention of Roon's name. Kol smirks just a bit. "Don't worry about me. I'll be right behind you," he says.

And I hear it in his voice—the resignation. I can hear him letting go of hope to stay with me. But I won't have that.

"No. No, you're going ahead of me. You're staying where I can see you." I want to take a few more minutes to let him rest. I want to push up his pant leg and look at his leg to see how bad it really is—but I don't dare. We need to go. And there's nothing I can do to help him here, anyway. "Noni, you lead the way. Then Morsk, Lees, Pek, and Seeri. Seeri, I'll send Kol in behind you, and I'll come in last. If you get too far ahead of us, call to me. We need to stay together."

The only answer is the singing of the water as it drips and pools. I watch Noni, so young but so strong, glance one last time at the circle of sunlight above our heads. Maybe she is soaking up the light before she plunges into darkness. Maybe she is wishing she could just make a run for it and leave the rest of us behind. Whatever she thinks, it's brief, and she turns back toward the black shadows where the rock underfoot drops down.

"You can stand for only about five paces," she says. "Then you need to duck. In another five paces, you need to crawl." I watch the back of her head—her black hair damp and matted—as she disappears into the dark. The sound of her sealskin pants dragging across the stone, the splash of running water as she crosses through the stream—these are the only signs that she is on her way through the passageway.

Just as I asked, Morsk goes next. He doesn't offer an opinion or even a glance back. Now it's Lees's turn.

"I'm scared," she says. She crouches down beside me, and I see Kol open his eyes to look at her. She turns to Kol instead of me. He has the answers she wants. "What did Roon say? When you said you were coming for me?"

"He doesn't know yet," Kol says. I know he's whispering intentionally, but his voice is a croak. "I left him in our camp when I came here. Someone needed to stay with our mother. But I never said where I was going, so he'll be really surprised when you get back to him."

"And why didn't Chev come?"

And there it is—the question that I don't want to answer. Right before I have to send her into the dark. Right before

I have to send her into a place she's afraid to go.

I look over her shoulder at Seeri. It's nearly impossible to see her face in the gray light that fills this room, but I can see her mouth. It is a hard, flat line. I wonder if she is thinking of Chev, and the fact she will never see him again.

Is she bracing herself for Lees's reaction to my answer? Is she hoping I will lie?

I wish I could lie—I wish I could pretend that a lie is justified here, but I can't. "Chev did come," I say. My throat is thick. My words break apart like sobs. "But he died. Dora and Anki killed him."

Lees's eyes grow wide, their dark centers melting as her eyes fill with tears. "They did?"

"Yes."

"Then they will kill *us*. They'll kill us too—"

"No, they won't. We're going to get back home to our camp. And if they make it back to our camp, they'll have to face the council of elders. The Bosha are rejoining the Olen. They won't get away with this—"

"But what if they never come back to our camp? What if they run away?"

Of course, I've already thought of this. I've asked myself this same question. Could I leave this island without doling out the punishment I know Dora and Anki deserve? Could I take the chance that they might abandon clan life and never return to face the elders?

Would they dare to come back to the clan, expecting to find support for what they've done? And can I be sure they will find none?

"We need to get out of here first. Then we can worry about that," I say, and this time my voice is strong. "That's what Chev wanted. He wanted you and me to come home. On our own terms. Because he loved us."

Lees's eyes touch mine. There is a hint of skepticism there. I can see she wonders if Chev used the word *love* or if that's my interpretation, but she decides not to ask. "All right," she says. "And you'll be the High Elder now?"

"Yes."

I see her eyes drift back toward the place Kol lies on the ground beside me. There's a question in her eyes. *What about your betrothal?* But she knows not to ask about that now.

She turns and slides around Seeri. I can hear her boots splashing in the trickling stream under her feet, her hands scratching on the rock. "Hello?" she breathes into the dark.

"Right here." It's Morsk's voice, coming from farther down the passageway. "Right in front of you."

"And I'm right behind you," Pek calls. There's something protective in his voice. I appreciate it—of course I do—but it also makes it plain to me that he wants to keep an eye on Morsk. Even crawling through the rock in the dark, he doesn't trust him getting too close to Lees.

Seeri turns to me. "I'm next," she says. She steps into the

shadow, then turns and comes back quickly into the light. She draws in a deep breath. "You're doing well," she says. "You're a good leader. Chev would be proud of you. So would Father."

Before I can answer, she slides back into the dark and out of my view.

I turn back to Kol. "Ready?" I ask. I try to smile—try to push some hint of light into my eyes—but it extinguishes when he shakes his head in reply. "Kol. Stop. You're next."

"No," he says. "I don't think I am." He presses his eyes closed, and when he opens them again, they sharpen so much, they pierce me. "I'm not going with you."

NINETEEN

"**I** won't let you do this to me—"

"Mya, I'm not doing anything *to you*—"

"Then *for* me. However you see it. But I won't have it. You're not going to sacrifice yourself for what you think is my good—"

"That's not what this is—"

"So I can get away and save myself and the others. You think you're helping me succeed, but you're still forcing me to fail. Because nothing about this will be a success if you don't come with me."

Kol sits forward and I can see the pain in his eyes. The whites are shot through with red, and the always-warm brown has chilled to the shade of cold earth. It's as if his fever has stolen the warmth from every other aspect of him. Like it's feeding on the warmth in his eyes, his voice, his smile.

But not the warmth in his Spirit. That's still there. That's the thing pushing him to make a ridiculous decision because he thinks it's for my own good.

"Mya, I'm not as selfless as you think I am. I'm not planning to stay behind to die—I'm not begging you to abandon me. I want my future too much." He manages a smile, though it's weak and thin and holds no joy at all. "I'm betrothed to the smartest, most beautiful girl I've ever met. Do you think I'm ready to let that slip away?" Kol pauses, and I wonder if he's thinking what I'm thinking—that now that I will be expected to fill the High Elder role in my own clan, our betrothal may no longer be possible. If we marry, one of us will need to join the other's clan. One of us will have to step aside. But can either of us do that? Can either of us let our love for each other be more important than our love for our clans?

"I'll come. I'll be right behind you." Kol makes this promise, even as he winces and lies back down, letting out a long, slow exhale through clenched teeth.

I'm not sure if I believe what he says. He's not speaking the truth about our betrothal. How can I believe that he's speaking the truth about anything?

"Leave one of the kayaks for me," he groans, "and I'll come. As soon as I can—"

"You must think I'm pretty foolish." I slide closer to him. I want him to feel me, even though his eyes are closed.

"You must think you can tell a girl she's smart and beautiful and she'll accept everything else you say, too. Say all you want—I'm not leaving you. I know you're very sick, but I've seen you worse. When you came to warn me and my clan about Lo's coming attack? When you pushed through the storm and came to me, freezing and only half-alive? You were much worse that day than you are now. And yet you recovered. You recovered and came with me, and you're coming with me now."

"That was different—"

"No, it wasn't—"

"I didn't have to be carried then."

I notice a twinge of pain ripple across Kol's face, but I'm not sure if it's his knee or his pride that's hurting. "Is this about Morsk?"

"I can't do it. Mya, I can't crawl—"

"Then you'll go backward. You can lie down and slide on your back—"

"Mya!" Kol sits up again, his back arching, his features contorting with pain. I had thought he was sitting forward before in an effort to be closer to me—to speak to me more privately—but now I realize he was moved by his body, not his heart.

Maybe he really isn't trying to sacrifice for me. Maybe he just can't go on.

"I'll follow you. I promise," he says. "Let me stay here until I get some strength back. You can all crawl through to the beach. I'll wait. When I can, I'll come through after you."

As Kol speaks, I lean closer. For just a moment, I force myself to consider it—I force myself to try to walk away. As the High Elder, I am obligated to ask what course would be best for the clan. What course is the right one for the greater good?

In that moment, the darkness in this cave cannot compare with the darkness that envelops my heart. The darkness I feel when I consider what might happen if I were to leave Kol here. When I consider my future as the High Elder of the Olen, if Kol never made it out of this cave.

Some rewards will never make up for the sacrifices made to achieve them. "We all go home," I say. "There's no other option. There's no option where I decide to leave someone behind. Not you, not Morsk, not anyone."

"Of course you can't leave Morsk—"

"What does that mean—"

"You might need him. Someone has to father the next Olen High Elder."

"Don't talk that way—"

"Mya," Kol says, his voice suddenly strong, "don't hold on to me now, only to let go of me later."

His eyes are closed. I think about his words as I notice the tightness of the skin across his cheeks. The puffiness of his dry lips.

I lean over him and touch his lips with mine—a kiss to

seal a promise. "I'm not leaving the High Elder of the Manu to die. You are needed—"

"And so are you—"

"So we're going out together. You must try. We can discuss the future of our betrothal and the future of our clans—we can even discuss who will marry Morsk—but not here. We can discuss all of that once we are home."

Kol struggles up onto his elbows and gives me an even look. No smile—not on his lips or in his eyes. "I can't go on, Mya. I can't make it." For the first time since he told me he wouldn't come with me, I know he is telling me the truth. "But for you, I promise to try."

He leans toward me, and seals his promise with a kiss.

I get up and walk toward the passageway, feeling the walls with my hands when it's too dark to see. Kol comes behind me, sliding across the floor backward, keeping his left leg straight at the knee. I tell him when the ceiling drops down, though it hardly matters to him. When the opening closes to a space barely wider than my shoulders, I stop.

It's not big, but it will have to be big enough.

Kol slides past me until he can go no farther. Lees calls to him from the other side of the opening, ready to help him through.

"Where's Seeri?" I ask.

"She's right here. I just . . . I wanted to be the one to help."

I almost argue with her—I almost tell her to go back to her place between Morsk and Pek—but then I change my mind. We came to this island together. She wants to play a part in getting us home.

"Can you thread your arms through first?" Lees asks, her voice a soft hum. "It's easiest if you slide forward, onto your hands. I'll be here to make sure your knee doesn't hit the floor." Lees's voice shakes as she gives him instructions. Maybe someone else wouldn't notice—she's trying so hard to stay calm—but I can hear the strain behind her words. For now she's trying to stay strong for everyone else. I think we all are, actually. But I marvel that Lees, my impulsive little sister, is able to succeed at it so well.

A sharp groan rolls out of Kol as he pushes his body through the tight space. As his knees rub against the rough rocks that line the gap into the passageway, I bite my lip. I almost pray, but I don't dare anger the Divine with another request.

Once Kol is through, it's my turn.

It's so dark, I can see Kol and Lees only as shadows. Every small sound hits me like a clap of thunder. I thread my arms through the opening. The floor of the passageway is lower than the floor I kneel on, and I tumble forward onto my hands. Lees catches me around the shoulders and I slump onto the stone floor. The thud of my hip is echoed by a low yowl from Black Dog.

"It's all right, boy." Noni's voice is soft and reassuring. "We're going to get out of here soon." The dog settles and quiets, and I try to settle too. My pulse hammers in my temples and my thoughts race, but I push those things away.

It's so quiet and still, and the walls of rock are so close around all of us, even Noni's hand stroking Black Dog's fur makes a sound. *Shh . . . shh . . . shh.*

My eyes have adjusted to the hazy light. We're in a narrow tunnel of rock. The sides curve and wrap above our heads, rounded and smooth like the inside of a hollowed-out bone. I can feel where flows of water have seeped in and dug channels into the rock—some wide, others narrow. In places, thin trickles still ripple along. A *drip . . . drip . . . drip . . .* reverberates, faint but persistent, lending us a faltering heartbeat.

The ceiling is too low to stand, but there's room to crawl—or slide, as Kol will need to do. The dog whines, and his voice sounds like my soul feels. We need to get moving.

"Noni, are you ready to lead us out?"

Her only reply is the shuffle of her pants along the floor, her quiet whisper of assurance to Black Dog. She slides away. I can barely distinguish her outline as she reaches a spot in the passageway that dims. She twists her shoulders and disappears around a tight turn.

I gulp in a sharp, quick breath. How will Kol maneuver

that bend in the rock? I say nothing. First we need to get him that far.

In front of us, Pek, Seeri, Morsk, and Lees all follow Noni and Black Dog, disappearing out of view. Kol and I draw closer to the turn, creeping along as he slides slowly on his back, pushing off again and again with his right foot. His eyes are on the rock above our heads—he hasn't seen the turn yet. But I'm sure he remembers what Noni described, and the sound each person makes as they pass through— grunts and groans mixed with the scrape of elbows and knees against rock—leaves little doubt of what's ahead.

When his shoulders finally touch the wall—when he can go no farther without contorting and curving to follow the bend—he looks back at me. The light filtering in from beyond the turn illuminates the right side of his face like the glow from a dying fire. He squints at me, as if trying to read my face.

"And now?"

"Like you did back there. You'll need to thread your arms through first. Then your shoulders. Twist your upper body through, then let your hips follow—"

"Pull my hips through. Like escaping a capsized kayak."

I think for a moment. "Yes. Like that."

A long, rippling sigh pours out through his lips. "And you'll be right behind me?"

"Of course."

"All right then."

The yellow glow of light shrinks to a dull gray haze when his body begins to slide through, filling the narrow space. His head and shoulders disappear, and then I hear his voice. "It's wider in here," he says. "It's another room, but smaller than the first one. It's a bulge in the passageway— like a mouse passing through a snake."

I bite my lips, suppressing a smile. "Thanks, but I'd rather not think of it that way," I say.

Kol's body rolls over, until he's lying on his right hip. Then his belt, hips, thighs all slide through. When his feet disappear, I know it's my turn.

Looking around the corner, I see the open room with its higher ceiling and wider floor. Beyond Kol, Noni and the dog huddle against a small opening that I hope leads to the outside.

But I doubt it. If we were that close, sounds would filter in—gulls and wind—and the light would be brighter. If we were that close, Noni wouldn't be able to keep the dog from running out. "How much farther?" I ask, calling as I take my first crawling step around the turn.

"Not too far. Ten paces . . . maybe twelve."

"Then start through. Just be careful. Let Seeri go first. She can be sure it's clear before she climbs out onto the ground. But don't wait. I'm almost there."

I try to crawl another few steps forward, but I have to

stop. My hips won't fit. I slide back a half step, sitting back on my heels. I notice Kol's eyes on me. It feels wrong to go backward—to go away from the only way out—but I have no choice. I slide back until only my head and shoulders are on Kol's side of the turn. I twist. I angle my torso to slide forward again.

Now I've found the right position. Now I can slide my body through. I reach with my left hand to crawl forward, but all at once the ground drops away.

Everything shudders—the walls, the ceiling, the floor as it crumbles and caves into black space. I feel Kol's feet fall against my hands as they tumble into the ever-widening hole that opens where the ground just was.

Black Dog howls, and Noni screams, but both voices sound muted and far above us. The light goes out, then returns, as a new gap in the rock opens over our heads. Sunlight pours in, and with it, water.

We must be right at the edge of the creek. The gap in the ground above us becomes the lip of a waterfall as a torrent splashes against the folded and crumpled rock.

"Go!" I snap. "All of you—get out before the water rises."

And they go. I can't see them—the quake has broken this room away from the passageway—but I hear them moving, shuffling along the stone, the sound fading as they draw farther away.

But Kol doesn't move, and neither do I. Instead he lunges forward from where he sits, splashing his hands into the water and clawing at the floor.

My arms and his legs are already submerged—hidden under dark water—but I don't need to see them to know. The pressure of the rock digging into my wrists tells me. The way Kol frantically claws at the ground beneath the water tells me.

The shifting rock has pinned us both in place.

And the water is rising fast.

TWENTY

The sun reflects off the moving surface, throwing a rippling pattern of gold against the walls. Interwoven lines of light shimmer and glow like a golden spiderweb. I crane my neck and twist in place, both hands wedged tight between rocks that fell with such force, they feel like they have always been here.

Like they will never move again.

The ceiling overhead is broken open to the ground, and above it, a clear blue sky. Tall grass clings to a strip of dirt that hangs into the gap above our heads, like a torn hide in the roof of a hut.

This same gap that lets in the sky lets in the creek. Water splashes over the lip, filling our room of stone.

I lie facedown, my weight on my wrists and elbows, as cold water creeps up to my chest and over my shoulders. I struggle, trying to stay calm. Trying and failing as I thrash harder and faster in the deepening water.

But nothing moves. The more the water rises, the heavier the weight against my wrists. The surface licks at my chin, and Kol calls out my name. "Mya!"

I glance up and I see his face has gone the gray of ash left in the hearth long after the flame has burned away. His eyes are red and sunken, his cheeks gaunt. I've never seen so much fear on his face. Fear for me, because even though he is caught just as firmly as I am, his head is much higher above the surface.

For now, at least. Who knows how long it will take for the water to be over my head and threatening his?

"Can you get your legs under you?"

"I'm trying," I say, but the words are drowned out by the gurgling of the water and the breath that wheezes out of me. "I can't get a foothold." I gulp in a few more quick breaths and my head swims like I'm on a rocking boat out on the sea.

I need to stay calm. I need to think.

My right hand is pinned beneath my left, and I can straighten and stretch the fingers of that hand. I do, and beneath the rock, space opens up at the ends of my fingertips. They wiggle, pressed on by swirling water, but nothing else. Despite the voice in my head screaming at me to pull my wrists up, I fight against my instincts and push them deeper into the rocks.

And something gives. My right arm slides forward, and I splash through the surface, landing on my elbow. My face plunges under the water.

Don't panic, I tell myself. *Remember who you are. You are Olen's daughter. You are Chev's sister. The Olen High Elder. You are in control.*

And my heart, pounding like a burial drum, calms just a bit. I slide my arm forward again, sliding even farther into the rising flood. My shoulders submerge, and I think I hear Kol's voice shout my name again, but I can't be sure.

My eyes open into murky blackness, but through the blackness I see Kol's legs. I see his hands. He reaches beyond the rocks that hold his ankles firm, stretching his open hands toward me, trying to pull me up.

His fingers graze my left forearm. He comes closer, stirring the water, and his fingers wrap around my sleeve. He grabs hold and he pulls.

My right wrist twists between the rocks, and something gives. A stone shifts; another slides down to take its place.

And a small space opens. My wrists gain some freedom of motion and I know this is it. The best chance I'll get. Maybe the only chance I'll get.

I pull and Kol pulls, and I twist and he twists, and my wrists slide out from the rocks. I fly up and out of the water and gasp. My chest burns, even as it aches with cold. But I am free.

Kol lets out a sound, something like a cry of pain, but when I turn my gaze to his face, he's smiling. The sound comes again. This time it's clearly a cry of joy, so sharp and strong I feel it push against me; I feel it pierce my skin. It cuts through my red and bleeding arms, flowing into my veins.

His smile softens. He leans back against the wall of rock behind him, half sitting, half lying, and he smiles at me the way he did the day we became betrothed—the day he placed the honey in my hands. The look in his eyes is like pure sunlight, though at this point there is no sunlight left in our little room. The gap above our heads no longer lets in a piece of the sky, a vent to the air. Water fills the gap now, pouring in at every angle, from every side. It spills along the walls and splashes onto Kol's head as he leans against rock.

The top of his head is not far from the gap where the water pours in. Maybe just the width of two hands separates him from the way out.

Yet how can that matter? It might as well be the width of a thousand hands; Kol is pinned so firmly to the floor. The only way to get him out is to free him, the way we freed me.

I return his smile. I want to say something—I can think of so many things I want to say—but I won't say them now. *Save them for later,* I tell myself. *There will be plenty of time after today.*

But then Kol starts to speak. He leans forward, and I think he is saying that I should climb—try to make it up through the gap before . . .

But the rest is lost to me. His voice is drowned out by the hum of water as I dive back under to the place where his legs are pinned below.

I trace his left leg to the floor. His foot is wedged in a gap between two large shoulders of rock. My hands run over the surface of each one—they are broad and wide, like the backs of two short-faced bears lying side by side. This is a different kind of trap—different from the smaller rocks that held my wrists in place. Moving the boulders that pin his legs to the floor will take all the strength I have.

Even that may not be enough.

Liquid cold tears at my skin like the claws of a saber-toothed cat. It holds me in its grasp. It peels away my warmth like a sharpened blade slicing meat from bone. The bare skin of my hands and face, the covered skin of my arms and chest—every piece of me aches, every piece of me burns with cold.

Every pulse is like a scream, every heartbeat an order to swim up to the surface and breathe. But I won't yield. As the water runs in, time runs out. And Kol is no closer to escape than he was when I dove down.

My hands thread between the rocks, wedge around his legs, seeking any knob or notch to grab hold of. Nothing.

Smooth stone wraps all the way around, as far as I can reach. I work my fingers around his ankles, down to the soles of his boots. Pushing . . . pulling . . . I manage the smallest of movements. His left leg slides up the width of one of my clawing fingers. His right leg slides out from under his left about twice as far. A victory so small, so insignificant, but it's enough for me to allow myself a moment at the surface to breathe.

The moment I break through to the air I hear Kol's voice shouting at me. I think I may have heard it under the surface as well, but the desperate screams of my body and mind overwhelmed it. Now it can't be ignored. His words ring against the rippling surface that climbs ever higher. They shiver against the close walls. The room shudders with his words—*foolish*, and *too late*, and *save yourself*.

I cough, spitting water and silt from my lips. I don't dare answer his shouted demands. I don't dare take time to argue. Instead I try to give him the kind of smile he gave me, and I soak in the image of his face one more time.

Then I swim back down, fast.

My hands go right to his legs, squeezing around them and easing into the gap between the rocks. I lean hard, wedging my arm as far into the dark space as I can. I claw at the stone, fighting to stay down, leveraging all my strength, holding myself underwater as I fight to lift this impossibly heavy boulder up and away.

And the effort is answered by the tiniest shifting of weight.

The rock on my left slides ever so slightly farther to the left. Kol's ankle writhes under the pressure of my hand. I feel a tiny shiver of movement, the smallest advance toward our goal. Kol pulls his knee just a hair toward his chest.

My heart gallops. I feel the weight of a hundred running mammoths. They stampede by, breaking my selfish will against these rocks as they pass. My will to save myself, my will to escape at any cost. Those things are torn and broken, splintering into pieces that sink to the bottom and disappear.

I let go of it all. I let go of the fear, I let go of the instinct to save myself, to scramble up through the hole overhead and say that I tried my best. I open my clenched heart, and let go of everything that won't help us both get out of here alive.

I see Kol's legs pinned against the rocks, and I know that I am pinned here too. I feel his bruised and broken knee, and I know that I am bruised and broken too. I turn over and slide my leg under his leg, wedging myself in as tightly as I can, pushing the heel of my foot against the rock that pushes on his.

Because I know this is the end, one way or another.

I wriggle my leg deeper into the chasm, and my face angles upward toward the surface. I see his chin, his mouth, the back of his tilting head, already under the water. My leg wedges deeper still into the rock, and I twist my knee, driving it into the boulder until I feel like it will shatter into dust.

A heavy weight crushes down on my chest. The water around me grows a little bit darker. Not breathing becomes a little bit easier.

And then the boulder gives.

It rocks away, tilting and tumbling, sending a wave through the water that forces us both up, bobbing away from the floor and up to the surface.

For the first few moments, air fills my gaping mouth and dim light fills my eyes. But then a choke rises in my throat. My chest refuses to rise. My vision fills with a murky smudge of silt, growing darker as I sink farther down.

My eyes sweep the cave floor. Bubbles rise from the shifting rocks, but Kol is gone. He made it out.

Now I need to make it out, too.

The floor of the cave comes up as I sink, and I feel my shoulders, my back, my head settle against the stones. I stare up at the surface, at the small circle of light that floats just above me, when all at once I see Kol's face come into view.

An arm wraps around my waist, a hand slides down my back, and I am rising. My face warms, my chest aches, and my knee throbs as Kol pushes me up through falling water into the open air. Someone grabs me under the arms and hauls me onto the grass.

I roll onto my side and gag, water pouring from my mouth and my nose. I tremble all down my body, my eyes pressed closed, when someone touches my hand.

A second shudder runs from head to foot, and the hand tightens around mine. A third, and an icy, wet arm sweeps me into an icy, wet embrace.

I open my eyes. The harsh sun is cold and bright at the edges of my vision, but then my gaze warms. Everything about Kol is warm, but his eyes burn. The sun sets a fire in each of them, and I can feel their heat.

"Don't ever do that again," he says. His lips are close to my ear and his breath heats my skin. I turn my face toward him and bring my lips to his.

At first his kiss is soft, but like the light in his eyes, it's filled with its own warmth. Heat runs down my spine. With each beat of my heart it spreads—into my chest, down my arms, over my legs, all the way down to my toes.

Fighting against my will one more time, I pull back from him and tip my head to look him in the eyes. "I will do it again—"

"That was foolish, Mya. You could have died—"

"You're welcome," I say.

"I *do* thank you," he says. "But—"

"Whatever you intend to say, please don't say it." I pull

back a little more. "You smiled at me—just after we got me free—"

"I was happy. I knew you were safe."

"Yet you would deny me the same happiness? You would deny me the satisfaction—the joy of saving *you*? No. That's something you can't take from me." I kiss him once more, and his lips are already dry and hot with fever. Fear flickers back to life at my core, where I had almost extinguished it. I'm reminded that I haven't saved him at all.

Not yet.

I roll onto my side and find Pek and Seeri kneeling beside us. Behind them, the creek splashes in and around newly exposed rocks, following a fresh-cut course across the ground.

Pek's eyes sweep over Kol. "I'm going to give you my tunic," he says. "You're too sick to be wearing wet clothes—"

"Pek—"

"Yours will dry quickly on me, once we're moving again."

Kol doesn't offer another word of protest. He knows his brother is right. Pek pulls his tunic over his head while I tug Kol's up over his shoulders. The skin across his chest is bright red with cold.

Pek squats beside me and I'm suddenly in the way. Reluctantly, I leave Kol in Pek's hands and climb to my feet. Seeri jumps up with me and pulls me into an embrace. "If I'd lost you, too . . . ," she whispers into my ear. But then she pulls back, shivering with cold. "Your skin feels like ice."

"I'll warm up," I say. "Like Pek said—as soon as we're moving again—"

"Kol won't be able to walk on his own," Pek says, still squatting beside his brother. "We'll have to carry him."

Seeri's eyes drop to the ground. They sweep over Kol and she covers her mouth with her hand. I drop my eyes to his face and all at once I see him the way she sees him.

How can those bone-white lips be the lips I just kissed? How can those dim eyes be the eyes that just warmed me to my toes?

"He's getting worse," Seeri says, and something in her words flares up anger in me that I have to tamp back down. *It's not an accusation*, I tell myself. *She is not saying that you failed.* I want to scream, to defend myself, to shriek that I am doing everything that I can. But I know better. I know I can't let this be about me. Defensiveness is just a distraction, and I can't indulge in even the smallest distraction right now.

Seeri drops to her knees and picks up Kol's hand. "If only we had a fire . . ." Her eyes scan the ground, as if searching for firewood, but then she looks up and meets my gaze.

And there it is. I find in her eyes what I was dreading to find there. Fear. A fear that matches my own. A fear that tells me that my panic is justified—the panic that at this moment runs over my skin like a thousand tiny spiders.

"We need to go," I say as Seeri scrambles to her feet. "Even if we have to carry Kol, we need to get out of the open." I look around, realizing that I'm not sure where we are. "Lees and Noni said we would come out near the beach," I say.

"We're not far," Seeri answers. "I think just beyond this cliff is the sea."

The sea.

Of course. My mind has been a jumble since Kol and I climbed out of the water, but I remember now the purpose of crawling through the rock. It was a passage to the sea.

Not far from where Seeri and I stand I see Morsk, Lees, and Noni. Their backs are to us, and they are watching Black Dog. I stop and watch him, too. He is running along the edge of the cliff.

And I know that below that cliff is a beach. A beach that holds our tent, our food, and just a bit farther away, on the beach facing east . . .

Boats.

TWENTY-ONE

It doesn't take long for all of us to assemble at the top of the cliff. Pek carries Kol over his shoulder, but Kol doesn't complain. I think he'd rather accept help from Pek than from anyone else. We stand in a clump facing north, Kol leaning against his brother, with the sun dipping over our left shoulders in the west. The day is growing late and hunger gnaws at me. No one says anything, but I'm sure everyone is hungry.

The ledge below us drops straight down to the water, but to our right, a strip of sand extends from the base of the cliff out into the sea. This is the beach—the far northern edge of it at least—where Lees, Noni, and I set up our camp last night. Squinting, I can see the shadowy outline of the tent in the distance. The kayak Lees and I came in is only a little farther east, tucked up against the wall of rock. According to Seeri, the two double kayaks she came in with Kol, Chev, and Pek are on the eastern shore of the island, too.

"What about the boats the Bosha came in?" I ask Morsk. "You were following them. Did you see where they left them?"

"Right beside the kayaks your family came in."

"And your boat?"

"In the same place."

My thoughts race. If we can reach them safely, there are enough boats in one place to get us all out of here. But would we be able to make it to the boats if we started down this cliff now? Or would picking our way down in the open, under a sun that's still high in the sky, leave us too exposed? We will have to go slow, finding the best way down to the sand while Pek carries Kol. If the Bosha are nearby, we'd be completely vulnerable to an attack.

I glance around at the others. Everyone except Kol, Noni, and me still have spears by their sides. I doubt Noni ever had one, and mine and Kol's were lost when the passageway collapsed. Both Pek and Noni carry packs.

"Pek?" I try to speak quietly into his ear. "Do you have any food in that pack?"

"I do," he says, "and I'm more than happy to share it."

"I have food, too," says Noni, "though it's not much."

"Let's find a place out of sight," I say, noticing what sparse choices we have for getting under cover. The trees facing the north coast are few, and those are thin and spindly. Still, Pek finds a place where there is shade enough to conceal us. Everyone is excited about the prospect of food, and the mood is lighter than it's been all day. Only Noni still stands at the bare edge of the cliff looking out.

"Come sit," I say. "Everyone's hungry. I know you must be, too."

"I am," she says, but her eyes don't leave the beach. They stay fixed on something in the distance. I turn to see what it is that has her so entranced, and I see what she sees. A man, walking toward the base of the cliff. My breath catches in my throat.

"Is that your father?" I ask, sweeping her behind me.

"No, but I know him," she says. "He's my uncle."

"Your father's brother?" I ask. Fear ripples under my skin at the thought that Noni's father might have found her.

"My mother's brother," she answers. We both watch him as he follows the curve of the shore. All at once he looks up at us and throws his arms up to wave. "I don't know how he found us here."

I stand staring at the form of the approaching man, wondering if he's a danger, and wishing I had a spear. I remember the man who pursued Lees and me out to sea in a kayak from the Tama's shore. I can see even from this distance that this is not that man—his hair is much longer— but that doesn't mean Noni's uncle doesn't intend to do her harm. He reaches the base of the cliff and begins to climb. "Noni!" he calls. "I've come to warn you!"

"I trust him," she murmurs.

We watch him climb—not coming straight up but choosing to pick a path that winds up the cliff. Still, despite this easier route, he struggles. I watch him grope for handholds as if he were weak, as if he were a man much older than he appears.

"Something's wrong," Noni says. "I'm going down."

I watch him advance up the cliff as she works her way down, panic growing inside me. We should not be out in the open, exposed to the Bosha. Noni should not be climbing down this cliff, even if she does trust this man. I start down a few steps behind her, my eyes on her uncle, when suddenly he falls forward, landing on his face on the sand. A long dart protrudes from his back.

I glance over my shoulder at the clump of trees where the others are huddled. Kol lies on the ground, but Morsk sees me. He gets up. As I descend the cliff, I hear him coming over the ledge above me.

Noni reaches her uncle. He's still alive, but won't be for long. His hands grip Noni's arm. "I had to warn you," he says. "I had to warn you and your mother."

"But how did you know—"

"Your father has been looking for you. He knew a boat was gone." The poor man chokes. Blood spills over his lips.

Morsk hurries to our sides and helps pull the man upright. He leans over and spits blood into the sand. "When he didn't find even a sign of you up the river, he turned his attention to the sea. He's had people out searching the coast. But—" He gasps and coughs, and I draw Noni away, as if I mean to protect her from the horror of watching her uncle die. But she pulls away from me and moves closer to him. She wants to hear every word he came to say.

"He noticed a branch with green leaves that came in on a wave. 'Islands.' That was what he said that day. He had seen two paddlers heading out to sea. He said they knew where the island was. He said this proved it. . . ." This time, mercifully, his voice trails off instead of breaking into a hack.

I swallow hard. The paddlers he saw were me and Lees. "We gave you away," I say. "It was us—"

"I don't care. I would be dead by now if it weren't for you, anyway."

I doubt this is true, but if Noni hoped it would make me feel better, it does. "Who attacked you?" I ask. "Did Noni's father—"

"No." He coughs again, and this time I think he's died. He stills. Noni sets a hand on his, and he opens his sunken eyes. "Protect her, please," he says to Morsk. "Protect her and her mother."

In reply, Morsk simply nods. I see him swallow hard.

"This dart. It was thrown by someone here on the island.

I never saw who it was, but they are here. They are already here, and they will kill to get her back." He chokes again, gasping for air. His eyes meet Noni's one last time. "Be careful. Be careful."

He lies back against the sand. For a moment his breathing comes in a rough pant, and then it stops. His chest stills, and the hand clenched around Noni's wrist slides to the ground.

He is dead.

"I'm so sorry, Noni," Morsk says. I notice a knot in his throat as he speaks.

She leans over and kisses her uncle on the brow. "He was my mother's favorite. Now he's going to her." Tears spill from her eyes and she turns her face away.

"The dart was thrown by someone here on this island," I repeat aloud to myself.

"So her father is already here?" Morsk sets a hand on the dart, rocks Noni's uncle forward, and tugs hard to pull it loose. With it out, the dead man's body is able to lie flat against the sand.

Noni slumps against his chest. "That's better," she sobs.

Something about the dart is familiar to me. I take it from Morsk's hand. His eyes stay on it, too. "You've seen darts like this before, haven't you?" He nods. We grew up in the same clan. "Noni, does your clan use darts?"

"Sometimes."

"What do you carve them from?"

"Bone."

I hold up the dart to the light. "This is spruce," I say. "I know the design. This is Bosha made."

We leave Noni's uncle at the base of the cliff and rejoin the group. They've shared some food, but they've also stood at the edge of the cliff. They are anxious to ask about the man who died.

"So the Bosha are not far," Pek says.

"But why would they want to kill my uncle?" Noni asks, passing me her pack so I can try to get some food into Kol.

"I don't think they knew who he was," I answer. "They probably thought he was one of us."

Kol is awake, but very weak. He accepts a sliver of dried mammoth, but takes only a small bite. "You should let me go look for feverweed," Noni says. But I can't let her go now, even though I know Kol needs it.

"Soon," I say. "When I can go with you."

"So the Bosha are close, armed, and ready to kill," Pek says. "And Noni's father's clan is coming, too."

"We need to go—to get down the cliff and to the boats before the Bosha find us and before the Tama attack." I say all this—not as much to let the others know my plan as to clarify it for myself. The sun is sliding toward the sea, and though we still have a long time before dark, we don't want to push out onto the sea when the day is mostly gone.

"But if the Tama come for Noni, I want you to know I will defend her. I will protect her like I would if she were of the Olen clan. But she's not, so I can't ask any of you to do the same."

"I would do the same." It's Kol. The first words he's said since Pek carried him across the ground. "I may not be well enough to defend her. But I would."

"I would, too," says Pek.

"We all would, Mya." Seeri leans forward and clasps my hand. "You aren't asking us to do anything we don't want to do." My gaze moves to Lees, and then to Morsk. They both nod in agreement.

"Who wouldn't defend a child in danger?" Lees asks.

Chev might not, I think to myself. Not that Chev was cruel or unfeeling, but he lived by the rule of clan first. He might not have defended Noni if he thought it risked the safety of members of his own clan. He may have forbidden others from defending her, too.

Am I already failing in Chev's place? Or were his rules for leadership all wrong? Right now is not the time to ask these questions. Instead, I look around the group, assessing weapons and skills. "Since we all agree that we will protect each other and Noni, here's what I think we should do."

I outline my plan—Lees will stay back with Kol and Noni. She will be left with a spear, an atlatl, and darts, but they will be expected to stay out of sight under these trees.

Morsk, Pek, Seeri, and I will climb down the cliff wall and move up the beach to the boats. We will each row back one of the boats so we can get all of us off the island tonight.

Pek is on his feet almost before I stop speaking—one hand reaching for his spear while the other tugs Seeri to her feet. Morsk has yet to sit. His eyes have been locked on the sea the whole time.

"Before you go," Lees starts, "I have a comment on your plan."

"We'll be careful—"

"I think I should go, and you should stay with Kol."

My back is turned to Lees—I'm leaning over Kol, my hand pressed to his scalding cheek—but when I turn I see something unfamiliar in her eyes. She hands me her spear. "You'll need this. I'll take a set of darts and an atlatl instead. But you should stay with Kol. I would want to stay if Roon were the one sick. He needs you." There's a heaviness in her voice I've never heard before, and I realize the thing in her eyes is concern. Not the childish kind of concern I've seen there before, like the look she gets when she fears she's missing out, but the concern that I am doing the wrong thing by leaving her with Kol.

By leaving Kol with anyone but me.

"It's too dangerous—"

"Staying here to defend the two of them is *just as dangerous*. Noni's never even held a spear—"

"That's not true," Noni blurts out, but I know what Lees means. She can't be depended on to help if they were found.

"The trip to the boats will be much more dangerous—"

"Will it?" It's Seeri who interjects now. "I don't know. Honestly, Mya, I think I would be less worried about Lees if she were with me, Pek, and Morsk than if she were left behind to defend two defenseless people."

I study Seeri. Is this really what she thinks? Or does she think Kol might die and I should be here if he does?

I know he won't die—he can't die—but I bend down beside him and he turns to me. His eyes see me, but I don't think he's heard anything we've said. His eyes flutter, move to the sky, and fall closed again.

"All right then. I'll stay. But I want a signal. If any of us gets into trouble, we'll set a fire. If we see smoke, we'll know it's a call for help."

"But won't smoke draw everyone else who's stalking us, too?" Pek asks.

"I'd be happy to have them all out in the open at last," Seeri says. "It would be better than fearing every shadow."

With these words in my ears I walk with them to the edge of the cliff, wondering where the Bosha might be at this moment and when they might attack. I watch Pek, Morsk, and Lees drop over the ledge one by one and start down. Seeri goes last. "Don't worry about us," she says, pulling me into an awkward hug. "Take care of Kol. We won't be long."

I stay low to the ground and watch her descend. When she is halfway to the bottom of the cliff, I creep back into the shade of the trees and find Kol alone.

Noni is gone.

TWENTY-TWO

Kol lies on the ground, but he does not lie still. He tosses restlessly, like a dreamer caught in a nightmare. Every part of his body is in motion except for his left leg.

From just beyond the edge of this clump of trees, Black Dog howls. I crouch down and slide toward the sound, Lees's spear balanced on my shoulder. Black Dog howls once more and I am up, running toward the sound.

I see her even before I reach the edge of this meager stand of stunted trees. She lies on her back beside a clump of plants with deeply serrated leaves. Feverweed. Handfuls of stalks yanked straight from the dirt litter the trampled grass. Noni lies still, a dart sticking out of her neck. Black Dog runs in circles around her until he hears my foot on the ground.

I drop down, crawling on hands and knees to the edge of the trees. Noni looks at me, moving just her eyes. She is alert—alert enough to know she is in danger. My gaze sweeps the open space around her, but I see no one. *Where did her attackers come from*, I wonder, *and where did they go? Are they hiding, waiting for me to come out into the open?* It doesn't matter; I have to go to her. With the spear balanced on one shoulder, I slink across the ground to her side.

Blood runs from both wounds in her throat—where the dart went in and where the tip came out. She is bleeding hard. "I had some," she says, and her chest rises and falls like the sea in a storm. "I dropped it—"

"Shush," I say. I gather the plants that are scattered on the ground. "I've got it." I scoop her into my arms—she is so light—but I'm exhausted. My steps are slow, and with each one I turn and look over both shoulders.

"I didn't see anyone," Noni says. Her voice gurgles, like she's underwater. As I carry her, Black Dog runs in front, but then stops and lifts his head. He sniffs the air. I hesitate, wondering if he smells the scent of the person who attacked Noni. I don't move until the dog runs again, returning to Kol's side.

I lay Noni beside him on the mossy soil. When I brush my fingers across Kol's forehead, they burn. His fever must be rising. His body has gone still. I think maybe he's fallen back to sleep, or whatever approximation of sleep his high fever will allow.

I check Noni's wounds. "I'm going to leave the dart in

place," I say. "It will bleed less."

"Pack the feverweed all around it." Even with blood running from an open wound, she still wants to tell me how to use the plant. I'm happy for it—she is still awake, and I so desperately want her to stay that way. "I promise you it will stop the bleeding." I follow her instructions, hoping these leaves will do even a fraction of what she claims they will. "But give some to Kol. That's why I went out there. To get it for him."

Noni tells me to wad up a few leaves and press them between Kol's teeth. I whisper to him, telling him to bite down on it, and though his eyes stay pressed shut, he does as I say. I ration the remaining supply of leaves, setting some aside to dress Noni's wound again later.

I listen for any sound that might suggest someone is nearby, planning to attack. I hear nothing but waves below the cliff and the wind rustling the leaves. "The person who did this—you saw nothing at all? You didn't hear a voice?"

"Nothing." She sighs, but pain tears at the edges of the sound. Her breath rattles, and when it stops, something else rattles, too. A crunch, like a foot on the ground. Noni's eyes move to my face. Her head nods. She's heard it, too. I pick up the spear, stretch to my full height, and turn in place, searching for any movement beyond the trees.

I pause, holding still and silent, and listen again. My attention catches on another rustling sound, like footsteps coming through the trees. Noni looks up too, and this time, so does Black Dog.

My imagination might play tricks on me—Noni's might play tricks on her—but I trust the dog's senses. Lees's spear rolls in my hand, my grip ready, as I turn in the direction of the sound.

I see nothing . . . nothing . . . until all at once a dark shape is hurtling toward me. . . . A person running, a spear raised over her shoulder. In the pale light of the dying day, I see her face. Anki. She slows, and I see her eyes. Her gaze locks on my face as she cocks her arm back at the elbow and throws.

But her aim is compromised. The clutter of trees and the tricks of the shadows confuse her throw, and her spear bounces off the bent branch of a poplar that twists up through the shade. I don't know what other weapons she might have, but I know I need to retrieve that spear before she does. I take off toward the place where it lies, not far beyond the circle of ground where Black Dog keeps watch over Noni and Kol.

I tear over the ground, Anki running hard from the other direction. I am so close, much closer than she is. I reach the spear, trading Lees's to my other hand in favor of this larger, fiercer weapon. My feet plant, my arm rises over my shoulder, and I measure my aim.

A violent shudder tears through me, as if my will has

torn in two. I ready myself to take a life—something that feels so wrong—while I revel in the privilege of ending the person who ended Chev. The two sides of my heart struggle, wrestling inside me, right up until Anki stops. She pulls a long flint blade from her belt. Black Dog appears at my heels, growling through bared teeth, and Anki aims the knife at the dog. The memory of Chev's knife clutched in that same hand rushes back, and my resolve hardens.

The spear flies from my hand and finds its home, deep in Anki's thigh. I know at the moment the spear pierces the hide of her pants that I've hit the mark I sought. Blood runs, pulsing, over her knee and down her calf. Thick, heavy blood, so dark it's almost black. It won't take long until she has nothing left to bleed.

Still she struggles forward, her face a knot of concentration and rage. "You may think that you will win. That I will die and you will have beaten me." She takes a few stumbling steps, and my eyes move to Noni, vulnerable on the ground.

Black Dog watches, sniffing the air, as if he recognizes the scent of Anki's blood.

"Yes, you may think that you've won," she says. "I certainly won't last." She reaches down to press her fingers into the wound. The flow of blood doesn't slow. It runs out over her hands, painting them red up to her wrists. "But I don't need to survive to get what I want. I just need to kill you."

Even as she threatens me, her legs give out and she

collapses, landing in a thicket of thorns that tear small red gashes in her cheeks. She hardly seems to notice. Instead she struggles to her knees, grabs the spear with both hands, and pulls it out, leaving a gaping hole in her leg that goes all the way through muscle to bone. "Thank you for returning my spear," she says. She braces all her weight on it and forces herself to her feet.

She raises the spear, steadying herself against a tree.

But there is no strength left in her, and she drops back to the ground, the spear still clasped in her fist.

For a long stretch of time I stand there, not making a move toward Anki or away. A breeze picks up, swirling the branches above my head. Could it be the movement of her Spirit as it leaves her? As the gust fades, I force myself to slide toward her. We are too short on weapons. I cannot leave this spear—even covered in her blood—cast aside on the ground.

As I tug it free from Anki's hand, I think again of my brother's knife—the one I'd seen her treating like a toy—the one she took from his body when he died. And I think of Dora's words to her daughter—*You know better than to steal from the dead.* Does taking this spear make me no better than Anki?

But then I turn and see Noni and Kol lying side by side on the hard ground. Both of them weak. Both nearly defenseless.

I grasp the spear. I will return it to her clan when I see

them again. I am not stealing from the dead, but for now I am borrowing this spear.

Back under the trees that overhang Kol and Noni, I slide to the ground.

"Is she dead?"

I startle at the sound of Kol's voice. "You're awake."

"I am."

I drag myself to his side. His eyes are open, and in the thin light of the fading day, I see a bit of fire in them. His head is damp with sweat. "Your fever's coming down."

"Maybe the plant is working."

I slide over to Noni's side. Blood still leaks around the feverweed packed around the dart, but after seeing Anki's leg, this doesn't scare me nearly as much as it did.

Kol sits up. "I thought I would die today," he says. "And do you know what I feared?" He leans forward. Through the deepening shade, I can just barely see the shape of Kol's mouth, a straight even line with only a hint of a curl at the corners. "I feared that I would never get the chance to marry you. That I would never get the chance to be your husband."

I flinch at Kol's words, and I hope he doesn't see. I've feared the same thing today. I've feared that we would never marry. But not because Kol would die, but because Chev has died, because Arem has died. I feared our new duties to our clans would tear our betrothal apart. That the need to lead separate, independent clans would mean we would have to stay separate and independent, too.

But Kol hasn't thought of this. Or if he has, that's not what he wants to talk about now.

"I wasn't afraid of you living a long life without me," he continues. "I wasn't afraid even that you would forget me. You would marry someone else someday. It would be better if you did forget.

"But I was concerned about one small thing. I was worried I would never get to dance the wedding dance with you."

The sun has sunk so low that it gives little warmth. Cold seeps up from the hard ground. Yet despite the chill, my body warms. My hips turn, tilting me toward Kol. I lean in, almost close enough to kiss his lips. "We could dance right now," I say. Heat runs down my spine. I lean closer.

Just as my cool lips press against the heat of Kol's, a sound snaps my head around.

The sound of a dart sticking into the ground.

I tear myself from Kol and spring to my feet. A spruce dart identical to the one that pierced Noni sticks up at an angle just an arm's length away. I pivot, searching the darkness that spreads in every direction, broken by only the smallest swaths of light. I see nothing, nothing, nothing . . . but then another dart lands a bit farther from my feet, but a bit closer to Kol. My gaze flicks to the place it came from and I see her—Dora—her bright white hair glowing in the scattered twilight. She is running hard straight for us through the trees.

She must be out of darts. She shoulders a spear, and she is closing in, nearing the distance she needs to make the strike. I lunge for Anki's spear. The shaft, sticky with blood, feels right in my hand.

I step out, putting distance between me and Kol. I know what she wants. She's not here to kill Kol; she's here to kill me. And despite the shadows, despite the trees, despite the way she seems to struggle to get a clear view of me, she is determined to take the shot. So I encourage it. I step out just far enough for the slanting rays of the sun to slash across my face. Her steps slow . . . she takes three sliding steps forward and releases the spear.

Even before it's out of her hand, I'm diving back into the shade, toward Kol and toward the ground. The shot falls just short, nicking my calf as I fall.

I look up, and my eyes meet Dora's. She smiles, the same meek smile I first saw when she climbed out of the kayak on the shore of the Manu's camp, her arms laden with sealskin to help them rebuild the camp her son had tried to destroy.

A smile that is a lie.

Her eyes are on her spear just a few paces from my feet. She has no hope of retrieving it before I can get off a shot. Judging by her smile, she's out of darts, too.

"You're making a mistake," Dora says. "I know you think I came here to kill you, but I didn't. I came here to stop you from marrying a boy from the clan that killed your mother. She was a friend of mine, and if I have to kill him to honor her memory, that's what I'll do."

Dora stops. Her eyes cast a quick glance over her shoulder. She's thinking about escape. "Even in your last moments," I say, "you're still a liar." She pauses, hesitates, just long enough for me to raise Anki's spear. Then she turns and runs back the way she came—back toward the cliff.

As I chase her, I hear her suck in heavy, labored breaths. She's still winded from the hard climb up the cliff from the beach. The evening air grows colder—the north wind sweeps over the cliff from the sea—and my own lungs burn. My eyes tear and my cheeks sting, but I never slow.

Within ten paces of the cliff wall, I catch up to her. I am well within range. I think of my sisters on the beach heading for the boats, maybe even coming back with them by now. I think of the possibility Dora has her own boat at the base of the cliff, maybe loaded with other weapons. How if I don't stop her, she could reach the others faster than I could.

And I throw the spear.

It sails true to its target, but she drops to the ground and rolls just in time. It grazes her hip and bounces in the dirt.

From where I stand, I assess the distances. She is closer

to the dropped spear than I am. She could be armed before me. She sees it too. Her eyes give away her desperate need to reach it, but her mouth, twisted in pain, gives away the extent of the wound on her hip.

Dora raises herself on one knee, lunging for Anki's spear. Time slows, and I notice small details—the curl of the grass under the hand of the wind, the shadows of birds flying west toward the sun. I think of those birds—I wonder if they are black shags, flying to their nests out at sea. And I notice a sound, the howl of a dog, and a voice calling my name.

I turn and look back, just a momentary glance over my shoulder. Kol stands, leaning on the shaft of Lees's spear like a walking stick. "Use this," he says, and he holds it out to me.

And so I turn and run, knowing that as I run to retrieve Lees's spear, Dora is retrieving Anki's.

My feet fly over the ground. I feel like an elk or a deer. I grab the spear and spin. Dora is struggling to rise to her feet. Blood pours from her hip. She moves slowly, getting only to her knees before I am closing the space between us, preparing to take the shot. She wobbles, climbs to her full height, shifts her gaze from me to Anki's spear and then to the cliff behind her.

She makes her choice and staggers toward the cliff.

I am still chasing her—still closing the distance in hopes of making the shot—when she plunges over the edge and down to the sea below.

I have to look. I have to be sure I see Dora's body broken on the rocks or floating in the tide.

But the tide has come in. The rocks have disappeared. High water splashes against the base of the cliff wall. I do not see a kayak waiting for her. And I do not see Dora's body.

I stand looking out at the sea for a long time, but I never see a sign of any living thing.

I don't find Kol at the edge of the trees where he gave me the spear. Instead I find him back at Noni's side. He has found Noni's pack, and he's searching for something.

"We need to signal them," Kol says, pulling something small from the pack. "We need to set the signal fire—"

"What *you* need to do is stay out of sight. Move farther back from the cliff, away from the beach and sea. Take Noni and Black Dog with you—"

"And you will do what?" Kol asks, getting to his feet. He's shaky and avoids putting weight on his left leg, but he stands. "Give the Bosha the chance to kill you? You agreed to use a signal. It was your idea."

"He's right." It's Noni's voice. Her eyes are open. She's found the feverweed and packed a bit more around her wounds.

I recognize the thing in Kol's hand—a fire starter. "We'll find a place near the edge of the trees—a place where the fire will be seen," Kol says. "Noni says she can walk that far."

Kol turns, expecting me to follow. But from beyond the ledge a sound rolls up, mixing with the beat of the waves that whip against the cliff. It echoes back again—not the sound of water on water, but rock falling on rock.

Rocks are falling, and I can't help but worry that someone is making them fall. Maybe Dora survived after all. Maybe it's Noni's father.

I stride to the edge of the trees, peering through the eerie glow of twilight. Motion shifts at the ridge where the ground drops away. A silhouette takes shape, climbing to the top of the cliff face and rising up into the slanting light, stretching to the full height of a man.

Thern. He stands and unfolds his arm, and in his hand is an atlatl. He loads a dart. His focus shifts—I wonder if he is searching for me, or Kol, or even Anki or Dora—but then something in his movements strikes me as halting. He lifts his other hand, drawing it over his eyes, and I know he is blinded by the setting sun over my shoulder.

For one small moment—a moment no wider than the breadth of a single hair on my head—I feel relieved. He can't see to shoot the dart. He doesn't have a clear view.

But then the moment dissolves like foam on a wave, and Thern takes the shot anyway. The atlatl comes forward and the dart flies straight. He's luckier than Anki, and nothing deflects his shot. But it flies wide, sailing past the place I stand, landing somewhere in the trees behind me.

I turn. Kol still stands with the fire starter in his hand, but his eyes are on Thern. I wonder if he—like me—is wondering where the others are. Hoping that they are still on the beach with the boats. That nothing has happened to them, and they are still coming.

"Go set the fire," I say. "Keep this near you." I toss Lees's smaller spear onto the ground beside him, but keep Anki's with me.

Thern loads another dart. His arm cocks back, the dart stabbing the sky as he readies his throw. I hesitate for only a moment, knowing that I will have only one shot. I squat down, hoping I can't be seen in the undergrowth, and I raise Anki's spear to my shoulder.

Thern's attention sweeps left to right, scanning the trees, searching for a target. Is it possible he does not see me? He takes a tentative step into the space between us.

He may not see me yet, but I have only another moment or two before he does.

My hand goes damp with sweat, the heavy shaft of Anki's spear slipping in my grip. Thern takes a half step closer, then another. With each step, the time I have to prepare my shot contracts, but the chance I have of landing the shot grows. So I wait.

Behind Thern, something moves. Something calls my

attention to the ledge that drops to the sea. A shadow that bends and changes—one moment long and flat to the ground, the next crouching, then straightening into a man. Just as Thern did before him.

Morsk.

He hurries to his feet, raises his spear overhead, and locks his eyes on the place where I crouch. Unlike Thern, he sees my hiding place.

And he is running hard right for me.

TWENTY-THREE

Morsk flies across the open grass, his eyes locked on mine, his spear ready.

My heart pounds in my throat and in my temples. *Could I have misjudged Morsk completely? Could he have been helping Dora and Anki all along?*

But then Morsk sends his spear toward its goal—not me, but Thern. The shot is strong and accurate, but Morsk's target is quick. He drops to the ground and Morsk's spear flies over his back, landing in the dirt behind him.

This is my chance. Thern doesn't know I'm here. He believes Morsk to be his only opponent—an opponent who is completely unarmed.

Thern leaps up. Ignoring the dropped spear, he pulls another dart from the pack slung over his shoulder. He turns his attention to Morsk, who stands empty-handed with only the cliff behind him.

I know I will have only one shot before I'm exposed. While his attention stays fixed on Morsk, I creep closer. I don't want to squander my chance by rushing.

But Thern isn't ready to kill Morsk just yet. He has suffered five long years, and he wants to condemn Morsk for siding with the people he believes caused that suffering.

My family.

"You're willing to kill me," Thern says, "to save men who are already dead. Olen is dead. Chev is dead—"

"How do you know Chev is dead?" Morsk calls.

"Anki told me," Thern answers. "She told me she killed him herself. She is not far away. If I don't kill you, she surely will, just to punish you for your loyalty to him."

I want to shout to Thern that Anki has already been here, that she is already dead, and that he is next. But I hold all my words inside and stand to my full height. All I have to do is throw Anki's spear. I think of Anki dying in front of me, as I ready to take another life. My hand is damp on the spear. Anki killed my brother, but this isn't Anki. My arm shakes. My heart pounds in my chest. But then Thern takes aim at Morsk and I know I have to act.

My throw is straight. The spear sticks in Thern's back, not far below his left shoulder. He spins, and his wide eyes meet mine. He doesn't drop, doesn't even fall to his knees. His rage fuels him. Reaching around with his right hand, he plucks the spear from his back. A thin trickle of blood seeps from the wound, but Thern shows no sign of weakening.

"How lucky," Thern says. "I'd much rather kill you than Morsk." He readies the spear. My eyes find Morsk's dropped spear on the ground but I have no time to run to it. But I don't need to.

Over Thern's shoulder I see Morsk running toward him. He tackles him and the two men crumple to the ground before Thern can take the shot.

As they struggle, both of them reaching for Morsk's spear, I run to it and claim it. Thern's dropped atlatl is not far away. I hurry to scoop it from the grass, but Thern grabs at my ankles, tripping me as I run past. I fall, and Morsk's spear flies away from my clutching hands. Anki's lies only a few paces away, and the knowledge that I am completely unarmed sends a surge of fear through me. I clamber forward, my hand extended out in front of me. I am almost there when a dart lands just beyond my reaching fingers.

A shape shifts and stirs at the edge of the cliff. I look up to see a person standing right where Thern first appeared, and Morsk right after him. An empty atlatl hangs at her side.

Pada.

She laughs, a strange high sound. "Unarmed?" she asks. Her hand slides into her pack. Despite the fading light I can see the shape of the carved spruce dart, see her slide it into her atlatl. I dash toward Anki's spear. Just as my hand closes around it I hear a cry—sharp and edged with pain—burst into the air and scatter on the wind.

Pada drops to her knees, a dart protruding from her arm.

Not a dart of spruce like the Bosha make. Not of ivory like the Manu make. I remember Noni's answer when asked what the Tama use to carve darts. Bone.

The dart in Pada's arm is made of bone. This dart was thrown by a member of the Tama clan.

With Anki's spear in my hand, I climb to my feet, and I lose my breath. Behind Pada I see them coming. Boats—six kayaks—are heading for the bottom of the cliff. Just as her uncle warned, Noni's father is here.

"Get down!" Thern calls to Pada, and he lunges for his atlatl. A woman climbs over the ledge not far from where Pada stands. In her hand is her own empty atlatl. She reloads with a new dart and aims again at Pada.

I have no time to think. I can only react. Not to protect Pada, but to drive the Tama woman back—to protect all of us, but Noni most of all. I reach back and make the throw, hand over shoulder, and Anki's spear lands in the Tama fighter's shoulder, but it doesn't stick. My angle was bad, and it falls away. She drops to the ground and picks it up, her attention shifting from Pada to me. She reaches back, the spear held behind her ear, ready to repay my throw with one aimed right at my chest. But she's careful, deliberate. As she steadies her aim, I grab Morsk's dropped spear and send it flying toward her.

This second throw is much more accurate than my first, and much less tentative. The spear plunges deep into her side and she drops to her knees.

A flash of relief is washed away by panic when I see another figure—a man—scale the cliff, a dart already loaded and ready to throw.

It flies at me. I roll away, but not before it cuts my ear. But when I look back at the man who attacked me, I see him fall back, one of Thern's darts in his chest. He tries to get his feet beneath him, but he can't stop his momentum before he tumbles over the ledge.

While I try to pull myself together—try to sort friend from foe—Morsk runs past me. He grabs his weapon from the place it fell beside the woman I speared. He comes so close to her I fear she will throw him from the cliff, but she is too weak to do any harm. Instead she pulls Anki's spear from her side, drops it to the ground, and retreats back over the cliff wall.

Pada grabs the dropped spear. She turns to me, and I flinch. But she nods. "Thank you," is all she says as she tosses the spear to the ground at my feet. "More are coming," she adds. Loading her atlatl, she turns again to face the edge of the cliff.

The battle with the Tama has slowed just enough for me to take note of not just Pada's shift in allegiance, but Thern's too. A loaded atlatl in his hand, he has a clear shot at Morsk. A pivot would give him a shot at me. But he readies, like

Pada, for the next Tama over the wall.

But the next person to appear isn't a Tama fighter. It's my sister Seeri. She and the others must have seen the smoke of Kol's signal fire. Whatever might have delayed them, I'm glad they are here now. Seeri clambers over the ledge and hauls Lees up behind her. Pek appears at the very spot where the Tama woman disappeared, his spear on his shoulder as he ascends.

Just as they all clear the wall, Lees calls out. A dart sticks in her upper arm—a Tama dart that came from below. Seeri scoops her up and sweeps her behind her as two Tama men come over the ledge at once—one carrying a spear, the other reloading his atlatl.

Before I can think or weigh my actions, Anki's spear is out of my hand, heading for the man with the empty atlatl—the man whose dart protrudes from Lees's arm.

It flies true, but the man has already turned away to seek his next target. The spear lands squarely in the middle of his back, lodging right between his shoulder blades.

He drops to both knees. His atlatl and dart slip from his hand as he falls. The fear pressing down on my chest eases just a bit at the sight of his dropped weapon, and a deep breath rushes into my lungs.

Anki's spear stands out from his back at a hideous angle, like some grotesque and unnatural tusk. He flails, twists, and turns, but he cannot reach it. He cannot shake it loose. The more he tries, the thicker the trail of blood running down his back becomes. Turning in place, pivoting from his knees, he looks back to find his attacker. He sees me, but he also sees Thern and Pek, running right for him.

The man struggles to his feet, one hand searching the ground for his dropped atlatl. But he has no hope of finding his weapon—Thern is coming too fast.

Before the man can straighten to his full height, Thern is on him, knocking him face-first onto the ground. With both hands, Thern tugs Anki's spear from the man's back, blood flying from the point as he swings it like a club.

As Thern swings the spear, he connects with the other Tama man who climbed over the wall. Staggering from the blow, he drops his spear and retreats for the cliff. Pek grabs the dropped spear and raises it over his shoulder, but he never has to make the throw. Both men disappear over the ledge.

I drop to the ground, breathing so hard I feel faint. I glance around. Pada—a dart still in her arm—comforts Lees, who has pulled the dart from her own arm. Seeri is at Pek's side, checking a cut on his face. Winded and gulping for breath, Morsk and Thern kneel side by side at the edge of the cliff, watching the water below.

"They're paddling away," Morsk calls over his shoulder. "They're in retreat." He climbs to his feet just as Thern does, and Thern hands him his atlatl and pack of darts.

Morsk nods to Thern, and walks to Pada's side. Without a word, Pada nods and hands him her weapons, too.

"How?" I stammer. "How is it that there are not more—"

"There *were* more," Pek says. "We saw them coming while we waited below with the boats. We intercepted as many as we could, driving them back before they could climb the cliff. We turned quite a few around, but we couldn't stop them all. Then we saw your fire and we decided we better climb."

"Before we did, we slashed as many of their kayaks as we could," Seeri says. "Hopefully, we've bought some time before they can return." I step closer to the ledge and look out at the retreating Tama. Nearly every kayak carries an extra fighter, draped across the deck, hands and feet dragging through the water. A few boats struggle to stay afloat as two fighters cling to the sides.

"And our boats?" I ask.

"Tucked away in the dune grass, out of sight." Seeri actually smiles.

That's when the knot of fear around my heart loosens just enough for me to look back at the clump of trees. To seek out the glow of Kol and Noni's fire and know that they are both safe. I climb to my feet, ready to run back and thank them for setting the signal and tell them what has happened.

But only a scent of fire remains. No smoke rises from the trees.

Kol's fire is out.

TWENTY-FOUR

Before I can think, my feet are moving across the ground, carrying me back toward the edge of the trees, back to the place Kol and Noni set the signal fire. But then my thoughts slow me. I turn. The others are following—even Thern and Pada.

I stop. "You go and check," I say to Morsk. "I'll stay here. I need to talk with the Bosha."

Morsk hesitates. "We'll stay with her," Seeri says. "I have questions for them, too."

"Then I'll go with Morsk," Lees says. "Mya, if Kol needs you, I'll come right back."

She smiles at me, and the bond that brought us here—the need to protect each other—stretches between us like an unseen cord. I nod and Lees and Morsk hurry away. My heart tears as they go—I want to check on Kol and see him with my own eyes—but I need to deal with Thern and Pada first. As the High Elder, I need to decide what's to be done with them.

"We're unarmed," Pada says. "We turned our weapons over to Morsk."

I run my eyes over her and Thern. Their hands are empty. Morsk has their packs. "Knives?" I ask.

Pada lifts up the hem of her tunic to show me that there is nothing tucked into her belt. Thern does the same. When he turns to show me his back, I see the trail of blood that runs from the place I drove a spear into his shoulder. "You saved our lives," Thern says, even as I wonder how serious the wound I gave him might be.

"You tried to kill me and Morsk," I say. "How can I trust you now?"

"You tried to kill us too," Thern says, running a hand over his wounded shoulder. His fingers come away red, but the bleeding has slowed. "But then you defended us. You saved both of us. I don't know why you did it—I never thought I'd owe my life to an Olen—but we owe our lives to you now."

"Who were those fighters?" Pada asks.

"The Tama clan. There's a girl hiding on this island. They killed her mother and now they're coming for her."

"And you would fight to protect her?"

"I would."

Pada winces, touching the wound in her arm, and for a

moment I see something familiar in her—the girl I looked up to when I was small. "So then," she says. "What we believed about you was wrong—"

"What you believed?" Seeri asks. "What did you believe?"

Thern turns to her, but when he takes a stride in her direction, Pek comes between them. "You can answer her from where you are," he says.

A flash of something lights in Thern's eyes—anger or defensiveness—but it leaves as quickly as it came. "Lo and Orn, and then Dora and Anki, talked about Chev and his family as if they cared only for themselves," Thern says. "We believed that the Olen clan had no compassion for anyone—would never help anyone outside their clan—no matter how bad their need. But when Mya and Morsk came to our aid—risking their lives to save ours—"

"It became clear that everything we've been told about the Olen is a lie," Pada says.

"You fought to defend us. We fought to defend you, too," Thern adds. "And we promise to defend you from now on." A slight smile curls the corners of Thern's lips, and I'm reminded of his speech at the meeting of clans.

"You asked Chev to be the High Elder of the Bosha again," I say. "But you weren't sincere with that request—"

"He *was* sincere in asking on behalf of the Bosha," says Pada. "They sent us to ask Chev to be their High Elder. They wanted Chev to take them back. They still do. They had no idea what Dora and Anki were planning. Only Thern and I knew. Only Thern and I supported them." She pauses, looking down at her empty hands. "Lo was my cousin," she says. "I guess I trusted her too much." When she looks up, her eyes are damp. "We were family."

I glance at Seeri, who gives me a small nod. I turn to Pek, too, and he does the same. He even takes a step back so he is no longer standing between Thern and Seeri.

"All right," I say, "but while we're here you'll remain unarmed."

I turn toward the place Morsk and Lees went in search of Kol and Noni, the need to see Kol growing more urgent the longer we are separated. But even as I hurry toward Kol, my thoughts spin with memories of my brother, Chev, and the belief he lived by—clan always comes first. I can't help but wonder if my brother would have come to Pada and Thern's aid, or if he would have allowed the Tama to kill them.

We are almost to the trees when Morsk comes out, striding toward me. My heart rises in my throat, but he puts up a hand when he sees my face. "They're all right—both awake—but they are both weak. Travel tonight might be difficult for them—"

I push past Morsk and run back to the place where Lees bends over Kol and Noni. Noni is sitting up, propped against a tree, but Kol is stretched out on the ground. His eyes are closed. I rush to him, and he opens his eyes when I touch his cheek. His skin is hot. His eyes open and close twice before he sees me. "Mya," he says. "They came. Pek and the others. The signal fire worked." The faintest of smiles flickers across his lips before his eyes close again.

"We need more feverweed," I say. "I'll go gather some. Morsk, come with me—"

"Of course—"

"Pada, Lees, Thern—each of you needs to rest and heal. Everyone will need to row, even the injured. We'll dress your wounds when we return with the feverweed." My eyes shift to Seeri and Pek.

"Don't worry about Thern and Pada," Pek says. "Resting is all they're going to do. Seeri and I will make sure of it. And we'll keep watch for Dora and Anki."

Kol's eyes fly open. He's more alert than I knew. "Dora and Anki are dead," he says before letting his eyes close again. "Mya killed them both."

A taut silence stretches as if every breath is held, until all at once the wind gusts. The leaves shiver. "Anki is dead?" Lees gasps. "Mya, you've avenged our brother."

She runs to me and throws both arms around my shoulders. I stiffen. I don't want to be forced to talk about what happened.

I don't want to be praised for taking another life. But also, I don't want to admit how good it felt. How satisfying it was to take the life of the person who killed someone I love.

"They attacked us," I say. "I responded." My voice shakes.

Seeri comes up beside me and wraps her arms around both Lees and me, so that I am at the center of a tangle of my sisters' arms, protected from the stares of the others. Only Lees and Seeri can truly understand my heart right now, so I let them shelter me for a moment more before I pull back and break away.

"I'll restart the fire," Pek says. "When you come back, you can sit and rest." I walk away with Morsk, relieved that nothing else is said.

Morsk is quick to recognize feverweed, and together we gather enough to treat Kol, Noni, and the other injured. Except to compare leaves to be sure we are gathering the right plants, we don't speak at all, and I'm so grateful Morsk doesn't try to make me talk.

By the time we return to the others, they have organized a camp. We have no pelts to use as beds, but the ground has been cleared around the fire so that Pada, Lees, and Thern can lie down beside Noni and Kol. Seeri and Pek work together, cutting clothing away, cleaning wounds, and packing them with feverweed. Kol gets a ration of leaves to chew. By the time everyone is resting, the sky is a deep blue and the ground is swathed in shade. The fire gives the only light.

"I'll take the first watch," I say, and I'm relieved when no one argues. Everyone is exhausted. I am, too, but I know I won't sleep. The pounding in my pulse that started when my spear pierced Anki's thigh has yet to slow.

I stretch out beside Kol, watching him sleep. "I hope the feverweed helps," I murmur, more to myself than to anyone else.

But Kol turns to me and smiles. "I think it does."

"You're awake?"

"Mm-hmm. I think my fever broke." Kol sits up and reaches over me for the waterskin. His hand brushes mine. His skin is cool. "I'm feeling so much better, I think I'll sit up with you to keep watch."

"Kol, the reason we're staying here is to let you rest—"

"I've been resting. Now I want to be with my betrothed." He props himself on one elbow, trying so hard to appear comfortable and relaxed, but his breathing is still labored and sweat covers his brow. I'm not fooled. He may be improving but he is far from well.

Still, I'm selfish with him. I want him to stay awake so I can have him to myself. With everyone asleep, the fire glowing beside us, I'm taken back to the time we huddled together in the cave above the sea. The first time—the time he came to me half frozen and I had to use my own body heat to warm him.

I think about that night, my bare skin pressed against Kol's, and I lean forward until my lips are hovering beside his. "I want to kiss you," I whisper, "but I want you to rest. I'm torn."

Kol leans forward, tipping me back, blocking the light of the fire with his shadow. "I'm not torn at all," he says, and then his lips press against mine. They are warm but not with fever—with urgency. His kiss is searching; it holds a question and his lips move over mine as if he intends to draw out my answer. My lips respond, silently giving him whatever answer he seeks. My back arches as his hand slides under my waist. Encircled in his arms, I can't help but wish that he would never let me go.

His lips trace down my throat to my collarbone, then back up to my ear. "I've been waiting too long to kiss you like that," he whispers. His breath is warm. I'm reminded that he is still not well—he still needs rest—and I gently pull back, sliding from his arms.

He smiles a teasing smile. "You don't want me to kiss you?"

"I want you to rest."

"You're even more captivating when you're telling me what to do." His fingers brush hair from my eyes. "You make a wonderful High Elder, Mya. People want to follow you."

My heart flutters. These words of Kol's are the highest of praise and the saddest of revelations. "If only that were not true. If only I could walk away from the role of High Elder—"

"Don't say that," Kol says, drawing back. The sudden

firelight that falls across my face burns my eyes. All at once they swim with tears. "You don't mean it. So don't say it. I don't expect you to walk away from anything. I'm not asking you to—"

"And I'm not asking *you*," I say.

We both fall silent, and yet my head rings with its own thunder, as if the hopelessness of our situation were a sound only I can hear.

"But maybe I should ask you," I start. I know I am dragging the both of us out onto a dangerous ledge with these words, but I also know the right answer from Kol could make everything good again. "If I asked you, what would you do? If I asked you to leave the role of High Elder of the Manu behind and come to me?"

Kol rolls onto his back and stares up at the sky. It's still not dark enough to reveal the fires of the dead. "I would give up almost anything to come to you," Kol says. And he says no more.

"You need to sleep." I wish we'd never talked at all. I wish he had just kissed me and said nothing. "We can talk when we get home."

He doesn't answer. Maybe he's fallen back to sleep. Maybe he just doesn't want to respond. Either way, I am alone.

The night passes quickly, the sky darkening to obsidian, the stars giving off their heatless light. Too far away, I think.

The dead who warm themselves beside those fires—my father, my mother, my brother—they are too far away to lend me any warmth.

The sky is still dark when someone stirs. I'm squatting beside the fire, feeding it another few pieces of wood, when I hear Morsk clear his throat.

"Your turn to sleep," he says. "You'll be useless paddling home if you're exhausted."

"Thank you," I say. I stretch out beside Kol, hesitating for only a moment before I press myself against him. Before I can decide it's the wrong thing to do, I am asleep.

My sleep is restless and short. As soon as the sky begins to lighten, my eyes are open. My cheek rests against the base of Kol's neck. His skin is still cool. I pull away from him and sit up. Morsk startles and swings around. His spear slides in his hand.

"It's just me," I say, and he lets out a nervous laugh. The sound soothes me, and I realize my nerves are on edge, too.

"There's something troubling me," Morsk says. "Now that you're awake, I can do something about it."

"What is it?"

"I want to go bring back Chev's body. I want us to bring him home." He shuffles his feet and a cloud of dirt stirs. I can see where his boots have crossed the same ten steps of bare ground over and over. Pacing. Thinking about the body of his friend left behind in a lonely place.

"I want Chev brought home, too, but can you find him?"

I ask. "And if you do, can you bring him back?"

"I'll carry him. I'll rest when I have to—"

"But can you find him?"

Morsk walks to the edge of the stand of trees, his back to the lightening sky in the east. "It was on the western side of the island, not far from the stream. I remember hearing it. I think if I climb down to the beach from here, then climb the trail that goes up toward the south, I'll come to the place I found you. . . ."

He goes quiet, and I know we are both remembering that moment, when I discovered him over Chev's body and accused him of being my brother's murderer. "Go," I say. "But come back before the sun is well up. I want to leave while the day is still very new."

Morsk draws me to my feet and embraces me. It's such a startling thing for him to do, and I'm suddenly back in my family's hut, with Morsk standing too close, making a proposition. I pull back.

"I'm sorry," he says. He drops his eyes and turns away. His bag slides over his shoulder and his spear rolls in his hand. "I know you can't accept the offer I made you," he says without turning back to face me.

"In a way I wish I could," I answer. I'm being far too honest, I realize, but I'm too tired to censor myself. "It would be the most selfless choice. I wish I had the strength to be that selfless."

"If you would make that choice, I would do my best to

make sure you never regretted it."

I answer him with silence. "I won't reply to that, Morsk. I'm betrothed to Kol—"

"For now you are—"

"For now I am. And I will be loyal to my betrothed. I shouldn't have replied to you at all." I say this so firmly I hope it puts an end to any more talk between us.

But Morsk isn't finished. "No matter what you decide," he starts. This time he turns. The firelight burns in his eyes and the heat in them makes my breath catch. His face glows with an intensity I've never seen in Morsk, except in the midst of battle. "Can I ask you to try to find some way that you can stay with the Olen? Whether you accept my proposition or not, the Olen need your leadership."

"I will try to stay with my clan," I say softly. "My clan means more to me than anything else."

Morsk raises his eyes, scans our makeshift camp, nods, and leaves. As he goes, he calls over his shoulder, "Be watchful."

"We will," calls a voice from behind me. "You be watchful too."

I turn, but I know who the voice belongs to. I know who is sitting up awake, listening to my conversation with Morsk.

Kol.

TWENTY-FIVE

"Listening in?" I ask, and I immediately regret it. Why would I take an accusatory tone when I'm the one who should be accused? But I realize that's always been my way with Kol. I've always pushed him away rather than admit when I've been wrong. I did it when I wouldn't forgive the Manu for my mother's death, and I'm doing it again now.

"I couldn't help but hear," he says, "but maybe it's for my own good. We all need to know where we stand, Mya." Kol must be improving. There's only the slightest drag of illness in his voice. Warmth rushes through my chest at the thought that he may soon recover, despite the fact he may also never forgive me for what he heard me say to Morsk. "If you're considering Morsk's proposition to father the next Olen High Elder with you, I should probably be the first to know."

"If you're trying to hurt me," I say, turning slowly to face him, "you're doing a wonderful job."

Kol is sitting up, his arms crossed against his chest. "If I'm trying to hurt *you*?" he asks. "I'm only trying to protect myself, Mya. It's becoming more and more clear that you have no intention of leaving the role of High Elder to Seeri and coming to join the Manu with me."

"Seeri is not ready to lead," I say. I glance at the place where she sleeps. She doesn't stir. "She may be someday, but she is not now. You saw her reaction to Anki and Dora in the woods. She acted rashly—"

"She was trying to avenge your brother—"

"But she was going about it all wrong! She might have killed Anki, but Dora would have certainly killed one of us. Which of us would you have been willing to sacrifice to have that revenge, Kol? Would you have sacrificed Seeri? What about Pek?" I notice my voice rising in anger and I force myself to stop and take a breath. I turn away from Kol. It's too hard to say these words while looking at him. "Seeri wasn't thinking. And that's just one example. Seeri is not ready to take on the role of High Elder."

"But you are?"

"Are *you*?"

"I have to be. The Divine has chosen me—"

"And she has chosen me too."

Kol and I both go quiet. I notice the other noises all around us—the sounds of the island waking up. Birdsong.

Wings fluttering up to high branches.

"I'm sorry," Kol says after a long stretch of silence. He climbs to his feet, moves to my side, and takes my hand. For the first time since he's been on the island, I see the warmth I've come to expect in his rich brown eyes. "I shouldn't condemn you for your unwillingness to do something that I'm unwilling to do, as well. You can't walk away from your clan at the time they need you most. I can't do that either." He pauses. His hand moves to my chin. His thumb traces my bottom lip but he only studies my face. He does not kiss me. Not now. Perhaps not ever again. "I suppose the next thing to say is that our betrothal is . . . what was it you called Seeri and Pek when we first met? *An impossibility.* Perhaps we've become the impossibility now."

"Are you trying to break our betrothal?" I ask. "Is that what you're saying to me? That our betrothal is over?"

"I don't think we need to break our betrothal," Kol says. "If you must remain the High Elder of the Olen, and I must remain the High Elder of the Manu, I think it may already be broken. I don't know if there is a way to repair it."

I can't hear these words from Kol's lips. I lean against him and cover his mouth with mine, silencing him with a kiss. But he draws away.

"Mya," he says. There's an apology in his voice. Regret. But then he looks into my eyes and I see a war of emotions on his face. He wants to let go—he's trying to let go—but he's losing. His hands grip my upper arms, holding me away, but it lasts only a moment before he pulls me back against him, pressing a line of kisses along my hair. His lips stop at my ear. "I don't know how to do this. I don't know how to let you go." His mouth moves to mine. Heat binds our lips together, but the kiss is brief. "Even though you may already be gone," he says.

For a long moment I stand silently slumped against him, my head on his shoulder. Then I tip my head back and look into his face. "There is another option," I say.

He leans away. To see me better, I think, but maybe to put distance between us.

"Our clans could merge," I say.

Even as the words slip from my lips, I know how unlikely it is to work. I know his father never wanted a merger. Even when he sought an alliance with our clan, he made it clear a merger was unacceptable. To Arem, merging with another clan meant being absorbed by them.

It was always the same with Chev. He never wanted to merge with any clan, with the exception of the Bosha, because we were one clan already. To him, a merger with the Bosha meant an absorption of the Bosha. Exactly what he and Arem never wanted for the Olen and the Manu.

"Who would lead? Would you be the High Elder, or would I be?"

"We would both be," I say.

"So your clan would follow you and mine would follow

me? How is that a merger?"

"Kol . . ." I can't stand the practical tone of his voice. Yet as I think through the consequences a merger presents, I realize that perhaps it is a completely impractical suggestion.

"It's not that I haven't considered the idea of our clans blending, Mya. But I can't see how it would preserve anything. The Divine made us separate. Traditions, dances, songs, stories—so much would be lost by both our clans if we were no longer independent."

I think about this—about the independence that would be lost. If the Manu were to combine with the Olen, could I allow the Olen to follow Kol, even if they were following me, too? What if Kol and I differed on a decision? Could I allow him to override me? Could I allow my clan to follow him instead of me? I don't think I could.

It would mean the end of the Olen, and the Olen cannot be allowed to end.

"What about the Bosha? Do the Olen still intend to accept them back?"

"That was my brother's wish when he died—"

"Because I don't think the Manu could ever merge with a clan that accepted the Bosha. They have done too much harm to us. A merger that included them . . . I'm afraid it could never be possible."

So there, I think. *The first instance where we could not lead as one.*

"I know you want me to say I would walk away from the

Bosha to merge with the Manu," I say. "But I can't give you the answer you want." I slide out of his arms. The day is brightening. The others are starting to stir. "Though I wish so much that I could."

He holds me at arm's length. "Don't say that. Don't. Because you don't really mean it."

"I *do* mean it. But the decision isn't mine to make. I could be selfish and say that what we want is all that matters, but *you know* a High Elder can't decide like that. Though I honestly wish that I could."

"Just like your brother wished he could let Lees marry Roon."

He drops his hands to his sides. This mention of my brother—of my brother's regret at having to make hard decisions for the clan—feels like a double insult. An insult against my brother for the way he led and against me for being like him.

A voice comes from beyond the trees. A groan of someone carrying a heavy load. Morsk. Without another word to me, Kol walks away to wake his brother.

I step beyond the shade, striding toward the place where Morsk has placed the body of my brother on the ground. Leaves still stick to his parka and hair. I'd hoped he would look like he did when he first died—like he was only sleeping—but his skin is so sickly gray there's no pretending he is anything but dead.

I drop to my knees beside Chev's shoulder. I wonder how he would feel if he knew how I was suffering under the burden of leadership. Would he sympathize with me, pity me? Or would he feel I'd gotten what I deserved for undermining his authority and taking Lees away?

I look at his face and I remind myself that he came here to bring us back. I remind myself that he loved me, and I feel the sympathy he would give me if he were here.

It doesn't take long before we are ready to climb down to the boats. Before we do, I tell them all I have an idea I hope will help us avoid the Tama. "Rather than rowing directly east and then turning south when we come to shore," I say, "I propose we row south for a distance before we cut in toward the coast. It will be riskier—without a view of the shoreline, the chance of disorientation is greater—"

"But it will help us avoid the eyes of the Tama," Kol says.

I'm relieved when everyone agrees.

Morsk and Pek work together to carry Chev's body down the cliff, then Anki's. Noni has gotten enough strength back that she is able to climb down without help. Kol follows her, with Seeri right behind him carrying Black Dog. Then Lees starts down the cliff—Thern ahead of her and Pada behind.

I'm last to descend the rock face. It's slow going, but I'm in no hurry. This day we will return the body of Anki to the Bosha and tell them of Dora's death. Thern and Pada will admit to their clan what they did to help Dora and

Anki seek revenge. What will the Bosha do? Will they react with shock and shame? Will they punish Thern and Pada? Or is Kol right not to trust them at all? Could it be that all the Bosha elders have been on the side of Dora and Anki all along?

I could go back on the promise Chev made. I could say that as High Elder, I refuse to allow the Bosha to rejoin our clan.

And Kol would have made his first decision on behalf of my clan. I would have allowed someone outside the clan to decide the best course of action for the Olen.

What's so bad about that? What's so bad about letting Kol influence the Olen's relationship with the Bosha? Doesn't he have the best interests of the Olen at heart?

I remember when I pushed out with Lees, Kol agreed to speak with Chev on my behalf. He said he was happy to speak for me. *I'm your betrothed. Our interests are one now. Our actions are one.* Isn't that what he had said? So why can't that extend to decisions for the clan?

I talk to myself about all these things, telling myself it's my choice to make. But I know it's not.

I could never let another clan's High Elder have a say in the Olen leadership. Not even Kol. It puts the survival of the Olen as a separate and independent clan in jeopardy, and the survival of the Olen is too valuable to risk.

These are the thoughts that loop through my mind as I

push out a double kayak that I will share with Lees, just as we did the day we left. When we pushed out that day I was hoping to teach my brother a lesson. Today I head home, feeling that he is the one who taught me.

TWENTY-SIX

Once we have all boarded the boats—Anki's body lying in a canoe paddled by Morsk and Thern, and Chev's body lying in another paddled by Pek, Pada, and Kol—I begin watching the sea for signs of the Tama. If they've been waiting for a moment to attack and take Noni back, now would be the time.

Noni shares a double kayak with Seeri, but we are all vigilant. Lees and I stay to one side of them and the canoes stay to the other. Even once we are far enough south that we feel safe enough to row closer to shore, I still throw frequent looks over my shoulder. I notice Lees does, too. But the water is always empty. Seabirds dive for their meals, but otherwise, the sea rolls unbroken to the horizon.

Nothing to be afraid of, I tell myself. But fear hovers over me, like a shag that won't fly far from its young.

And so I row. All day, as the sun rises and crosses over

into the western sky, I row, and I try not to think.

We are in sight of the Manu's bay when Lees calls out to me. "You look at him so often," she says.

"Who?" I call back, though I know. As we've traveled south, I've stayed aware of Kol's canoe, whether they were ahead of us or behind. I've tried to gauge how well he was by watching the movement of his oar. At times he seemed strong; at others I thought he might drop the oar into the sea.

"Your betrothed, of course," Lees shrieks. "I can't blame you. I would be the same way. I can't wait until Roon and I are betrothed." Her voice scatters on the wind, breaking on the waves. Of course she assumes she will soon be betrothed to Roon, and why shouldn't she be? Chev was ready to agree to it, too. So Lees will become betrothed, but my betrothal will be broken. I should have just accepted Morsk's proposition and never gone away.

If I had stayed—if I'd taken Lees's place and agreed to marry Morsk—would Chev still be alive? This question has haunted my thoughts since I found him on the ground, his throat slashed with his own knife. If we'd never gone to the island I feel he would be alive, but I can't forget who's really to blame for his death. I can't let my guilt confuse me.

Still, I feel the loss of my brother covering me like a shadow. The sun hits my face, but it has no warmth.

When I first glimpse the bay that opens beside the Manu's

camp, my heart begins to thrash inside my chest as if it is trying to escape. I imagine the questions we will face from both clans camped on that bay—the Bosha on the western shore and the Manu on the east.

We do not linger at the Bosha camp. I climb from the kayak to speak briefly with the elders, but I say little. I will let Thern and Pada explain to their own clan the events that led to Dora and Anki's deaths. The events that led to Chev's death. As the elders learn that Chev was killed, I see their reactions—grief and fear. I hear the questions they murmur to Thern and Pada as I go—will the Olen still accept them back? Will Chev's sister honor his promise?

I climb back into the boat, my heart pounding with hope. I hope that I was right to trust in Pada and Thern's word. Hope that my brother was right to take the Bosha back.

My heart has finally calmed by the time we reach the shore of the Manu camp, but then it grows heavy like a stone in my chest when I see the clan come to meet us on the beach. I imagine someone must have spotted our boats on the opposite shore and word must have spread that Kol and Pek, gone two days, have returned.

If there's a buzz in the crowd, it quiets as soon as Kol climbs out of the canoe and throws his arms around his mother. He speaks into her ear, just a few words, and as Lees and I approach the shore, I watch her run into the water.

She stands at the edge of the canoe and looks down at the body of my brother, and she lets out a cry that breaks my stone heart in two.

Mala's cry is like an echo—the twin sound to the cry I hold inside, the cry I've yet to let out. Hearing it feels dangerous, like the pain inside me might take flight and leap from my throat, answering the call of its own. So I push the pain down. I'm the Olen High Elder now. I can't let my weakness show.

Once the boat I share with Lees is close to shore I scramble out, anxious to climb the steep bank and escape the cold sea. Someone reaches for me and I look up to see Mala. She has hurried onto shore ahead of me and is ready to haul me up.

I think back to the last time I stood on this bank—just days ago when I came for my betrothal—and Mala pulled me into her arms. I was protective of my emotions that day. Like today. Like every day. I didn't want my weakness to show.

And I regretted it.

I put both my hands in Mala's and let her pull me to her, tugging me up the slope and into her embrace. I know how much I need this comfort, how much I need a mother's embrace. I surrender to it. I let the cry I've been holding inside finally escape, muffled and muted against Mala's shoulder.

Once Kol's whole clan has joined us and we are all huddled together around the hearth in the Manu's meeting place, the long story is told. About Noni and her mother. About Chev and how he died. About our trek across the island, Kol's illness, and our battles with the Bosha and the Tama. When the whole story has been told and there's nothing more to say, Mala brings out food. She fusses over Noni, who stays very quiet and very close to Lees. The children squeal over Black Dog. Mala feeds us until we are all full, and I can tell by the foods she shares, especially the honeyed roots, that she is trying to comfort us—to comfort me—without words.

After the meal, no one from Kol's clan leaves the meeting place. Instead, everyone stays—everyone crowds around me and my sisters—and they all share their memories of Chev. I know they have the best intentions, and yet with each story the pain inside me grows, like it's nourished by words. I sit as long as I can, though I ache to retreat into our family's hut and hide.

You can't do that ever again, a voice inside me says. Chev's voice. *You're the High Elder now, and a High Elder does not hide.*

But I do hide. I hide inside myself, even when I'm in plain sight.

The sun slides west against a pale blue sky, but it seems to stay fixed in one place—the evening goes on and on. Finally, the sun hovers above the treetops on the western hills, and the crowd begins to thin. Urar, the Manu healer, comes and sits by me. He tells me he has been to the shore. He has chanted over the body of my brother, which still lies along the bottom of the canoe. He asked the Divine to watch over Chev until he can be buried when we finally reach our home.

"The Spirits in the sea are caring for him now," Urar says. "He is cradled by the sea. The Spirits will keep the body cold and well until he can be buried."

And then Urar reminds me of a thought I have been hiding from. "I could rub the body with red ocher," he offers, "unless you think the Olen healer would like to prepare the body himself."

The Olen healer—Yano—the man my brother loves. *Loved.* The man he loved until he died.

All at once I feel as if the ground has slid out from beneath me. As if I've been standing on the edge of a cliff of shifting rocks and now they are tumbling to the sea. A wave crashes up, pulling me under. I feel it, feel myself drowning, even as I sit here and calmly stare into Urar's face. "I think it would be best if you did it," I say. But my voice is wet and choked, like I am speaking underwater. "I would appreciate it so much if I could take him home already prepared."

"Of course," Urar says. His eyes reach out to Kol, calling to him from across the meeting space. I can see what his expression says. *She needs you.* He can't know that I have hurt Kol too much for him to want to come and comfort me.

To my surprise, Kol does come to my side. "My mother wishes to speak to me, but it shouldn't take long," he says. "After, would you walk with me?"

A light behind Kol's eyes flickers for just a moment, like a flame flaring up in a breeze, then just as quickly dies down again. But the brief moment it was there is enough. "Yes," I say. "I would."

While Kol is gone, a woman of his clan approaches me. She is maybe a little older than Mala, her hair a mix of black and gray. She stretches out her cupped hand, and in it she holds an obsidian spear point. I can tell instantly that it was carved by Chev.

"This was given to me by your brother," the woman says. "I had admired the workmanship of the one on his own spear, and the blade on his knife. He thanked me, and we talked about other things. But the next time he came to our camp, he brought this one as a gift for me."

This story surprises me. It doesn't sound like something Chev would do. But then, as I turn the spear point in my hand it catches the light, and for an instant, I see my brother's eye reflected back at me. I see him in every careful cut made to the stone, and I realize I am being too hard on my brother's memory.

He enjoyed attention, yes. He liked to be admired for his

craftsmanship, and he liked his work to be acknowledged. But he also was frequently generous. He insisted we bring a feast for Kol to this camp when he realized he'd been rude. And he'd painstakingly worked this spear point for a member of another clan, simply because she'd admired one of his own.

My throat goes dry, even as tears fill my eyes. I lay the point in the palm of the woman's hand, and she folds her fingers over it carefully. She pats my hand and walks away, straight into her hut, presumably to tuck away this gift my brother made for her.

With no one else hovering to speak to me, I decide to take advantage of the chance to duck out of sight for just a moment. But as I pass the door to Kol's hut, I hear his voice and then his mother's, and my steps slow.

If I hadn't meant to listen, that changes when I hear my own name.

"This isn't about Mya."

"You're right," his mother answers. "It's about you. And your father. And every other Manu—every Manu who's ever lived, and every one who's yet to live. It matters that much."

I stand still a moment longer, but when Kol replies he's too quiet to hear, and Pek and Seeri are coming close. I can hear their voices. They are heading to the door of Kol's family's hut, and I try to appear to be going there, too.

"Are you all right?" Pek asks. I remember the tears in my eyes.

"Yes. Just taking a moment—"

"There you are." It's Kol's voice. He's just pushed back the hide that hangs in the doorway of his hut. His mother steps out behind him. Her face glows in the sun that still hangs in the west. Still, her expression stays cool. "I have a few items of clothing I think will fit Noni," she says. "She can change out of those torn pants."

"She'll like that," I say. We all turn to see Noni and Lees in the center of the meeting place. Black Dog is putting on a show, retrieving sticks. Mala walks toward her as Pek and Seeri duck inside the hut.

Kol and I are alone.

"Are you still willing to walk with me?" He smiles, and my blood crackles and sparks. My heart jumps as if it's startled by his voice.

Without a word about where we would go, we both head up the trail to the meadow.

As we walk, I'm reminded of the tunic I still wear—my betrothal tunic. A strip of trim has loosened at the hem, but the pattern on the front is unchanged. "Do you recognize it?" I ask, just as we reach the field of grasses and flowers that inspired the tunic's design. "Did you know—"

"I knew. Of course I knew. I recognized the colors, and the shapes of the blades moving in the wind." His finger alights on the tunic just below my chest and traces a seam where a section of caribou is stitched to a piece of otter. His hand stops just below my navel and his fingers fan across my stomach. "It's beautiful."

We both stand motionless, as all around us the sun sets the whole meadow ablaze in light. The north wind gusts loud in our ears, every stalk of grass flattens under its weight, and yet the stillness of Kol's eyes staring unflinchingly into mine is all I know. A tumultuous silence. An unruly stillness.

Then Kol drops his hand to his side, I slide my eyes to the sky, and everything comes back into motion.

"My mother and I talked," Kol says, leading me farther up the path, walking into the wind. I think of his father. The last time either of us passed through here was the day he died. "I told her you and I had discussed a merger of our clans."

I stop. The words I heard through the walls of the hut come back to me. *It's about every Manu who's ever lived. Every one who's yet to live.* "She's against it," I say.

"She is." His hand swings at his side and he hooks a few of my fingers in his. "And I listened to her. But nothing she said could convince me. Nothing made me sure that a future together was impossible." He stops. Tilts his head at the lowering sun. "It's too late in the day for bees, but . . ."

We both stretch out on the tall grass. Purple and white

flowers—so small from above—stretch past the corners of my eyes, reaching for the broad blue expanse of the sky. I feel like we are floating side by side in water, like the grass is a wave upon the sea.

"I can't say yes to a merger of our clans," I say. I have to say it. It's the truth.

"Not now, or not ever?"

I lie still, let my eyes fall shut. "I feel like it's not my decision to make," I say. "It's like trying to decide if the sun should rise. Or if the sea should freeze, or melt again in the spring. It's not my decision to make. It was decided by the Divine, a long time ago."

"Well, then that's a shame," Kol says. "Because I brought you here to tell you that I've made the decision to do whatever you choose. If you choose a merger, we will merge. If you choose not to, then we won't . . . and I suppose then our betrothal will end."

We lie there and listen, as if listening for bees, but Kol is right—it's too late in the day. The sky hardens from blue to gray. Kol stands and holds out his hand. "It's late. We need to go back."

I climb to my feet, resisting the urge to wrap my arms around his neck. "I decide that the sun will not set," I say.

"Be careful. Even things that the Divine decided long ago can change. A winter storm can come in the spring. A cavern can be torn open to become a stream. Even the

Divine can change her mind." Kol's face is momentarily striped with black and gold, as slanting streaks of sun mix with shadows. Something shimmers there—a meaningful twist of his lips—but by the time I really see him his hair falls across his eyes and his face is lost in darkness.

He takes a few strides and I watch him go, letting his words repeat in my head. *A cavern can be torn open to become a stream. . . . Even the Divine can change her mind.*

I stand still so long, I have to hurry to catch him. We walk the rest of the way back to camp in silence.

TWENTY-SEVEN

In the morning we board the boats early, but not so early that Mala doesn't make sure we eat first. "It will be a long day," she says. "A long, sad day, and hunger will only make it worse."

We will take six boats—Mala herself will come. "To be present at your brother's burial," she says, squeezing my hand. I smile at this gesture, and though a part of me wants to flinch away, I don't.

Urar, the Manu healer, reluctantly agrees that Kol is well enough to paddle, though he would prefer he travel in one of the canoes, rowed by an oarsman.

"My mother and Noni will ride in the canoe," Kol says. "I'd rather paddle with Mya." I startle a bit at this, having assumed I'd once again travel with Lees, but before I can speak Lees is at the water's edge, climbing into a double kayak with Roon.

Urar helps Noni into the canoe. "Don't forget to look," he says. He's asked her endless questions about feverweed, and though they went hiking with Lees and Roon, they found none near the Manu camp. Kol has even promised to take him north to the island to gather it if none is found closer, so I hope some is found. I shudder at the thought of any of them heading back into Tama territory.

The trip south to our camp passes quickly, and with every new landmark—the frozen waterfalls that run to the sea, the first tree-covered ridges—the blood in my veins seems to heat. The wind calms, and the air thickens against my skin as we get closer. I should be happy to be home, yet when the rocky cliffs that border our bay first come into view, my throat tightens and I gulp in deep breaths.

Soon I will have to look into the eyes of Yano and tell him his lover is dead.

Kol and I are still far out on the sea when the first boat lands on the beach. It's the canoe that carries Mala and Noni. Kayaks paddled by Seeri and Pek and then Shava and Kesh are next. Heads lean together. Hands point out to the second canoe. People are learning about my brother's death. Members of my clan are gathering—even from this distance I recognize Ela, Yano's sister. She raises her head and shades her eyes with her hand. Her gaze sweeps over the sea.

She is looking for me.

When we land, she comes to the side of our kayak. She

sees me with Kol and her eyes crinkle—I suddenly realize she knows we're betrothed. She doesn't congratulate us, though, of course. She's already heard about my brother.

"I'll go bring Yano," she says. "Do you want to come with me? To speak with him?" Her eyes swim with tears. Her fingers tug at the hem of her tunic. "I just can't believe it. I can't believe . . ."

Ela's tears change her—they transform her into the little girl she used to be. I remember that girl so clearly, the girl who shed tears over the smallest things but stopped almost as easily. But this is not a small thing. These tears will not stop when the sun comes out or someone takes her for a walk. We aren't children anymore.

We find Yano in the hut he shares with my brother, carving a mask. It's a wolf—a mask commonly used in weddings—and I realize he's carving it for me. When he sees me in the doorway his face lights up—the ember of concentration in his eyes catches and glows into something more diffuse and warm. "You're back," he says, his voice floating up, his tone light, but it lasts only as long as it takes for him to register our faces. Then his eyes tighten. His mouth thins.

"What's happened?"

I try to speak. I'm not sure how to say what I have to say. I haven't planned the words. "It's Chev," I start.

That's all I get to say. Yano is past me and out of the hut.

I wonder who he will find first. Who will be the one to tell him? But it doesn't matter. Ela's tears told him. My sunken eyes told him.

He already knows.

When Ela and I return to the beach, Yano is in the water, leaning into the canoe. His tunic, hands, and face are smeared with the red ocher that covers Chev's body. Morsk, Lees, and Seeri stand together on the sand, their posture tense, as if they are on the verge of movement. As if they are about to stride into the shallow water and bring Yano back. I notice all of them drip seawater from the knees down and I know that they aren't about to go after him—they already have. But unlike Yano, the frigid water chased them back.

But not Kol. Kol still stands beside Yano, holding his arm. Holding him up.

I stride right into the water. My gaze falls on my brother, lying in the canoe. The red ocher changes him—removes the familiar from his face—and I am so grateful for it.

As I approach I hear Kol's voice, his words a low murmur. Coaxing . . . coaxing. But Yano ignores him as if he can't hear. He bends at the waist, leans to Chev's ear, his own voice a murmur I can't understand.

"Yano," I say when I see Kol shivering, his body rigid with cold. "Please, help me. Kol has been sick. He's been burning with fever. I know he won't come out of the water until you do. I know he won't leave you. So please, for Kol's sake. Please come up onto the sand so Kol can get warm."

Yano may love my brother, but he is also a healer. He looks at Kol, as if he's noticing him next to him for the first time. His head falls forward—part nod, part defeat—and he lets Kol lead him up onto the bank.

Soon everyone is gathered in our meeting place, under the canopy. The midday meal is served, but no one is thinking about food. Everyone is talking, sharing stories about Chev, about all the ways he was like our father, the ideal High Elder.

I know these stories are meant to soothe me, but they do just the opposite. I feel like a fish held in the talons of an eagle. Every time someone speaks my brother's name, I feel a little more of my flesh ripped away, the bones of my memories exposed. Soon I will be picked clean, with nothing left to call my own.

But if I'm hurting, at least I'm not alone. My sisters sit in a circle around me. Yano and Ela are directly across from me, beside a large fire. *It must be warm*, I think. Yet Yano still shivers as if he were standing in the water beside the canoe. My own hands are still cramped with cold.

My eyes search the crowd, and though I don't want to admit it to myself, I know I am looking for Kol. He must be here. He is so good at this—so comfortable comforting others. But he's not here. Could he be sick? Could the cold water have brought back his fever?

Getting to my feet, I pick my way through the crowd, heading for Ela's hut, the place where Kol and his family are sleeping tonight. But even before I reach the ring of huts, I meet Kol coming the other way.

"I was looking for you," I say. A softness lifts Kol's eyes for just long enough for me to see he isn't sick.

"I needed to step away . . ." He sees the question in my eyes, though he must know I would never ask. "It's too soon, I think. My father—we gathered around to talk like this about him just days ago." Kol shakes his head in the way he does when he wants to shake off a feeling or a memory. He glances at me, then away.

Is he holding himself away from me because of last night? Does he think I've all but rejected the idea of a merger? Or is it the memory of his father as he says, or even something else?

"I'll be right there, if you want to go back," I say. "I think I need a moment away from it all myself."

"I understand," he says, and then he's gone, leaving a wake of confusion behind him.

Passing the hut Chev shared with Yano—the place where Chev's body has been laid until his burial tomorrow—I hesitate. If there is one person I wish to speak to now, it's Chev. I push through the door of the hut before I can question myself.

Seal oil burns on moss wicks in two shallow stone lamps. My fingers trace along the wall of the hut as I enter, skimming the edge of the room. Everything glows the color of warmth—the lamplight, the red ocher—but still my blood lies frozen under my skin.

"Chev," I say. I stop. If I could talk to him, if I could ask one thing, what would it be? If I had only one question?

"I don't want this," I say. "The Divine has called me to a role I don't want." I pause. I wonder how many times Chev had the same thought. *How many times did he wish the weight of leadership could be carried by someone else?* "I am trying to do as you would have me do, to lead as you would lead, to put the clan first, at all costs." A sob leaps up in my throat but I swallow it down. "But the cost is so high." This last word is like breath from my mouth. Like mist on cold water. Insubstantial.

Meaningless.

"So this is sacrifice," I say. "This is how you lived." I swallow again, and my throat burns. "I'm sorry I didn't acknowledge you more." My eyes move to the door. The hut feels small. I am all at once in the doorway, brushing back the hide, stepping into the sunlight.

Yano stands just beside the door. One glance at his face tells me he heard every word I said.

"Kol is looking for you," he says. "I think he wants you to take a walk with him—"

"We took a walk yesterday—"

"I think he wants to talk—"

"We have talked."

"Mya, come sit with me." He tugs me by the arm, dragging me back into his hut, right to my brother's side. "Sit," he says, but in a voice so soft no one could refuse. I fold myself onto a bearskin that covers the floor beside my brother's feet.

"Mya, you are not the same person your brother was. Yet you have been called to lead. The Divine knows that you will choose what's best for the clan. Your brother would know that, too. But you need to do what you think would be best for the clan, even if it's not what you think Chev would want—"

"But it's not what I *think* he would want. It's what I *know* he wanted—"

"The Divine has called you. This is your time to lead." A hand rises to Yano's lips, then drops again. "Chev's time has passed." Yano blurs and loses shape. My eyes fill with tears at the cruel truth that Chev's time is over. "Remember," Yano says. His voice is like heat—I feel it more than hear it. "Sometimes what's best for the future is different from what was best for the past. I know Chev would want the clan to be strong but also for you to be happy, and for the people to thrive, no matter what the clan is called or who is said to be the High Elder."

My eyes meet Yano's. His face is swollen with emotions held back. He and I share a pain so deep, and yet he has brought me a different kind of peace. I don't know what I will do, but I know that I'm not alone. "Thank you," I try to say. The words don't come, but he sees them on my lips.

When I step out of Yano's hut, swiping the backs of my hands across my eyes, I find Kol, waiting for me.

TWENTY-EIGHT

"Would you walk with me?" I ask.

Kol's eyes curl at the corners, a momentary smile. "I was hoping to. I thought you might say no."

"I still might say no—"

"I meant to the walk—"

"We're still betrothed. We should spend time together—"

"While we can," Kol says. He holds out a hand and I take it. His palm is warm. I wrap my fingers around it like I'm enclosing some small, vulnerable thing that I want to keep alive.

"While we can," I echo. Kol has a spear, so I know he is thinking we will leave camp. "How well can you climb?" I ask. "Are you well enough to handle the climb up the ravine?"

"All the way to the cave," he says. "Where else would we go?"

The hike up into the ravine that leads to the cave is not an easy one, but today, with the sun out and the ground dry, it's nothing like it was on the day Lo attacked our clan. The water that runs down from the peaks forms a shallow and winding creek, but I remember the raging river that swept us away that day—the day Lo drowned. The memory of the sight of that white water has faded like a dream, but I remember the loud roar in my ears and the cold that cut right to my bones.

And I remember Kol standing over Lo's body when he pulled her from the stream. The memory of her ash-gray face and pale blue lips will never leave me.

Kol uses his spear as a walking stick, but I worry about his footing when we reach the place where the trail splits, the left side leading down to the creek, the right side becoming a hanging shelf of rock leading to the summit and the cave. "Are you sure?" I ask. Besides his spear, he carries a pack and a waterskin. He pauses at my question and offers me a drink.

"I'll carry this the rest of the way," I say, "and the pack too." I shrug it over my shoulder. It's light. "What's in here?"

"You'll see."

"A surprise then?"

"More like a memory."

We pass up the trail slowly, feet cautiously placed, spots of hidden ice carefully avoided. When at last we reach the summit overlooking the sea, I know that the worst part of the path to the cave still lies ahead of us.

"It's easier, I think, if you go down backward," I say, climbing over the ledge and descending onto the side of the cliff that faces the sea. The footholds are narrow, the handholds few. Two steps down and I am almost to the lip of rock that skirts the mouth of the cave, but my attention is on Kol as he climbs down the cliff above me. One more step and I am on the cave floor. I draw a deep breath when Kol drops in behind me.

Crawling back deeper into the cave, I'm surprised by how well I can see. "I remember it being much darker in here."

"It was raining both times we were here together," Kol says. "I remember the sound."

We sit side by side, facing the curved opening in the rock. Today, the sound of distant waves below filters in from outside, but I'm far more aware of the inhale and exhale of my own breath echoing off the close walls. My pulse quickens, my heart runs hard in my chest, and I tell myself these are the lingering effects of the climb down the cliff, but I doubt it. Kol moves beside me and I turn to watch him dig through the pack I've dropped on the floor.

He pulls out a fire starter.

This cave is used as a lookout point, and a supply of wood is already stacked against the wall. He would have remembered that.

It isn't long before Kol has an ember glowing in the fire

pit. He stretches out on his side, his face close to the glowing tinder, his lips pursed as he blows breath into the flames. I watch his mouth, moving like he's sharing a secret, and I want to know his secrets, too.

I stretch out beside him. He startles.

"So why did we come here?" I ask. "Did you want to talk? Or . . . something else?"

Kol laughs, a nervous sound in his throat. "I came here with you to spend time with you. For now, we're still betrothed, and you said it yourself—that's what betrothed couples do." The fire catches. He turns to lie flat on his back, still stretched out across the ground. He doesn't make a move to sit up, so I slide closer to him, propping myself on an elbow.

"That's one thing they do," I say.

I watch Kol as warmth from the fire spreads across his face, creating shadows in the hollows beneath his cheekbones, setting circles of light in the blacks of both eyes. A smile climbs from his lips to those eyes. The blacks cool when I lean over him, shielding his face from the light, my mouth hovering over his.

"I'm not ready to kiss you," he says. His smile widens and his eyes flash when I pull back. "Not just yet, at least." He draws his legs in and sits up, reaching for the pack again. "I brought something for you—not really a gift. Something more symbolic."

His hand slides out of the pack, a pouch of honey tucked against his palm.

"I've been wanting to share honey with you again, ever since the evening you brought a cup of honey from the south to my hut." He pauses a moment, and I wonder if the same memories that light in my mind are lighting in his. "I wanted to kiss you that night—I wanted to taste the honey on your lips—but I missed the chance.

"I was hoping maybe I would get another chance today."

A flutter of nerves ripples through me as he places the pouch of honey in my hands. It's warm from his own. I notice the pouch is a bit larger and newer than the one he gave me as a betrothal gift—the one I'd refused when he'd tried to give it to me the first night we met.

A hollow bone serves as a spout, and I consider pouring a bit onto the tip of a finger. But that's not what I did on the evening we're re-creating. I turn the pouch in my hand, feeling the fullness of it, and I let my gaze sweep over Kol for just a moment. The playful smile on his lips only fans my nerves. I look away.

Tilting my head back, I close my eyes as I hold the pouch above my open mouth. The shock of taste on my tongue pulls a breath from my throat, a short gasp. I open my eyes, and as I lift my head, a drizzle of warm sweet liquid spills over my lower lip.

Kol doesn't hesitate. What he said must be true—he

must have been waiting for this chance since that night. His hands grasp my waist, pulling me toward him. His lips cover mine, and he drinks in every trace of honey that lingers there. His kiss deepens, his tongue tasting the inside of my lip.

His grip loosens, and he pulls away just enough to look into my eyes.

"Was it worth the wait?" I ask. My voice bubbles out of me. It's the happiest sound I've made in a long time.

"It was even better than I'd hoped."

"It is remarkably good honey," I say. "The sweetest I've ever had."

"I would agree."

"Whose is it, then?" I ask. "Yours or mine? Gathered in the north, or the south?"

"Hmmm, good question. Let me sample it again." He reaches for the pouch, but I pull it away. "Let me."

His eyes pinch—he's not sure what I plan to do and he's strangely wary. I slide closer to him. "Lie back," I say.

"I'm trusting you," he answers, that half smile I know so well flickering in the firelight. His eyes close and he slides back, stretching against the stone floor once more.

"Hold still," I say, my voice so low it makes no echo even in this cave. The snap of wood on the fire almost drowns out my words. The fragrance of the honey mixes with the smoke. The scent warms me.

Kol's lips are parted but my hand is shaking, and the first drips from the spout fall on his cheek. My lips find the place and I kiss the honey away. I try—and miss—again, this time leaving a sticky trail across his chin.

"I think you're missing on purpose," he murmurs as my lips move over the warm skin of his face, tracing sweet lines left by my nervous hand.

"Maybe," I whisper back. My fingers are sticky, and a trail of honey smudges Kol's skin as my hands slide down his throat. I lean over and touch the spot with my lips.

But then I hesitate. Am I taking this too far?

Maybe—just for a little while—it's all right to be playful. Maybe for a few moments we can stop being two High Elders and be nothing more than each other's betrotheds. My lips flutter over Kol's skin and I kiss the last of the honey away.

Kol pulls me down beside him, finding my lips with his. His kiss is slow and searching. Heat ripples across my skin like a vibration on the head of a drum. His hand draws back my hair and he leans close to my ear. When he speaks, his words stir my hair against my neck. "I wish this never had to end."

I pull gently away, not so much to separate us as to look into his face. His skin glows in the firelight, but around him the room is growing dim. It's getting late. I know we will need to leave, to return to camp soon. Even by saying he wished this would never end, Kol has admitted he knows it must.

I want to speak, to hear my own voice say out loud the truth that is thrashing inside me like something savage. That at this moment, I know I love him.

But I can't say that, even if I know it to be true. I can't tell Kol I love him if I'm going to refuse a merger. If I'm going to become the High Elder of the Olen, even as he becomes the High Elder of the Manu. It wouldn't be fair. So instead of the words *I love you*, I say, "We should really get back."

"We should," he says. I notice that he also makes no declaration of his feelings. I can't be surprised—it would be unfair to expect him to speak about his feelings for me while I choose to stay silent on mine for him. But he also hasn't mentioned the topic of a merger at all.

Perhaps he's given up on the idea already.

Kol opens his pack, reaches for the pouch of honey, and I set it in his hand. "You didn't tell me," I say. "Is it from the north or the south?"

His face opens, like a secret is about to be released to me. "Neither. Or really, both. This is what you get when you combine both together. The Manu and the Olen, mixed together as one."

"Merged," I say.

"You could say that."

"Well, in the case of honey, it works very well." I feel a

wave of relief to learn that Kol is still hoping for a merger, even though I'm still unsure of what I think is best for my clan. I want so much to do as Yano says and choose a path for the future without relying on the past. I wish I could believe that the past shouldn't control the future, but for now I'm not sure what I believe. With Kol's taste and scent all over me, in this moment I'm not sure my judgment would be clear anyway. I notice my teeth biting into my lower lip. "Ready?"

"You first," he says.

So I slide toward the mouth of the cave as Kol extinguishes the fire. The sound of the sizzling coals washes me in a diffuse sadness, and I try to push it from my mind by bracing myself for the coming climb back up to the summit of the cliff. I stare out at the sea and I stop. A chill chases away all of Kol's warmth.

Two boats are approaching from the north.

"Kol," I say. "Boats. Kayaks." I look harder and I recognize the shape of the kayaks. I recognize the design. "Bosha," I say.

Kol comes to sit beside me to watch the two kayaks come closer into view. The paddlers don't notice us high on the cliff, and we stay still, letting them approach. I don't want to react too soon. But it doesn't take long for me to recognize the paddlers.

Thern and Pada.

"I'm going to confront them," I say. "Give me your spear—"

"Mya, no—"

"We have only one weapon, Kol, and you're not well enough—"

"I just don't want you to react too quickly. You don't even know why they're here."

"I do know," I say, reaching for Kol's spear. "Look at what they each carry on the deck of their boat."

As they get closer, almost to the base of the cliff, everything comes into view. Thern's hands red with cold. Pada's hair, sticking to her forehead from the spray.

And on the deck of both kayaks, an atlatl and a pack of darts.

TWENTY-NINE

Watching them approach, my mind flies to my family. Lees and Seeri, unaware that there's any danger nearby, are probably in camp right now, helping with the evening meal or telling stories about the island. Fear yields to resolve as I start down the cliff, Kol's spear in my hand, to confront them. I don't need to look up to know Kol is right behind me.

"Mya," he calls.

"Kol, you can't stop me—"

"I'm not trying to." His eyes move to the boats, almost directly in front of us. "Listen, you can talk to them without going all the way down to them. Stay out of range."

He's right. They would have to throw their darts up from the boats. Even with an atlatl, that won't be easy.

Stopping on a narrow shelf of rock, I turn to face the sea. Kol keeps descending until he is beside me. "You couldn't really have believed I'd stay behind," he says.

When they are almost directly below the place we stand, yet almost certainly too far away to make an accurate shot with a dart, I call out to Thern and Pada. Looking up, they see us, and then something strange happens. They wave their arms and call back to us, smiling and paddling our way.

"We're so glad we found you," calls Pada. She picks up her atlatl and waves it over her head, and my thoughts spin, trying to make sense of it all—she and Thern here, weapons in hand, calling to us like friends. "Can you come down? We need to tell you something," she says, shouting to be heard over the waves. "We've come to bring a warning."

I turn to Kol, but he must want to trust them as much as I do. He's climbing down before I can ask a question. My eyes move between Kol's hands gripping the rock, Thern's hands gripping his paddle, and Pada's hands, still gripping the atlatl. She doesn't see me, but I hold Kol's spear angled at her chest, ready to throw it as soon as she makes a move for the darts. But she never does.

As I watch, Pada sets the atlatl down and picks up her paddle, moving closer to the place where Kol stops, just above the rocks that break the surface of the water. "Kol!" she calls out, his name carried on the sea breeze like a song. "You've recovered! You look so much better." And when

I hear this—when I hear the joy carried by her words—I know she is telling the truth. They haven't come here to do us harm.

They've come to warn us.

By the time I reach the wet and slippery rocks and crouch beside Kol, both of us shivering in the spray, Thern and Pada have paddled as close to the cliff as the rocks will allow. "We've come to tell you Dora is alive," Thern calls over the waves. "She is helping the Tama. She brought Noni's father and a group of Tama fighters to the Bosha camp and promised to help them find Noni."

I think of the last time I saw Dora, when she leapt into the sea. I remember waiting to see her body on the waves, but she never surfaced. I had worried that she might have survived the jump. Now I know that I was right.

"When will they be here?" I call out. I think of Noni in camp, unguarded. No one knowing she needs to be guarded.

"They are already here," Pada answers. "Not far north, waiting for dark. We volunteered to help find you and fight for the Tama, but it was a lie. We wanted them to bring us along so we could help defend you. Tonight, we told them we would scout ahead, to find the best way into your camp. We will go back and say we found nothing, but they will come anyway. They are all armed with atlatls and darts, just like these."

"How many in all?" Kol asks.

"Ten, counting the two of us."

"All in kayaks?" I ask.

"Yes, but they are not strong on the sea."

I remember this—Noni told us her mother ran away out to sea because their clan wasn't accustomed to paddling in the open water. "We won't wait for them to come to us," I say. "We'll come to them. We'll warn them that Noni is not going back with them and tell them to turn back, but if they advance, we'll stop them with force."

As I say these words, I imagine what my brother would say. Would he approve, or would he tell me that sending Noni home would be the best way to protect the clan? I'm not sure, but I realize all at once that it doesn't matter. Chev is not here to decide. I'm here, and defending Noni is the only choice I have.

I turn to Kol. I can't compel him to help. This isn't his clan and Noni is practically a stranger to him. He sees the question in my eyes. "Don't even ask," he says. "You know I'm with you. I'll do anything to help you protect Noni."

"It's not just Noni you're protecting," Thern calls. The tide is coming in and the waves pound the cliff. He and Pada dig in their paddles to stay back from the rocks. "Dora struck a deal with Noni's father—she brings him to Noni if he helps her kill Mya and her sisters."

A wave thunders against the cliff, but it can't drown

out Thern's words or the ringing that starts in my ears. "It doesn't matter," I call back. "Whether they're coming for Noni, or me, or any of us—if they're coming for Black Dog—they're not getting what they want."

"We'll go back and watch for you," Pada says. "And we'll be ready to fight."

Before I can shout a thank-you across the waves, she and Thern are gone.

The climb back up the cliff, the hike back down the ravine— it all passes like a cloud threading across the sky. By the time I notice where we are, we're back at the ring of huts. The drum calls the clan to the evening meal. Kol and I hurry to the meeting place, and when we find his mother, we call her aside. "We need to speak in Mya's hut," Kol says. Mala's eyes sharpen. She can hear the fight in Kol's voice. She finds her other sons while Kol and I gather Morsk, Yano and Ela, Seeri, Lees, Noni, and Shava. The council of elders are scattered throughout the clan, sitting and eating, and I work my way through the gathered crowd, tapping my brother's most trusted advisors and friends on the shoulder.

Once we are assembled in the crowded hut, I tell the story in as few words as possible. "My intention," I start, then, glancing at Kol, I start again. "Our intention is to cut them off before they reach the camp," I say. "But we have to prepare. The clan needs to be ready to defeat an enemy the way we defeated the Bosha."

The silence expands, pushing against the walls of the hut. Morsk speaks, his voice ringing through the quiet room. "We'll stop them," he says. "I'm coming with you."

"And me," says Pek.

"And me and Roon, too." My eyes move to Lees. Her usually soft face is hard with determination.

Before I can answer her, Kol is speaking. "I don't know about Roon. He might be too young—"

"Then I'm going without Roon," says Lees. "You can't stop me from helping defend my friend—"

"But this is about more than Noni," I say. "This is about you, too. Dora wants to kill *you*."

"Then even better. You certainly can't tell me I can't defend *myself*."

"Kol," Roon says, "if she goes, I go."

I stand staring at my sister as everyone else begins to move. People are anxious. "Morsk, Pek, Seeri, Kesh— you'll come with Kol and me to meet the Tama on the water. Thern and Pada will side with us, too—"

"Which gives us eight to their eight," Kol says. "One more would give us the advantage in number. Two more and we would be even stronger."

"I won't choose from among the Olen elders," I say. I look into faces—the husband and wife who served as rowers for our betrothal trip, a woman I know to be an excellent hunter—they all wait to be told what to do. Chev would have told them. Self-doubt creeps into my thoughts, and I long for my mother's voice, telling me she believes in me. I find myself turning to Mala. She's not my mother—she's not even clan—but I trust her. "Roon and Lees wish to volunteer and they have experience on the sea, but they are so young," I say.

"I can't tell you what to do to protect your own clan. You need to decide for Lees, and Kol needs to decide for Roon—"

"But you're Roon's mother."

"And Kol is his High Elder. I can only say that as a mother, I'm scared."

"Well, as High Elder of the Manu," Kol says, drawing a deep breath and letting it out as a sigh, "I believe Roon should go. I'm sorry, Mother. I agree that he's young. Probably too young. But I've seen him paddle for days. He's strong on the water."

"Mya," says Lees, "please. Roon's a stronger paddler with me than alone."

I let this sink in. Lees and I were partners in the kayak to and from the island. At the worst times when I was the most tired, she came through with the push to keep us going. I watched her and Roon travel down the coast from the Manu camp. She isn't wrong.

She would offer little help on her own, but with Roon,

she makes a difference. They are stronger together. "All right," I say. "You and Roon can share a double kayak, but you are there for a show of force and not to engage in fighting. You are to stay in the back—"

My words break off. Lees and Roon are already out of the hut, heading for the beach.

"Any others who wish to come with us to confront the Tama, we welcome you. We'll be armed with atlatls and darts—the weapon of choice of the Tama and the easiest to fire from a kayak." The husband-and-wife rowers—Evet and Niki—step forward. They were my brother's close friends. My eyes meet Niki's and I remember the last time I looked at her, as she helped steady me as I climbed from the canoe on the Manu's shore—and I think how her steady hand will help me again. She nods at me as she and Evet duck out of the hut.

"Those who stay onshore need to alert the rest of the clan and ready a defense. Spears must be distributed. Every member of the clan should be armed with some sort of weapon—a knife or even rocks—and *all* must be able to defend themselves if the Tama reach the camp."

"They'll never reach the camp," Morsk says so low it's no more than a whisper, as if the words weren't meant for me, but were between him and the Divine.

"I'll help hand out weapons." It's Shava's voice. She gets to her feet and steps to my side. "I'll make sure the strongest hunters are armed with spears. I know I'm not Olen or even Manu yet, but Thern and Pada are helping out on the water. A Bosha should help onshore, too." Shava has tears in her eyes. I don't pull back when she embraces me. "Good luck, my future sister." I nod my head against her hair. She pulls back, and slips out of the hut.

It isn't long before Mala, Kol, Noni, and I are left alone in the hut. "You don't need to do this," Noni says. Her voice shakes but her eyes are dry. I think she must have learned a long time ago how to hold back her tears. "I could hide from my father. I could run away again."

"This isn't just about you," I say. "It's about me and my sisters, too." Then I stop myself. There's more that she should know. "But if it were just about you, we would still stop your father. We would do whatever was necessary to defend you."

I say this without hesitating, without listening for my brother's whispered advice before I speak or his hushed rebuke after. For the first time since Chev died, I am trusting myself to be the High Elder.

I turn to Mala, and this time it's me who draws us into an embrace. Then I have Kol's hand, and we are hurrying to the beach.

On the water we are ten in all: Kol, Morsk, and I are out front, with Pek, Seeri, and Kesh forming a second row, all in single kayaks. And in back, Lees and Roon in one double kayak, Niki and Evet in another. We paddle hard as the sun drops into a ridge of clouds that sit upon the western horizon, spreading a diffuse light. Thern and Pada had said the Tama were waiting for darkness to strike. We need to reach them first.

We pass the cave in the cliffs where Thern and Pada found us. The high waves that crashed against the rocks have quieted—the tide is going back out. It makes travel easier and quicker, as ten paddles stab the water, pushing us farther and farther toward danger. Still, rather than rising, my fears ease as we get closer to the Tama. I feel the camp growing safer and safer the farther we leave it behind.

Like Thern and Pada, we each carry an atlatl on the deck of our kayaks. We each carry a supply of darts. I glance at the pack of darts looped over Kol's shoulders—ten in all—and I hope we have enough. Kol and I also found harpoons in the kayaks we took, left over from the last hunt for walrus or seals. Others may also carry them. We left them on board in case we were to need them, the ropes coiled at our feet.

We don't go far beyond the cave before Kol points to the shore with his paddle—the Tama are camped in the open on a low bluff. It isn't long before they see us too, and Thern and Pada sprint for their own boats. They paddle hard, leaving the shore and gliding like birds on the water, coming right for me.

I remind myself that they can be trusted—that they are coming to fight for us, not against. Still, my fear that we've been tricked ebbs only when they reach me and turn, lining up against the Tama by my side.

"The one in the middle is the High Elder," Pada calls over the wind, as we all bob on the surface, waiting like prey. The Tama aren't far behind the Bosha. Once they realize they've been betrayed and we've been warned, they scramble down to their boats. A flash of white catches my eye and I see her—Dora—boarding a kayak right beside Noni's father. Perhaps spurred by rage at having been fooled by Thern and Pada, they move astonishingly fast and paddle much more skillfully than I'd hoped. They head right for us. It won't be long before they have reached the place where we wait.

While he is still far enough off that a dart should not reach me, but close enough to hear, I call out to Noni's father. "High Elder of the Tama," I shout, suddenly aware that I don't even know the man's name. So be it. I'd rather not know the name of such a man. "We're here to tell you that Noni will not be returning to your clan. You may not proceed to our land. Turn back now and we won't pursue you. But be warned—we are prepared to defend her and ourselves."

"I will not take orders from a woman who believes she can steal my property from me," calls Noni's father. I recognize him as the man who chased Lees and me out to sea. "I will retrieve my daughter, even if we have to kill every member of your clan to do it."

With that he digs hard with his paddle, heading fast toward Kol.

THIRTY

My eyes linger on Noni's father while fear surges inside me like a gust of wind. I see him like I see things in a dream: inexact, smeared by memory. His face shining red, his sharp stare piercing like a knife, I see him pursuing me and Lees out to sea.

With a jolt the dream fades, the past yields to the present, and I move forward with all the strength in me. My arms work the paddle in my hands, pushing the surface as if burying that remembered threat. That memory cannot hurt me now. The real threat is the man with a loaded atlatl right in front of me, the man who will take Kol from me if I do not act.

My eyes on him, my arms digging hard at the sea, I know that now is the time to ready my shot. I slow my strokes, pull up my paddle, and reach for a dart. My fingers are just wrapping around it when a searing pain smashes through my temple. A thud reverberates inside my head, like something heavy dropped to the ground, and everything goes dark.

Although I sit in a boat atop the waves, I feel as if my feet have gone out from under me. I reach out a hand to hold on to the sky as the kayak flips and the surface comes up to meet me.

Upside down, I hold in my breath as I hold in my cry, reminding myself that water has tried, and failed, to beat me. The pack with my darts and atlatl slides from my arm, but I sweep out a hand just in time to catch it before it sinks.

Above me the hull of a boat floats like a cloud in a storm-darkened sky—a flatter, wider hull than those of the Olen or Manu. The pain in my head fades and the darkness rolls away from my sight, and I know it's a Tama boat. I reach up, the water blurs as silt and sand churn around my flailing arms, but finally my hands find the skin at the front of the Tama boat.

How long have I been submerged? When my clutching hands grab at the sealskin, my fingers digging in like they're digging into air itself, I know it's been too long. I pull the skin toward me, lifting my body and righting my kayak. My face breaks into the day, the boat in my grip tips toward me and over, and I see a Tama woman's face wide with fear as she flips into the sea.

I catch my breath. I am upright. My paddle is too far to

reach, so I grab the paddle of the Tama boat and row as hard as I can toward the place I last saw Kol.

But he's not there. In that place I see Morsk, a dart protruding from a spot under his arm. He's chasing something—a kayak receding toward the shore. Noni's father. Behind them both, in a kayak with a slash across the deck, I spot Kol.

Kol sees me. He gestures, telling me to get down. I do as he says, folding my chest over my legs. As I watch, Kol loads a dart into his atlatl and throws it at a target beyond my right shoulder.

A cry mixes with the slap of the waves against paddles and boats. I turn to see a face I've seen so many times before, a face that draws bile up my throat.

Dora's eyes bore into me as she tugs Kol's dart from her side, just below her rib cage. Blood spurts from the wound, spattering the deck of her kayak before being rinsed away by the spray. Her mouth twists into a grimace of pain. One gnarled hand curls into a knot around Kol's dart, while the other reaches for her atlatl. As I watch, she loads the bloody dart and aims at me.

I know I don't have time to row far enough to escape her reach. Even with blood pouring from her side, she could make the shot. It won't take much strength or skilled aim. I am too close to avoid her.

She reels back. I have only one choice. At the moment

her arm begins to come forward, I roll my kayak and again plunge into the sea.

The sea was cold before. This time the water bites into my skin like teeth. My hands, my throat, my face ache like they are being shredded by the jaws of a cat.

I watch, but I don't see the dart break the surface. I wonder if she held the shot. Wary, I know I can't resurface where I am. A dart could pierce me before I was able to draw my first breath.

I reach for the knife in my belt. I don't have much time. I cut through the sash that holds me in the seat and swim out, letting the harpoon that was tucked by my feet slide into my waiting hands. Kicking hard, I shoot to the bottom of Dora's kayak and slash at the hull with the knife in my right hand and the harpoon in my left. When a gash hangs down and blood from her wound starts to tint the sea pink, I pull myself up on the side of her boat. She spins to face me, and when she does I pull my body up onto the deck. The boat is narrow and slippery, the hole I cut causing it to toss unsteadily in the waves. I struggle first to get my balance, then to hang on without falling. But once I have myself in position—once I am straddling the kayak right in front of her, a knife in one hand and a harpoon in the other—Dora knows she's lost. She grabs at the bag of darts on her half-submerged deck and tries to use one like a knife, stabbing at my hands and arms. My skin tears and burns, but it's too late for her. The boat tips backward, weighed down by seawater filling the hull, and all she can do is grab at the sash to try to escape.

Her hands slide on the knot in the cordage. She's panicking, clawing at the sash.

And then she's gone, pulled down by the boat as it sinks.

I know I need to get out of the sea before the cold steals the life from me. But I can't help but swim down, sweeping the bottom for a glimpse of her. After all, I thought she was drowned once before. My lungs ache, and my legs are going numb. And I see her.

The boat touches the bottom and then floats up again, bobbing right below the surface, carried by the force of the waves. Dora, held in the seat by the sash, has gone still. A cloud of blood flows from her side.

I break the surface and find my kayak. Flipping it over, I drag myself out of the cold waves and climb on top, straddling the deck. My feet hang over the sides, dipping now and then into the sea, but wrapped in sealskin boots they resist the cold. But my hands, face, and neck ache as they thaw in the air.

I search for a paddle, finding one floating on the waves. The only way to reach it is to paddle with my hands, exposing them to the frigid water again. Still, I'm helpless without an oar, so I do what I must. Just as I reach it I hear my name. It's Seeri's voice. The one-word cry bursts out of her like a scream for help.

I have to paddle in a circle to see her—she and Pek are almost directly to my back. When I get turned, I know why she called out. Two Tama kayaks have targeted Roon and Lees, and they are coming fast toward either side of their boat. Both Tama fighters hold a knife in their teeth, keeping their hands free to row. Roon and Lees appear to have lost a paddle, and Roon is struggling to get them away as Lees hurries to load a dart.

But even if Lees were to succeed and get the dart loaded quickly, which boat would she target? She could load and fire only once before her time is up. Seeri waves to me—her hands are empty. She is either out of darts or her pack has tumbled overboard into the sea.

My bag of darts is still over my shoulder. I might be able to target one of the Tama kayaks if Lees targets the other. But one dart would have to be perfectly placed to stop the approaching kayak. If they can still paddle, they will have plenty of opportunity to attack with their knives.

Then I remember the harpoon—the harpoon tied to a length of rope—resting in my lap. I load it into my atlatl as quickly as I can. I hardly have time to aim. It flies over my shoulder, soaring toward the closer target, and it finds its home in the side of the boat.

The harpoon cuts right though the sealskin hide of the hull, just below the waterline. Tugging on the rope as hard as I am able, the boat jerks off course and flips before the harpoon comes loose. Lees lands her dart in the shoulder of the other Tama fighter. That boat turns and circles back, and Pek, waiting not far off, sends a second dart plunging into the man's back.

A voice calls into the wind . . . *Fall back!* Noni's father holds a paddle high in the air. A signal.

For one brief moment I think that the Tama are calling for retreat. Several of their wounded are paddling farther away, pulling out of range of our darts. Blood flows from arms and necks. Darts protrude from shoulders and backs.

But then I see that the Tama High Elder is under attack. A boat is bearing down on him.

Kol.

The High Elder is too far away for me to see clearly, but something is definitely wrong. He paddles awkwardly, as if he has the use of only one arm. I watch Kol, and as I do I notice several places where blood seeps from gashes in his tunic. Still, he rows hard toward his target. Morsk is not far away. Noni's father raises his paddle again and I realize he isn't calling retreat, not really.

He's calling all the Tama to his defense.

Thern and Pada, though, won't let them pass. Two Tama fighters are blocked, unable to maneuver around much more experienced paddlers. Niki and Evet, in their double kayak, have speed on their side, but though they hurry toward Kol, Morsk, and the Tama High Elder, the distance they have to cross is great.

I paddle closer, too, hoping to see Kol finish Noni's

father, but wanting to be close enough to help if he needs me. He holds his atlatl, loaded with his harpoon, all the while paddling to get close enough to know the shot is certain.

Morsk is not far behind Kol now, but a Tama is also closing fast. Kol surveys the water, takes stock of the paddlers and where they all are, growing ever closer to his goal. He glances back at Morsk just once before sending the harpoon sailing over his shoulder.

It hits the High Elder's back, slipping through his body like a knife sliding through water. I see him grasp at something at his waist and I realize it's the point of the harpoon. It has come straight through.

He drops his paddle, slumping forward. Kol turns, looking for Morsk. But instead of Morsk, a Tama fighter is right beside him. Too far away to help, I watch as the Tama raises a hand and brings it down. He raises it again and I see the dart in his hand. Another stabbing cut down through the air and he raises it again. This time I'm close enough to see that it drips with Kol's blood.

I paddle harder, digging at the water as fast as I can, but Morsk is closer. He glides across the water like a bird through the air, a sudden burst of strength carrying him to Kol. He reaches him, ramming the Tama boat and sending it over. The hull of the boat turns up, and the tumult of the struggle all at once goes still.

Morsk paddles a short distance away, waiting and watching for the boat to right on the waves. Even the other Tama, paddling to the side of their High Elder, slow, waiting for the boat to flip.

The longer it stays capsized, the more I suspect this Tama will never surface. All the other fighters from his clan have retreated, dragging the boat holding Noni's father into shore. A red wake trails his kayak. There is no doubt Noni's father is dead.

Finally, when this last remaining Tama kayak has stayed inverted for so long, Morsk turns to look at Kol. He calls to him, asking if he's too injured to paddle back.

I wait for Kol's reply, my heart skipping nervously in my chest at the thought of how badly Kol might be hurt. Wishing to be able to check his injuries, to see for myself if any would threaten his life.

"I can row," Kol calls. "I have plenty of wounds, but none of them is deep."

I am almost to Morsk, almost to the overturned kayak, when a figure springs up out of the sea. The man from the inverted boat, holding a knife. He climbs the side of Morsk's kayak and plunges the knife down. I see a flick of his wrist, the knife drawn across Morsk's throat.

Everything changes—the wind blows harder, the waves crash higher. Blood runs down from Morsk's neck, coating his shoulders and chest. I load my atlatl, take aim. The dart flies, lands in the Tama man's chest. Once. Twice. Three times.

My eyes sweep from boat to boat to boat, and I see that Kol and Pek both hold empty atlatls. They both shot just as I did. Three darts stick deep into the Tama fighter's chest.

Pulling one free, he tips backward. His balance is lost. He slides from the side of Morsk's kayak, painting three stripes of blood on the deck as he disappears into the sea.

Paddling, climbing—I've taken the Tama man's place on the deck of Morsk's boat before I know how I got there. His blood smears on my hands and on my tunic. I grab Morsk's shoulders, call his name, slide him back in the seat.

But he won't answer me, won't open his eyes.

THIRTY-ONE

I hover over Morsk, talking to him, repeating his name, as Kol paddles closer, pulling his kayak alongside us. I don't need to hear Kol's voice to know what he will say. Maybe I hear him, maybe I hear only the waves and the wind and the thrumming beat of a drum in my temples.

It doesn't matter what I hear. I already know Morsk is dead.

I want to stay slumped over Morsk's body, but I know I cannot. The Tama may have killed Morsk, but we killed their High Elder. We killed Dora and others of their own clan. They've retreated for now, but they may return. We need to head back to our camp before they can follow us.

I raise my head. Kol's heavy gaze rests on my face. Blood flows from two gashes in his shoulder and seeps from a smaller wound in his lower arm. "Can you row?" I call.

He doesn't answer, except to nod. His blood-smeared

face wears an expression like a shattered blade. Sharp, but no longer lethal.

I turn around, still sitting on top of Morsk's kayak. It's a larger boat than mine, and it handles the extra weight of my body well enough. Snatching Morsk's paddle from the sea, I turn the boat in a slow circle.

Each member of the Olen, Manu, and Bosha who came with us is watching me. Many are injured—blood smears across tunics, hands, faces—but they are all here. Morsk is the only one we lost.

When we row into our bay, our clan is waiting. Lookouts standing along the cliffs must have seen us while we were still out to sea, because when we reach the beach, the clan is there, ready to come to our aid. They crash into the shallow water to pull us from the boats and help us to shore. Mala runs to Kol, then Kesh, before her eyes fall on me. When she sees Morsk, his body slumped in the seat, she splashes through the waves and comes to my side. Two cold hands wipe blood from my cheeks before reaching around me and pulling my head to her shoulder.

I don't remember ever being more grateful for a mother's embrace.

It's late, but the clan will not rest tonight. Everyone stays up, sitting in the meeting place around a fire in the hearth, talking about Morsk and his great deeds. For once, I don't want to hide in my hut. Instead, I need to take part in the storytelling, to make sure that everyone knows of the heroism of Morsk and how he died saving the High Elder of the Manu.

Kol and I take Noni aside. "He's dead," Kol tells her. "Your father died in the battle."

Her eyes squeeze shut, and she covers them briefly with her hands. Yet when she opens them again they are dry. She lifts her narrow chin—a child's chin in a child's face. Only her eyes are old. "Good," she says. "Thank you." And then, "Was he the one who killed Morsk?"

"No," Kol says. "Your father was already dead when Morsk died."

Noni nods. "I'm glad. I already hate him. If I knew he killed Morsk, I would hate myself, too."

"Don't say that," I tell her. My voice is so bright, like a spark flying from the flame. Noni jumps. "Don't ever blame yourself for what others have done."

Noni looks past me. "I won't," she says, but I'm not convinced she means it.

As everyone talks, I sit on the ground and lay my head against a stone beside the hearth. Looking up, I take in the canopy that covers us, the work of Morsk's own hands. I recall the meal my clan had with Kol's family in this very space, and the way Lees had bragged about Morsk's skill in building the covering. Kol slides closer to my side. "There was a time when the sight of this canopy angered me," he says. "A time when I resented it. But never again. From tonight on, it will be a monument to the man who built it."

I draw a breath, thinking of the rivalry between Morsk and Kol at the very end of Morsk's life. I remember his proposition that we marry, and his promise to make sure I never regretted the decision if we did. But most of all, I remember why he did those things. "He loved the Olen clan," I say.

"He did," Kol answers. "He may have been saving me when he died, but he was out there to defend this clan. To defend the Olen and to defend its High Elder."

My heart seems to float in my chest. I feel as insubstantial as the smoke rising from the fire. These words are the gust of wind that scatters me. I realize that Morsk gave his life for the clan I lead, and I can't let it be for nothing.

In the morning I wake early, despite the fact I went to bed just before first light. As soon as I'm awake my sisters are up, making me wonder if they were waiting for me. Our brother and our friend will be buried at midday. I'm not surprised that they couldn't sleep.

Yano and his sister, Ela, as the clan healers, will arrange for the graves to be dug and make other preparations for the ceremony. "Please," I say to Ela, "don't let Yano help dig the graves. I'm sure there are others who can do it. And if it can be done without asking those who fought alongside

Morsk against the Tama, I think it would be right to spare them from that task."

"You are a good High Elder," Ela says. She surprises me—this isn't something I ever thought I would hear Ela say—and I'm both pleased and saddened at the same time. Saddened because I never wanted this role, and today more than any day I will not be able to deny that it is mine.

I wander out to the meeting place, but I find it empty. People not helping dig the graves have stayed in their huts. Grief is so much harder in the cold light of day, without the fire and the sheltering dark. Daylight exposes what should be here, but isn't.

I hope to see Kol, but his family stays away. "Maybe they're sleeping," says Pada, who, along with Thern, slept in the kitchen last night. I suppose she has noticed my eyes drift to the door of their borrowed hut too many times.

"Maybe," I say, but I doubt it. I imagine Mala wants some time with her sons. Perhaps she is talking to Kol about the future of the clans, perhaps telling him again that she believes a merger would be a mistake.

Or could she be saying something else? Could she be telling him that she's changed her mind about the idea of a merger? Could it be that she—like me—can't deny how well our clans worked together to drive the Tama away?

My thoughts are interrupted by Seeri. "You should come prepare for the ceremony," she says, tugging me by the hand.

She wears a plain tunic made from the stiff hide of an elk. I glance at the sky. The sun is already high up, half hidden behind a net of clouds. "You'll be standing at the head of the graves. Let me do your hair."

Back in the hut, I dress in a sealskin tunic that once belonged to our mother. It used to be quite big on me, but Ela took it and cut it down to my size after complaining that nothing I wore from her fit. It's open at the neck, and my carved ivory pendant—the one that had been my mother's, the symbol of our clan—hangs against my skin just above the laces.

When the sun is almost at its highest, Ela and Yano come to call me to the graves. "As the High Elder, you should lead the procession out of camp to the ridge," Ela says. I notice small things about her: bloodshot eyes. Red ocher staining the palms of her hands. "I'm going ahead," she says. "A few of the children are helping me carry the drum and the masks."

My stomach clenches at the thought of these things—all the necessary pieces of a burial. The drum, the masks. The bodies laid in pits lined with mammoth skins.

I'm glad I had nothing to eat because I don't think I could keep it down.

After she leaves I turn to Yano. His eyes are shadowed in violet. I suspect he hasn't had a moment of sleep since we brought Chev home. Looking at him now, he seems so alone without my brother, so small. "Ela said masks, not mask," I say. "Please tell me you're not doing the dance with her—"

"I want to," he says. "It's important. It hastens the rise of the dead to the Land Above the Sky. How could I do less for Chev than I would do for any other member of this clan?"

I choke down a sob. I can't break now. I need to stay as strong as Yano. "My brother always knew he was lucky to have you—"

Yano's eyes swim with tears. "No, I was the lucky one. I was so proud of him—I loved him very much."

"And he loved you just as much." I can't help but wonder if my brother told Yano how much he loved him. Somehow I think he did. I raise my hand to hide my tears. I start to turn away. But then I catch myself and turn back, my tear-filled eyes meeting Yano's. He stays with me until our tears have slowed.

The graves are dug on the ridge that overlooks the sea, in the very spot I stood with my brother and Kol to watch for the Bosha on the day Lo attacked our camp. A few of our clan are buried on ridges to the south, but I'm happy Yano and Ela chose this one for Chev and Morsk. This way I can imagine their Spirits watching over the sea, protecting their clan forever.

I don't see Kol or his family until we are climbing to the ridge. Perhaps they hang back out of respect for our clan.

I want to call Kol to my side, to ask him to stay by me as I preside over the ceremony, but I know I can't. This is my duty alone.

My knee buckles a bit when I see Chev and Morsk both covered in ocher, lying on the mammoth pelts at the bottom of their graves. Both are dressed as hunters. Morsk holds a spear in one hand and an atlatl in the other. Darts have been laid at his feet.

When I look down at my brother, I see in his hand a single weapon—his obsidian knife. The same one Anki stole from him after she killed him. The one Kol reclaimed and gave to Seeri to hold. Chev clutches the knife to his chest, the blade lying across his heart.

Though the drum beats right behind me and the dancers circle right before my eyes, I find my thoughts carrying me away. Maybe that's what you're meant to do at a burial, while the drum plays on and on.

I think of my father, my mother, my brother, and I wonder about the clan they share their camp with in the Land Above the Sky. Is Kol's father, Arem, a part of that clan? Do they all hunt together, and kayak on the Divine's endless sea? Does the same drum call them to meals? Do they share the same dances and songs?

After the burial, I lead the procession back to camp and everyone descends on the meeting space, tired and hungry. Mala heads into the kitchen and I hear her voice as she offers to help prepare the meal. I hesitate, unsure if I should intervene—I don't want her to feel she needs to feed my clan. She is our guest, after all. But Kol comes up behind me and touches me on the arm.

"Let her," he says, guessing my thoughts. "It makes her feel good. It makes her feel at home."

"She is at home."

"Is she?" I expect the half smile I so often see on Kol's face, but instead there's something else—closed lips in a flat line.

"Of course she is." I stop. Kol's eyes are dark. He's gone within himself. "I want to go down to the beach," I say.

Without asking why, Kol walks beside me. Together we sit down on the edge of the dunes. His eyes trace the horizon. I can't gauge his mood. Sad, yes—from the burial, I'm sure. But something else. Lost. Or hurt.

"This view makes me think of death," I say. "I've never told anyone that before."

Kol lays his hand on mine. I turn my palm up to touch his and lace our fingers together. "The first time I stood here was the day we landed, after leaving your camp. My mother was in a kayak coming in behind me. I ran to her, but she was already dead, and Chev chased me away."

When I pause, Kol doesn't feel the need to fill the silence, and I'm grateful for that. The sea breeze that's rippled in all morning has sharpened to a cold wind. Kol moves closer to me. "My mother, my brother, Morsk. None of them died here at home. And before the burial I worried that I would always feel like they were still out there, trying to come to this shore."

I close my eyes momentarily and I see it, the place my mind traveled to while I stood at the head of the graves and the drum beat on and on. I see again the fires set by my loved ones in the Land Above the Sky.

"But now I see it differently. I see them together in a new place, with a new clan. A clan that includes your father and mine, maybe even Manu and Bosha from long ago. Great hunters, great leaders, not yearning to come to the place they left behind, but instead waiting for us to come to them."

"So you think that Bosha and Manu—the founder of your clan and the founder of mine—might live together in one clan in the Land Above the Sky?"

"I think maybe they do," I say.

"Does that mean . . . ?" Kol's voice flickers like a flame in the wind—faltering and flaring. "Are you thinking maybe then our clans might merge?"

"I think it might be too late for us to make that decision," I say.

A flinch runs from Kol's shoulder down the length of his arm to his hand. In response, I raise his hand to my lips. "I think the Divine may have already made that decision,"

I whisper, my lips never leaving his skin. Somehow he still understands my words. "I think you and I are already sharing the role of High Elder, with her blessing." I turn my eyes to his. "We worked together to get our families home from the island. We worked together to fight back the Tama. I can't deny that our clans are stronger—*we* are stronger—when we're together." I stifle a laugh against his palm. "Even our honey tastes sweeter together."

Kol turns toward me and there it is, that half smile. He leans close to me, pressing a kiss to the hollow just below my ear. "The Divine has heard my prayers," he whispers.

His breath is warm on my throat. His lips trace the line of my jaw, flutter over my chin, stopping to cover mine. We fall back against the dunes and he draws me into his arms. His kiss is light and playful, but I pull him closer, deepening the kiss until I feel my heart pounding against my chest as if it's trying to break into his. I tip my head back. My eyes sweep over Kol's face, but he keeps his gaze fixed on my mouth.

"Mya . . ." Kol swallows, and I feel the vibration run into me, he holds me so close and so still. "I need to tell you . . . I didn't want this just to . . . our clans . . . it's not . . ." His eyes move to mine, and something inside him opens wide and pulls me in. For a moment I'm scared, but then I let everything that is Kol surround me and enclose me. "Mya, I love you."

"And I love you. With all my heart." My words are half spoken, half gasped, but I know Kol understands.

I tilt my head forward, touching his brow with mine. Our bodies relax. The tension between us slowly unwinds as we settle into the sand.

"Now," I say, partly to myself, partly to Kol, and partly to the clan that right now is sharing a meal, not knowing the plans that are being made. "Now we just need to give our new clan a name."

THIRTY-TWO

Lying here on the sand wrapped in Kol's arms, I try to memorize every detail of this moment—the sound of the waves, the wind in the dunes, Kol's breath coming quick, his chest rising and falling against mine. When I stand on this beach from now on, these are the memories that will stir in me. This place will no longer remind me of death.

"I wonder," I say, thinking out loud, "if the Manu-Olen would be the best name."

"I like that," Kol says, "but maybe for a clan that's so new, we should choose new names. Names of the leaders we want to remember every time we say the clan's name." Kol slides away from me and sits up. He looks down at his hands, bruised and cut in the battle with the Tama. "What would you think of the Chev-Arem clan?"

Hearing the name of my brother, so soon after standing at his grave, brushes my nerves, and for a moment I'm unsure. But bound together with the name of Kol's father, it feels solid and strong, like rock beneath my feet. Like something to build on.

"It's not like we'll forget Manu or Olen or Bosha," Kol says. He watches my face closely. He must see that I am happy with the name, because a smile lights in his eyes. "Their stories will be told forever, their songs sung and their dances danced at all the celebrations of the Chev-Arem clan."

"Yes," I say. "Beginning with a wedding."

Four days. At first I say it's too long, but after the first two days are behind me, I say that we will never have enough time.

"You want the good luck," Ela says. "You want to be blessed by all that the Divine promises to those joined under a full moon. We could wait for the next one, I guess—"

"No," I say, my voice so quick and sharp, Ela laughs.

"I didn't think so." Her fingers dance across pieces of a tunic—my betrothal tunic—as together we work to increase the intricacy of the pattern into something worthy of a bride.

"It should still look like a meadow," I say, "but now it needs to have no boundaries. We can add to it a piece of the sea and the beach . . . and maybe a cave on a cliff."

"All that on this one tunic?" Ela asks. Her eyes reflect

the light of the seal oil lamp. It's far too dark in this hut to do this work, but still we persist. In two more days the wedding will be upon us and we will be out of time. "You may be right," I say. "What if we simply add a few sections to suggest a bee? Stripes of light and dark and two wings?"

"A bee?" Ela asks. "Why a bee?"

"Because bees make honey," I say. "Don't worry. Kol will understand."

While Ela and I work on my tunic, others work on bringing in the guests. Everyone wants to attend—the Olen, the Bosha, who will soon rejoin the Olen, and the Manu, too—so boats make the trip up and down the coast over and over. With every new arrival from the north the decision to merge is reaffirmed.

Before we told anyone else about the merger, I went with Kol straight from the beach to talk with his mother. We found her in the kitchen after the meal, and I hung back near the door as Kol approached her. My memory echoed with the words she said when she didn't know I could hear: *This is about every Manu who's ever lived. Every one who's yet to live.*

The words she'd used to tell Kol she opposed a merger.

But when Kol takes her hands in his and tells her we would like to create a new clan, he doesn't wait for her response. "It will be called the Chev-Arem clan," he says, "because we know it's what Chev and Father would want if they were here."

My fingers curled around the bearskin hanging in the doorway at my back. My teeth bit into my lip. Kol had nearly extinguished my smoldering fear of the future, but now it began to flicker to life again.

But then Mala threw her arms around Kol. "I was so burdened with grief before, I thought that keeping the Manu separate was something we owed to your father's memory. But I was wrong. What we owe his memory is a strong clan. He would be so happy to hear this. He would be so proud."

I swallowed my hot fear down and stepped closer. Mala turned to me, and a tremor of joy ran over my skin when I saw her smile.

By the third day, the camp buzzes like a hive. In the morning, groups leave camp to hunt and fish, and in the afternoon, they head out to gather. They come back with overflowing baskets—Shava and her mother, Thern and Pada, Kol's aunt, Ama, and her sons. Even Noni and Black Dog go along. Ama gives Noni a little extra attention, and her boys give extra attention to the dog. Noni doesn't seem to mind. She seems happy to be a part of something again. At night, they all sleep under the roof that Morsk erected over the meeting place.

The morning of the wedding comes, though my bridal

tunic is far from ready and I know it never will be. "It's beautiful," Ela says.

"Beautiful," echoes Mala, who has joined us in Ela's hut to help.

Today I let Mala do my hair. Like Ela did for my betrothal, she threads ivory beads into my braids, but today she adds tiny purple flowers gathered from our meadow, and tiny white feathers. "They will glow in the moonlight," she says.

I think of this—the moon will soon catch in the beads and feathers in my hair. And I know that by the time that happens—by the time the sky is dark and the moon is out—I will already be Kol's wife.

The ceremony will be held on the beach. It's the only open space in camp that has enough room for everyone to gather. Weddings call for a large fire, and when I smell the smoke floating on the breeze, my stomach swims. Mala must see my nerves in the way my eyelids flutter and my fingers rub the trim at my tunic's hem.

"Don't worry," she says. "Today, you can do no wrong. Today, everything is right."

When the sun is just beginning to set, painting a wide path of gold across the sea, Kol comes to the door of my hut to ask for me.

Pushing back the bearskin, I look out and see him framed by the twilight sky. His face glows in the fading sunlight, a star burning in each eye, and I'm transported back to the first night we met. The night he came to the door of my hut to offer me a pouch of honey. The path we stepped onto that day has led to this door. His lips curl—not into a half smile but into something much warmer and brighter, something I can't help but return. "Would you walk with me?" he asks, holding out his hand.

I place my hand in his, and together we walk the path to the beach. Kol leans his head toward my ear.

"Are you happy?" he asks.

"More happy than I've been since . . ." I stop myself. No. That's not right. "More happy than I've ever been."

When we reach the fire, we are greeted by our healers, Urar and Yano. Ela is hidden out of sight—she will soon appear in a mask. But for now we are compelled to sit while all the others of our clan stand. A drum plays an urgent beat, a beat that makes my heart quicken, and from Kesh's flute a melody floats over our heads, carrying our joy to the Divine.

When it's time, everyone takes a seat on pelts that have been scattered on the ground, and from behind us a dancer emerges in a wolf mask—Ela. She circles me and Kol, then winds between the two of us and the fire, bending low to look into our faces. I see her eyes, but behind the mask they seem distant and strange. I feel the power of the mask, transforming Ela into the thing it represents.

A wolf. To remind us of the bonds of the pack, a bond that can't be broken. I can't help but think of Black Dog and of Noni, and of all the ways that a pack is more than family or even clan. Ela's wolf eyes prick my heart, but I don't turn away. Not until she does. When she finally drops her head and turns, I shiver and look over at Kol. He smiles, but I can tell by his eyes that he saw the wolf in Ela, too.

At the end of the ceremony, Kol and I share a cup of mead. I catch Kol watching me as I peer over the rim of the cup. The liquid burns down my throat and warmth rises up through me, lightening my head. I place the cup in his hand. His head tips back and he drains the last of the liquid. I watch the muscles of his throat as he swallows and I know it is done.

We are wed.

Later, the musicians gather to play and lots of people press closer, ready to dance. The first song is the song of Manu—Kol's favorite. Kol leads me to a spot in the circle that forms.

"I don't know this dance," I say. Shame sends heat up my neck and I feel my ears burn. I would know it if I hadn't run away to hide in my hut the first night we met.

"Don't worry; it's easy," Seeri says. She and Pek push into the circle next to us, just as the first line is sung.

Manu was a hunter lost in a storm, wandering far from home . . .

My sister tries to teach me, but she makes so many mistakes, Pek tells her she needs more lessons herself. Their laughter fills me up, so much I feel it overflow my edges.

After the dancing has gone on for a long time, Kol leads me to a place a few steps away from the crowd. He brings an elk skin, and we wrap ourselves in it as we lie back against a dune.

The sky blazes pink and gold, edged in the red of blood and of flame. The sun's light fades from the sky as the moon rises behind us. Stars are coming out. Not bright white like in winter, but the dim shimmer of the stars of the summer sky—the sky that never goes completely black.

"It's a blessing," I say. Only the thin elk skin separates us from the cold sand, but I don't shiver. Lying next to Kol warms me. "It's a blessing that the Divine lets us look up and see the hearthfires of the dead. To know they are so close. Watching us. Waiting for us to join them."

"That's why I like the blackest nights—the darkest, obsidian skies of winter. When the world is coldest and darkest, the stars shine brightest."

I think about this. I have never liked winter, when the cold could kill so easily. When game is harder to find. I've always hated the short days, and the long, dark nights.

But this is a new way to think of the winter, with its obsidian night sky ablaze with stars. Certainly I have been through my share of loss, my share of darkness. And I've hated it. But maybe Kol is right. Maybe the darkness can connect me to the past—to those who've left me and lit their fires in the sky. I turn to Kol. His eyes sweep the sky, flitting from one star to the next like a honeybee flying flower to flower. I draw closer to him, and he wraps the elk pelt around the two of us and pulls me against him. His warmth is irresistible, and I stretch out along the length of his body.

I turn my face to the darkening sky. Darkness connects us to the past—to the dead—but the darkness I've lived through connects me to the living—and to the future—as well.

I have to let go—of my mother, of Chev, of everything that's behind me. Kol has to let go too. We are both the High Elders of this new clan now, and we have to keep our eyes on the way forward. The stars in the obsidian sky may be beautiful, but they show the past, not the future. I know I need to begin to let go of the past. It's the only way I can really take hold of Kol.

The musicians stop to catch their breath and the dancers reluctantly sit. Urar adds wood to the fire, promising to read the flames. The night air snaps and hisses. The blaze spreads and grows. Soon, this spot of the beach is as bright as day as the smoke billows and coils, stretching a thick rope into the sky.

I watch it—we all watch it—and no one speaks for a long

time. When the sliver of sun is completely gone, and the moon is high in the east, Lees jumps to her feet. "The moon is up and the sun is down—it's time to dance again."

I have never heard of this custom, and I suspect it's something Lees has only just made up. She pulls Roon to his feet, and others who never seem to tire join them.

I'm surprised when Kol pulls his warmth away from me and gets up, too. "Yes," he says. "I haven't danced the wedding dance with my bride yet."

I don't know how this dance was overlooked. Perhaps with all the songs and dances of three clans, no one has remembered to ask for it. But Kol has remembered. "Waiting for this dance helped keep me alive," he whispers in my ear.

A broad smile lights Kol's face, much brighter and more enchanted than the stars in the sky. They are pale and weak, too far away to offer heat. But Kol's smile holds the heat of a thousand suns.

Kol reaches out a hand, and I take it.

Kesh's flute is the first instrument I hear. The others join him, and we begin to carve a path in the sand, moving slowly around the circle with Seeri and Pek, Lees and Roon. The music quickens and they dance faster and faster, but after a few turns Kol and I slide out of their circle and make one of our own. Kol's leg is still healing, and we want to take our time.

But then Kol wraps both my hands in his. His grip is strong, his balance surprisingly sure. He tips his head back, looking up at the stars draped overhead, and he begins to spin—not quickly, not recklessly—but spinning all the same. He turns in place, holding me at arm's length, letting me whip around him like a stone tucked in a sling.

I look up to see what he sees, and I catch my breath. The stars—small, distinct, pale—smear together as we turn. They blend into a circle of light, a beacon, right above our heads. My mouth opens to drink in a deep breath of night, and tears spring to my eyes as a sound bursts from my throat.

A sound something like a sob, but also like a cry of joy.

ACKNOWLEDGMENTS

I like to believe that some books come into being through a wave of inspiration. Maybe one day I'll write a book like that. This book came into being through sheer determination, and I could never have gotten through that process alone.

I owe so much gratitude to my editor, Alexandra Cooper. This book exists because of your remarkable talent and your uncanny ability to recognize the heart of the story I'm trying to tell. Without you, I'd still be lost in the dark of that first draft. Thank you for lighting the way. I'm incredibly grateful to have an editor I trust so much.

I also am truly thankful for my literary agent, Josh Adams. I can't thank you enough, Josh, for believing in me as a writer before I believed in myself, and shepherding my work along some invisible path that only you can see. You have agenting superpowers, and I'm thankful you use them for the forces of good.

To the team at HarperCollins: thank you to Rosemary Brosnan, Alyssa Miele, Erin Fitzsimmons, Jessica Berg, Olivia Russo, Patty Rosati, Kim VandeWater for kicking things off, and Bess Braswell and her team. At Adams Literary: thank you to Tracey Adams and Samantha Bagood. I owe special thanks to Sean Freeman for the artwork on this book's striking cover.

Thank you to Stephanie Garber and Kat Zhang. You

are great writers and great friends, and I appreciate you so much. I never work alone because of your support.

Amie Kaufman, thank you for reading, blurbing, and cheering. Thanks for being an amazing example of a generous writer.

Luke Taylor, your positive energy has come through for me at all the right times. Thank you so much.

Sarah J. Maas, thank you for everything you did to make the launch of *Ivory and Bone* a success—the blurb, the event, and the encouragement. You can't possibly know the impact your help had.

Thanks to the contributors at PublishingCrawl.com (past and present) and the enthusiastic readers of the blog. Thank you to the many members of the Sweet Sixteens who made 2016 the best year to be a debut author.

I need to thank all the people who helped with the launch of *Ivory and Bone*, my book club friends, the great team at Barnes and Noble Neshaminy, and my church friends who supported me and made the *Ivory and Bone* release so wonderful.

Thank you to all the many bloggers, reviewers, book clubs, and friends who did so much in support of *Ivory and Bone* and encouraged me as I wrote *Obsidian and Stars*. Thank you to the great team at @IvoryandBonePH. Thanks to the people behind FairyLoot, LitJoy Crate, Expecto Booktronum, and Bookish Desires for supporting my debut. And thank you to the many enthusiastic readers who brighten every day for me.

I want to thank the experts in the field of archaeology whose nonfiction works informed the fictional world of these books. In particular, I want to thank David J. Meltzer, E. James Dixon, Tom D. Dillehay, James Adovasio, Jake Page, and E. C. Pielou.

To all the teachers, librarians, booksellers, and conference coordinators who support my writing and help me connect with readers, your hard work is appreciated. Thank you for the benefit of your expertise and time, and for all your efforts to encourage and nurture readers.

I want to thank my family. Thank you to my sister, Lori, for always listening and encouraging me. Thank you to my father and stepmother, for always believing in me. And to Nashville and Jeepster, thanks for ensuring there's never a dull moment at home.

Thank you also to Mia Bergstrom, for shining your amazing light into my life.

Thank you to my husband, Gary. You were my earliest inspiration, and I never would have tried if it weren't for you. Thank you to my son, Dylan. Your creative energy is contagious, and you inspire me with every single thing you do. Thanks to both of you for putting up with me as I struggled with this book. I love you so much.

And to the God of love and all creation, thank you for every person listed here, and all the other blessings that are far too many to name.